Fountain of SECRETS

JOSIE LITTON

BANTAM BOOKS

FOUNTAIN OF SECRETS
A Bantam Book / August 2003

Published by
Bantam Dell
A Division of Random House, Inc.
New York, New York

ISBN 0-553-58584-3

Manufactured in the United States of America
Published simultaneously in Canada

OPM 10 9 8 7 6 5 4 3 2 1

For all of you who
write to tell me of
missed meals, undone
laundry, and too-late
nights spent in the
world that springs from
my imagination to yours.
Thank you! Josie

Fountain of
SECRETS

CHAPTER I

Summer, 1837

IN THE MIDST OF PULLING HIS BOAT ABOVE THE tide line, Gavin Hawkforte straightened and glanced around. On a deserted shore, miles from any habitation, he was struck by the sense that someone was watching him, a sudden awareness that put his instincts on alert and sent his hand to the hilt of the short sword at his waist. Yet there was no one in sight, not in either direction along the strand of beach glittering in the midday sun.

Bare-chested, wearing only the pleated white kilt of an Akoran warrior, he finished securing the boat and stood to stretch, letting out the kinks of the long row over from the neighboring island. There was no wind this day. The air hung still and heavy on Deimatos and beyond it over Akora, the Fortress Kingdom wreathed in legend and mystery. Home to him for all that he was heir to a great title in England.

Thoughts for another time. The beach was a curve of gold, lapped by the azure waters of the Inland Sea. Palm trees were separated by low scrub grass and bushes bursting with scarlet hibiscus flowers. It was a pretty sight, belying the fearful history of the place.

Barefoot, carrying the canvas bag that held his equipment and a pair of wooden poles too large to fit in the bag, Gavin moved up the beach. At the tree line, he paused to put on his sandals, then continued. The ground quickly turned rocky, dotted by outcroppings of coarse black stone that looked as though it had been poured directly from the earth, as indeed it had.

He turned briefly, hazel eyes scanning the beach. The shore of Phobos, from which he had come, was just visible in the distance, and beyond it he could make out the vague thickness along the horizon that was the island of Tarbos. The three small islands of the Inland Sea were all that remained of the drowned heart of Akora, remnant of the night of fire and terror thousands of years before, when a volcanic explosion ripped the island apart.

A disaster and a tragedy, yet from it had come the world he knew and loved. The world beneath his feet, within the grasp of his hand. The world he feared to lose.

Again the strange, disquieting sensation of being watched swept over him. He paused and looked around, but saw nothing. Annoyance drove out unease. He was worried, had been for several months, but that was no excuse for his mind playing tricks on him. The sooner he got to work, the better.

If the map was right, the closest entrance to the caves lay along the overgrown path ahead of him. It looked as though no one had used it in years, which did not surprise him. Deimatos was uninhabited. No one had a reason to go there, at least not until now.

Caves were common on Deimatos, but many were no longer accessible, the entrances to them destroyed in the conflict that had raged there a quarter-century before. His parents and others of his family had been involved in that struggle and were lucky to have survived it. If his information was right, only a handful of entrances remained usable. He had to hope he was headed for one of them.

A little farther along, the path diverged, a fork cutting away sharply to the west. He glanced down the side path but kept going in his original direction, only to stop suddenly and turn back.

The grass growing over the fork of the path showed evidence of having been trampled. It had rained three days before, great bands of water and wind sweeping out of the west. Whatever he was looking at must be fresher than that.

An animal? He bent down, seeking any hoof or paw prints that might be present, but if they were, he could not make them out. Perhaps he should have paid better attention to the men in warrior training who were master trackers, instead of spending all his time wrestling and building siege engines.

Mindful that there might be something fairly large and not necessarily friendly on the island, Gavin went on. He was well armed and confident of his ability to see to his own safety. It was the safety of others—many, many others—that worried him.

Near the entrance to the caves, he stopped and set down his equipment. Drawing out his instruments, he placed them one by one on the level ground beside him, all the while keeping his attention alert for any sound, a hint of motion, anything that could explain what he was feeling.

The bag was unpacked when he heard a rustle behind him and to the left. Had there been wind, he would have thought it the cause. But there was none, not a breath.

He kept his back to the sound, but eased the blade of his sword from its scabbard. If it was an animal waiting for a moment to pounce, the beast was in for a nasty surprise.

When no attack came, he turned and surveyed the area around the cave. He saw nothing, but did note several large boulders and trees that could offer concealment.

Replacing his sword, he returned to work, but kept a careful watch. His measurements, he decided, would begin directly in front of the cave. Setting up the poles, the height of each known to him precisely, he stepped back, adjusted the sextant he had brought, and took a careful reading to the top of the hill above the cave. He noted the measurement in a notebook, then took it again to be sure.

He was adjusting the poles when a flicker of movement caught his attention. He saw—what? Very little, for the sun was shining directly into his eyes. All he could make out was a form that appeared to be human—slim, swift, seeming to appear and disappear in the same instant.

Not an animal, then, a person. A boy perhaps, judging by his size. What would a boy be doing on Deimatos?

Gavin set the poles down and put the sextant—precious instrument that it was—away carefully in the bag. That done, he called out, "I know you're here. Declare yourself."

When there was no response, he added sternly, "It is dishonorable to skulk in the grass."

Still nothing. Once more he spoke, and this time with a note of warning. "Do you wish me to think you an enemy?"

For a moment he thought this, too, would be ignored, but then, some thirty feet in front of him, a figure emerged from behind a rock outcropping. He shaded his eyes but still could make out only that the interloper was a few inches shorter than six feet, slim, wearing a tunic, and carrying a bow. Was he also clever enough to have positioned himself with his back to the sun? If he was old enough for warrior training, as his height suggested, he would know such tactics. But why use them against a fellow Akoran?

The boy stepped forward, head high, showing no sign of fear. "Who are you? What are you doing here?" he demanded.

Gavin frowned. The voice was at odds with what he thought he was seeing, belonging to a much younger boy who could not possibly have attained such height or, for that matter, such assurance.

A younger boy or . . .

A woman?

"Take off your sword." There was no mistaking it this time; he was dealing with a woman, for all that what she said made no sense. No man would allow a woman to disarm him.

The bow was raised, that much he could see. He had to presume it held an arrow.

"Take off your sword," the stranger said again. She spoke clearly and firmly, with no hint of fear.

He damn well would not. Indeed, it was all he could do not to draw his blade. He had to remind himself that she was a woman, never to be harmed according to the most sacred of all Akoran creeds. Summoning patience, Gavin said, "What are you going to do if I don't—shoot me?"

The arrow whooshed past his shoulder, missing him by no more than inches before striking the ground. She had another notched and ready in less than a heartbeat. "Understand," she said, "I do not miss. That was a demonstration. Take off your sword."

"This is ridiculous." He was genuinely angry now, and in that anger, he began walking toward her. "Unless you're a mad woman, you're not going to murder me in cold blood." Of course, there was always a possibility that she *was* mad, in which case he might be enjoying his last few moments in this world. For a man with a reputation for being unfailingly calm and controlled, it would be supremely ironic to die because of a fit of temper.

All the same, he truly was angry, and his mood was not improved when he moved close enough to see her more clearly. She wore not the ankle-length tunic of a woman, but the short tunic of a man, ending above her knees. Her hair was golden brown, braided, and tightly coiled around her head. Her skin was deeply tanned, suggesting she lived much of her life outside. She was slender, but her bare arms, holding the bow, were sleekly muscled. Her eyes were large and thickly fringed, her nose surprisingly pert, and her mouth—

Her mouth was full, lush, and positively enticing, for all that it was drawn in a hard line.

He was still staring at that mouth when she said, "I am not mad."

"I am infinitely relieved to hear it."

"If you come in peace, why do you need a sword?"

"Well . . . the truth of that is a little embarrassing."

As he spoke, he continued closing in on her. "When I put on this kilt this morning, I realized it was missing a clasp. I was in a hurry, and I figured my sword belt would hold it up fine. But now you want me to take the sword off and I'm thinking that if I do that, my kilt's going with it, and the fact is, I'm not wearing anything under—"

Her eyes were growing saucer-wide. They were, he saw, a deep, rich brown lit by fragments of gold. Rather more to the point, she was startled and distracted just long enough for him to close the remaining distance between them, take hold of both her arms, and twist the bow from her grasp.

"Damn you!" she cried out, struggling fiercely.

Gavin let her go at once, partly so as not to hurt her, but also mindful that she might very well feel no similar prohibition where he was concerned. All the same, the brief contact was enough to inform him that for all her dressing as a man and acting as one, she was most definitely a woman, lithe and slim, but perfectly rounded where it mattered most.

Kicking the bow beyond her reach at the same time he tried to dispense with such unwonted thoughts, he said, "The first lesson of warrior training is that you do not draw a weapon on an opponent for any reason other than to kill."

She watched him warily but still showed no sign of fear, as he duly noted. Indeed, disarmed, she held her ground with courage and spirit. "Are you saying I should have shot you?"

"I'm saying we should both behave like civilized people." This despite the fact that the feelings she provoked in him were anything but civilized. First anger and now something altogether different, for all that it was no less hot and raw. That was absurd. He was a gentleman—cultured, educated, a man of science and reason. Women were marvelous creatures, to be sure, and passion was one of Creation's great gifts—but in the proper place and at the proper time, always properly controlled.

He was not feeling controlled now—far from it. With an effort that should not have been necessary, he said, "My name is Gavin Hawkforte and yours is—?"

At the mention of his name, she drew back a little farther. Did he imagine it or did she pale slightly? Looking at him, she said, "Your mother is the Princess Kassandra of the House of Atreides and your father is the Hawk Lord, is that not so?"

This recitation of his lineage caught him off guard. He understood that he and his family were public figures, not only on Akora but also in England and elsewhere. Even so, the degree of awareness about them invariably took him by surprise. "He is called that here. In England he is the Earl of Hawkforte."

Her eyes flitted to the bow, but to her credit she did not attempt to reach for it. Returning her gaze fully to him, she asked, "Why have you come here?"

"In due time. I have told you my name. Now what is yours?"

She hesitated, but after a moment said, "I am called Persephone."

It was a strange name for anyone to give a child, recalling as it did the legend of the daughter of the Earth stolen away to the underworld. All the same, Gavin merely nodded. "Persephone . . . what brings you to Deimatos?"

"I was about to ask you that. I saw what you were doing. What need have you for surveying instruments?"

There was no mistaking the challenge of her words. Even so, he answered calmly. "I'm just taking a few measurements."

She frowned, and again glanced toward her bow, but still held her ground. "Do the Atreides intend to build on Deimatos?"

"Build? Of course not."

"The question is not so foolish as you would make it sound. What reason is there for surveying unless one intends to build?"

"There is no such intention. I'm merely following up on an earlier survey, doing some measurements for purposes of comparison. That's all."

Her laugh was dry and scoffing. "A prince of the House of Atreides doing the task of an artisan? That is difficult to believe."

"Why would it be? My brother, cousins, all of us do

all sorts of tasks. Even so, I have told you why I am here. Now I ask you the same." And woe betide her if she failed to answer. Lovely she might be, for all her unusual garb and manner, not to mention her decidedly unorthodox behavior. And lovelier she might seem with each passing moment. All the same, he would have his due, which meant courtesy and no more nonsense.

She was silent long enough for him to think she truly did not mean to answer, and for him to consider what he really could do about that. Finally, she said, "I live here. Deimatos is my home."

THIS TRULY WAS NOT POSSIBLE. SHE COULD not have been in the midst of what seemed a perfectly ordinary day only to find herself confronting so extraordinary a man. Such things did not happen in her simple, solitary life.

She had drawn a bow on a prince of the Atreides and lived to draw another breath. That alone was remarkable. As for the prince himself—

She must not! Just keep breathing, keep walking beside him, keep pretending that everything was all right. He had scarcely reacted to her announcement that she lived on Deimatos, but she was not fooled. He was a warrior, bred and trained. Such men were unfailingly dangerous, not in the least because they did not toss their thoughts around like crumbs for birds, but kept their own counsel, awaiting the most opportune moment to strike.

He had returned her bow. Having disarmed her, seemingly effortlessly, he had given her back the bow as they walked together toward the cave.

He had not hurt her. He could have easily, for though she was tall for a woman, he was taller yet. Moreover, the broad sweep of his bare chest and shoulders, rippling with muscle, mocked any thought that she could hope to challenge him and win.

He was, she guessed, about her own age, which would make him twenty-four or perhaps slightly older. One of the golden youth the people of Akora enjoyed so much, the children of the royal house of Atreides with its many branches. His hair was dark blonde, very thick and brushed back from his forehead to fall almost to his shoulders. His eyes were deep-set above a blade of a nose. The skin of his face was burnished by the sun and stretched tautly over hard bones. He was, she realized, supremely masculine in a way she had not encountered before.

But then, she had encountered so very few people in her life, preferring to keep her own company.

"I really am just taking measurements," he said when they reached the entrance to the cave. "And I mean you no harm whatsoever."

It would be so much easier to believe him, but doubts lingered. She did not know the Atreides, but she knew of them, had studied their extraordinary history as described in her precious books. For more than three thousand years, members of that family had ruled Akora in an unbroken line that spoke of their courage, tenacity, and, when necessary, ruthlessness. That one should appear here now could not be mere chance.

"All right . . ." she said slowly. "What are you measuring?"

"The elevation of various points around the island."

"To compare, you say?"

He nodded. "There was a survey done about a hundred years ago. I found the records of it in the palace library."

Despite herself, she smiled. "Oh, yes, the library."

"You know it?"

"I go there from time to time." The palace and its magnificent library dominated the royal city of Ilius, the city she shunned except at those times when the weight of solitude became crushing or the hunger for knowledge proved intolerable. She had thought to go there shortly, to tell the people she feared what she had learned. Now it seemed one of them had anticipated her.

"But you say you live here?" Gavin asked.

"I do live here," she corrected.

"With your family?"

He was bound to know, there really was no preventing it. Already she sensed he had a strong, seeking mind that would be no easier to stand against than the strength of his body.

"I have no family," she said, just as she spied the instrument in the open bag. "Is that a sextant?"

"Yes, it is. Everyone has a family."

"That statement is obviously incorrect, since I don't."

She thought her logic irrefutable, but it did not appear to impress him. "There are just over three hundred-and-fifty thousand people on Akora," he said. "With the exception of *xenos,* strangers newly arrived here, we are all related to one another in multiple ways. You are clearly Akoran, therefore you must be part of that web of relationships."

"If you say so. I say I have no family, at least none known to me. Why would you choose to retrace a century-old survey of this island?"

"How can you survive here alone?"

The question amused her, hinting as it did at an underlying belief among Akorans that she had discovered in her readings. Akora was the place "where warriors rule and woman serve." Women, it must be assumed, who were not capable of living or acting independently, but were instead dependent on their benevolent masters—the men—to care for them. The mere thought of such an existence made her skin crawl.

"I am very good at taking care of myself," she told him, and let a little of her pride show.

"Apparently so. How long have you lived here?"

"A long time. You ask too many questions, Atreides prince."

He ignored that and went on, all the while watching her with disconcerting intensity. "Then you must know this island very well."

Persephone nodded. "That is so."

He hesitated as though coming to a decision. Casually, as though the question was really of no importance, he asked, "Have you seen anything unusual happening here lately?"

She knew then, in a way she had been coming to know since realizing who he was and what he was doing. A prince of Akora come to Deimatos. Come to measure the earth and search for answers.

She had thought she would have to go to them, persuade them, convince them, but now she knew that would not be necessary.

All she had to do was show him.

"I have seen what I think is the real reason why you have come here."

She looked up into his eyes, seeing in them wisdom and strength, praying her vision was true.

Around them, the island lay wrapped in stillness. The fronds of the palm trees hung motionless, the scarlet blossoms of the hibiscus did not stir. Sunlight glinted off the azure sea and the golden beaches, over the green hills and the black outcroppings. Time itself seemed not to move, but it would, inevitably and relentlessly. There was no escape from it. They would be carried along to whatever fate awaited them and be forced to endure it as best they could.

Best, then, to confront the truth and hope this man could somehow help to ease the horror she feared was coming.

Quietly, into the stillness of the golden day, she said, "The volcano that tore Akora apart more than three thousand years ago is awakening."

CHAPTER II

S HOW ME," GAVIN SAID. HE DID NOT QUESTION
her statement or express any surprise. He merely
cut to the heart of it, demanding to be shown the evidence.

They went out of the bright day into the cave. Waiting
for his eyes to adjust, he was aware of Persephone taking
flint and tinder from a box near the cave entrance. She
struck them to ignite a spark and used it to light a small
lamp.

"The oil in this will last about two hours," she said.
Taking a second lamp, she handed it to him unlit.
"Keep this one in reserve. It is very dark through most
of the caves. To be lost in that darkness is to perish."

"You've explored these caves?" When she nodded,
he asked, "Alone?"

"I was very careful."

"Even so." The thought of her alone in circumstances where one false step or miscalculation could mean lingering death in the dark struck him hard, raised as he had been to always protect women. He had to resist the impulse to take hold of her and tell her forcefully how foolish she had been.

"If I had not explored them," Persephone said over her shoulder as she moved toward a passageway leading deeper into the caves, "I would not be able to show you what you are about to see."

He could not argue with that, therefore he did not try. But his conviction that her way of life was not safe took firm root.

They proceeded through a passageway that narrowed steadily as it branched downward. The air cooled, then began to warm again. The lamp cast a minimal circle of light. Gavin followed closely upon Persephone's heels, near enough to become vividly aware of her scent in the confines of the cave passage.

She smelled of sunshine and salt, of the blessed outdoors, and of wild roses.

Wild roses abounded throughout Akora: on the eastern island of Ilius where the royal city stood; to the west on Leios, island of plains, known for its magnificent horse breeding; and even on the three small islands in between.

On warm summer days, the scent of all those roses released into the balmy air was intoxicating. The women of Akora seemed to understand this, for they crafted from the roses a perfume of rare beauty and, it was said, enticement.

He doubted the woman who had come damn close to putting an arrow in him wore that perfume, for how would she come by it here on Deimatos? But she could gather rose petals, crush them, rubbing the oil into her skin or sprinkling it in water when she bathed. . . .

He was losing his mind. It was the result of months of strain, no doubt. All that roaming about Akora, measuring every hillock and cleft, worrying over the numbers that resulted, producing a report his family had looked at and uniformly suggested was an "interesting" starting point worthy of "further investigation," never mind that he thought it might signal a true emergency.

So here he was, lusting after a woman he had only just met, when he should have his mind on dire and urgent business.

He'd long held the suspicion that a man had two brains, one in the usual place, the other considerably lower and vastly simpler in its interest and direction. As scientific propositions went, his theory was unproven, but he was convinced it was right. In all honesty, was there a shred of evidence to refute him?

"We're almost there," Persephone said. She bent down as the ceiling of the passage dropped. He followed, having to crouch almost double before the passage widened again, disgorging them into a large cavern.

At least he thought it was large by the way her voice

echoed once they entered. The circle of light showed very little, only vast shadows seeming to vanish into infinity.

"I think there used to be much more extensive passageways near here," she said, "but they've been closed off by rock falls."

"The traitor Deilos trapped my mother and father here twenty-five years ago," Gavin said. "He and his men set off explosions in an attempt to kill them."

She was silent for a long moment. He could not see her face, for she had withdrawn into the darkness beyond the circle of light. "Did he?" she said, finally. "I was not aware of that."

"Afterward, my uncle, the Vanax Atreus, ordered that further passages deemed to be dangerous also be sealed."

At the far end of the cavern another passage continued downward. The scent of roses vanished, subsumed beneath the acrid aroma of molten rock. Slowly Gavin realized he could make out the walls of the passage more clearly, thanks not to the lamp Persephone carried, but because of the red glow in front of them.

They stepped out of the passage and onto a narrow ledge above a seething cauldron of lava, thin black crusts forming and dissolving over pools of molten fire. It stretched as far as their eyes could see and bubbled up against the edges of the very ledge where they stood. The thought flashed through Gavin's mind that he had entered Hades, for surely no place could resemble more the underworld of legend.

"When I first found this place," Persephone said, "the lava flow was very small."

"When was that?"

"Ten years ago."

"You have been on this island that long?" He was shocked, estimating that she could have been no more than thirteen or fourteen then.

"I came here with my mother shortly after I was born."

He looked away from the inferno, watching the play of shadows across her face. "Where is your mother now?"

"She died years ago. I chose to stay on here."

"I cannot begin to imagine why you did that, or why no one in your family intervened to stop you."

"I told you—"

"—you have no family. Yes, so you said. Perhaps it would be best for us to discuss this later."

"Or not at all. In the time I have been coming here, I have seen the lava flow wax and wane. That seems to be a natural process, perhaps one that has been going on for a very long time."

"There are lava flows beneath the palace," he told her. "They follow the same cycle and have never done any harm."

Persephone nodded. "But this is different. About four months ago, the lava here began to spread and it has not stopped. It is now far higher than I have ever seen it. Soon, I think, it will overtake this very ledge and begin to seep into the cave." She paused, staring into the fiery hell. "Or perhaps it will do far worse. Perhaps what we see here is only a warning of the terrible forces building up within the earth, preparing to destroy us."

He did not deny that possibility or the hideous images it conjured. How could he, when he had lived night and day for months with the fear of just such a tragedy looming over them? Instead, he asked, "Have you noticed other changes?"

"New pockets of lava have appeared elsewhere on the island, but so far they remain small."

Gavin crouched down, staring at the lava. It was what he had seen elsewhere, not entirely surprising in a group of islands that owed their existence to a volcano. Even so, its recent increase was ominous.

Something was stirring in Akora, something he was trying desperately to understand. But so far, none of his instruments and equations, his observations and analysis could lead him to any but the most obvious conclusion: The home he loved and the people he cherished were about to experience a catastrophic disaster. Or they were not. He simply didn't know which was true, at least not yet.

"Have you spoken of this to anyone?" he asked as he stood.

"I thought to go to Ilius but I have hesitated, not

knowing how I would convince anyone there to believe me."

He, who was so vastly closer to the seat of power, faced the same problem, but he refrained from saying so as they began retracing their steps. They had gone only a very little distance when Persephone suddenly stumbled. She reached out a hand toward the wall of the passage and might have caught herself had not Gavin done it for her.

Holding her, he was vividly aware of the heat and softness of her skin, of her sudden intake of breath and the way—just for an instant—she leaned into him. Her head rested tantalizingly on the bare curve of his shoulder before she straightened abruptly.

"I'm fine," she insisted.

"But you almost fell." For good measure, he added, "With the lamp."

"You have the other. Normally I would be carrying it myself."

"Little good it would do if your fall broke it as well, or if you were hurt or unconscious."

"Nothing of that sort has ever happened to me."

"And therefore you presume it cannot?"

In the faint, dancing light of the small flame, he could see her face, pale and strained. Quietly she said, "This is my home. I am safe here." Looking directly at him, she added, "Or at least I was."

With that she turned on her heel and strode swiftly from the cave, leaving him to follow her.

They were back out in the sunlight before she deigned to speak to him again. Glancing at the surveying equipment he had left in front of the cave, Persephone asked, "What have you found to lead you to the same conclusion I have reached?"

He stared at her without answering. She was entirely outside his experience. The women of his family were strong-willed and high-spirited, but they were also kind, genuinely caring, and—truth be told—adept at making a man happy for having made them happy.

The women of his acquaintance outside his family ran the gamut from interesting to inspid, but they all had one thing in common: a sensible desire to keep a prince of Akora, who was also heir to an earldom, in a pleasant frame of mind. He hadn't appreciated that quite as much as he did just now.

Prickly Persephone was an altogether different matter—wary, defensive, and just this side of rude. Not to mention that she was the only woman who had ever shot an arrow at him.

"Your conclusion that the volcano is awakening?" He saw no reason to satisfy her curiosity at once and good reason not to do so. "The answer to that is lengthy and the hour grows late. I need to set up camp."

"You are staying the night?" Her surprise could not have been more evident, nor could her obvious reluctance.

In return, he said coolly, "I had a long row over from Phobos and I have no intention of making the return trip today. Besides, I still have many measurements to take."

Of course he did, and she was being singularly ungracious by suggesting that Gavin's presence was less than welcome. That part, at least, was not true, or not entirely, at any rate. It wasn't his fault that he made her feel—what? Confused, distracted, enticed, anxious? All that and more. She wasn't used to dealing with people, but even so, she should have been able to manage better. And perhaps she would have if he hadn't been so . . . everything.

None of which made it acceptable for her to behave like a shrew.

"I'm sorry," she said, sounding grudging even to her own ears. "It's just that visitors never come here."

He shrugged, but she could tell his displeasure did not linger. Perhaps he truly was, as he seemed, a man not likely to indulge anger for very long, at least not without a very good cause.

"I don't mean to intrude on you," he said. "I'll camp on the beach, but tomorrow I would appreciate it if you could show me more of the island."

"There are crabs on the beach." She spoke before she could think better of it.

"Crabs?"

"Small blue crabs with very sharp pincers. They come out at night and they have a tendency to bite."

He winced and as quickly smiled. "Thank you for the warning. Perhaps you could suggest somewhere more comfortable?"

She hesitated, knowing full well what she should not do.

Then she did it anyway.

Let my spirit soar like a child's, free and unhindered. Let me dance amid motes of light and sing of joy.

Thus one of Akora's great poets had written in a work she cherished, perhaps all the more so because she had never been such a child.

Yet standing there in front of the cave in the waning light of afternoon, looking at the man who had appeared so improbably in her world, her spirit dared to lighten and even to leap.

"You'd better come with me."

At her invitation, if it truly could be considered that, he raised a brow but mercifully said nothing. In silence, they made their way from the caves, up into the hills toward the center of the island. The climb was steep, but the view, when they got to the top, was wondrous. Toward the west, the sun was setting over the island of Leios. Already the eastern sky above Ilius showed a sprinkling of stars. A crescent moon was rising, sending a ribbon of silver across the waters of the Inland Sea.

"Magnificent," Gavin said softly. He had set down his canvas bag and poles, and stood with his hands on his hips, surveying this new domain.

Her domain, Persephone reminded herself. Her home, where she had lived alone since her mother's death more than ten years before and to which she had never invited another human being.

She was suddenly nervous. What if he thought it a poor or, worse yet, foolish place? She had built almost all of it herself, using the carpentry skills her mother had taught her, her mother having learned them from her own father before her life was blighted by shame and grief. A good deal of experimentation and learning from mistakes was also involved, but Persephone was proud of what she had accomplished. Even so, she did not delude herself, nothing he saw could possibly compare with the glories that were so routine a part of his own life.

Yet he was looking round with what gave every appearance of real interest and growing surprise.

"Is that a . . . tree house?" he asked, staring at the structure perched high in a sturdy chestnut tree that rose thirty feet above the floor of the clearing.

"It is; I like to sit up there on warm days. There's usually a nice breeze."

"How did you get the wood up there?"

"Gears, pulleys, and sturdy rope. It wasn't hard."

He looked at her closely. "You understand all that? How to rig gears and pulleys to make lifting easier?"

"Is such skill presumed to be beyond the ken of women?"

"I didn't say that," he replied patiently. "You might

want to pull in those bristles. You don't actually need them, at least not around me."

The reprimand, if it could even be called that, made her flush. Yet she was not willing to back down, at least not entirely.

"Do not think me ignorant," she said, "because I have lived almost all my life on this island. I have always had books."

"That's fine, but you can't learn everything from books."

"All the same, I have learned a great deal, especially about Akoran life. For instance, I know full well that women are supposed to merely serve while it is warriors who rule."

He stared at her for a long moment before he suddenly, completely, and unexpectedly burst out laughing. " 'Where warriors rule and women serve,' is that what you believe?"

She looked at him narrowly, trying to discern what amused him so. "How could I not? Isn't that the first and most important law of Akora?"

"I suppose you could say that, but you do know there's a second part to it?" When she did not respond, he said, " 'No man may ever harm a woman.' That's the first thing any boy learns once he's old enough to understand anything at all. He learns it from his father and grandfather and uncles, from his older brothers if he has them, from his teachers, from the leaders in warrior training, from everyone. And he sees it in practice all around him. How long do you think it took the women to point out that being required only to serve would be harmful?"

"I don't know," she said, her eyes locked on his. He appeared entirely serious as he described a reality completely apart from anything she had ever known.

"Our best estimate is about two days," he said, deadpan. "That was more than three thousand years ago. We're still trying to work it out."

"But there are men who harm women." She knew that only too well. He could not convince her otherwise.

"That is true," he said quietly, "but they are very few and far between. We deal harshly with such criminals."

"Do you?" She knew of one they had dealt with harshly, but that was for entirely different reasons.

"Did your books not mention that?"

They had, but she had paid scant heed to what she assumed were mere words, having no power in real life. Yet she had believed other things readily enough. Perhaps she should open her mind to the possibility that all was not as she thought.

Certainly this Atreides prince was not. He looked at her in a way that made her all too aware of herself as a woman. She felt at once threatened and enticed, which made no sense at all. He spoke to her readily, as to an equal, and that fit with nothing she thought she knew. He was intelligent and he smiled easily.

As for his appearance—

There was no point dwelling on that. No point at all.

"I suppose you're hungry," she said. She certainly was, but that was no surprise. Her life was active and her appetite correspondingly healthy. Besides, she liked to cook.

"Starved," he admitted. "I caught a couple of fish on Phobos yesterday and they weren't bad, but nothing I cook seems to have much flavor."

"You cook?" The very notion surprised her. Surely he had servants for that.

"My family believes people should be able to take care of their own basic needs. That includes cooking."

"But you aren't any good at it?"

"I didn't say that. I can fix it so whatever I'm eating isn't actually raw."

The corners of her mouth twitched. "That's a start."

"The trouble is, what I end up with is usually charred or dry or otherwise unappetizing."

"I'll see if I can improve on that," she said and headed for the small cooking shed at the far end of the clearing.

Gavin followed. He was frankly fascinated. What he saw all around him spoke of years of hard work, determination, and more than a little ingenuity. Looked at a certain way, the cluster of small huts, each apparently with its own purpose, the neat garden, and the tree house seemed like a rustic paradise. He had to remind himself that they were the abode of one person who lived entirely alone. A man who liked solitude to pursue his own interests, he nonetheless could not imagine such an existence.

She made soup from sea urchins. With the soup she served a flat bread cooked in a stone oven and made from grains that grew wild on the island.

"It's amazing what grows here," she said as they ate. "I think Deimatos must have been inhabited at some point, because there are so many plants that seem to have returned to the wild after being cultivated."

"How do you know that?" he asked, tasting the soup that proved unexpectedly good. Granted, he was hungry, but even so, she had a fine hand with seasonings.

"Because they need more tending than truly wild plants do. They are very susceptible to weeds, for example, and they do far better when they are fertilized with seaweed and the bones of fish."

"It's possible," he acceded. "I haven't studied this island's history except for geological events. However, I do know it was in Deilos's family for a very long time."

She stood up abruptly and took their bowls—halves of palm nutshells—back to the kitchen shed. Returning, she set before him an iron kettle brimming with delectable aromas.

"*Marinos,*" he said with amazement. The fish stew was as close to a national dish of Akora as existed. Every family had its own favorite recipe. There were annual competitions to determine which was the best, but it seemed that everyone had his favorites.

Persephone, it seemed, had produced a champion.

"When did you make this?" he asked as he lifted a spoonful of the liquid, swimming with bits of seafood, spices, and vegetables.

"I set it to simmer this morning and returned several times to add liquid."

"While watching me?"

Even in the light of the setting sun, he could see that she flushed. "You must understand why I was wary of you?"

"Having been so much alone, you would be wary of anyone."

"I am not a hermit."

"Truly? Yet you live here cut off from human society."

"I can have the benefits of that society, such as they are, whenever I please."

"And how often is that? How often do you leave your solitude?"

"Several times a year. I go to Ilius for supplies, and that isn't all. I visit Phobos and Tarbos. Indeed, I suspect I know those islands as well as anyone."

"Good for you. What about Leios?"

"I have been there as well. It is a pretty place."

"But you always go alone?"

"Is that so hard for you to understand? Is it so improbable for a woman to be self-sufficient?"

He was a fair man and so he considered that. What was it about her life that so shocked and even saddened him? She had what many, especially in the England he knew, would regard as a paradise. And she certainly did not seem unhappy. To the contrary, she appeared to him to be a woman who was content within herself.

And there was the problem. Something in him, something essentially male, bridled at the notion that she could be content. Without a man, without the child or children such a man could give her, without all the small, daily interactions between men and women that wove the fabric of life.

"Self-sufficiency is good," he said, but grudgingly, not quite believing it.

She ladled more *marinos* into his bowl, in the process affording him what he knew to be a completely unintended glimpse of her breasts beneath the tunic.

Wonderful. He was reverting to randy boy, a stage he had not particularly enjoyed back when he was rightly in it.

"But . . ." she prompted.

"But humans, men as well as women, are social creatures. We all need one another, at least to some extent."

"As I said, I do go to Ilius and elsewhere."

"You did say that. Why did your mother come here?"

She looked away, and for an instant, he saw the deep shadows stirring within her.

"She had her reasons."

"It is hard to imagine what they might have been."

"Then you are fortunate, Atreides prince, that life

has spared you knowledge of the sorrows that can come upon people."

"My life is privileged," he admitted, "but I am not ignorant of the difficulties people can face."

She shrugged and stood, rising gracefully with her long legs unfolding beneath her. "If you say so. I rose early and am weary. I bid you good night."

Gavin sat a little while longer by the fire. He watched the glowing embers and thought of the lava in the cave. Thought also of Persephone, legend and woman, the one captive in the underworld, the other—what? Free and content as she wished to appear? Or captive of another sort, here on this island scarred by old treachery and new danger?

She went into one of the little huts and emerged with what looked like a folded blanket. Without further word to him, she climbed to the tree house where, it seemed, she meant to sleep.

He stretched out on the ground and after a while took the blanket he had brought from the canvas bag. Wrapped in it, he lay with his arms folded behind his head, looking up at the stars. They were a glory, to be sure, but he was more aware of the earth beneath him, still holding the warmth of day. He was a man for the earth, he thought, able to appreciate the beauty of the heavens, but always drawn back to this, the land of his birth.

Eldest son, heir to the great earldom of Hawkforte, he had nonetheless been born on Akora, his princess mother choosing to bring him into the world here.

Always, he had felt a special kinship to this place that he could not, for all that he tried, manage to feel for Hawkforte itself.

He would have to develop such a kinship eventually, for his responsibilities lay in England. But his love was for Akora, never more than now, when it might be in such deadly danger.

Akora, set apart from the world, proud in its solitude and sovereignty.

Persephone, alone, prickly in her determination to remain so.

He drifted off on the bosom of the earth, woman and land entwining in his mind until at last and uneasily, he slept.

CHAPTER III

T HAT'S IT," GAVIN SAID. "JUST HOLD IT STEADY."
He took a sighting with the sextant, checked
it, and recorded the measurement before walking over
to join Persephone.

Morning had brought soft rain that ceased while
they were having breakfast. Since then, the day had
brightened as ever-widening swathes of blue appeared
between the clouds that were speeding off to the east.
A light breeze blew from the west, carrying with it the
scent of the vast ocean beyond Akora.

Taking the survey rod from her, he said, "That
agrees with what we've been seeing. Compared to the
survey done a hundred years ago, there are points all
over the island that are now slightly elevated."

She nodded but did not meet his eyes. All morning,
she had felt both shy of him and ridiculous for doing

so. He had haunted her dreams in ways she did not care to recall. She had woken from them several times with a sense of amazement—that she was not alone, that he was there, that all this was happening.

Her awareness of him was constant, encompassing even the smallest detail. He had shaved earlier, using a small mirror propped up in the cleft of a tree branch, soap, and a razor taken from his kit. Having never seen a man shave before, she had tried not to watch, but without much success. When he was done, she had a disconcerting urge to run her hands over his smooth, square jaw . . . down over his broad shoulders to his chest rippled with powerful muscles . . . his skin so taut and golden in the sun . . .

She wrenched her mind back from its wayward path. "That cannot be good." They walked farther along the small river where they were measuring. Gavin had chosen the area because it was where Persephone told him several of the new small lava pools had appeared. It was also almost in the precise center of Deimatos, where the land rose to its highest point.

"I wish we knew more about volcanoes," he said. "Knowledge of them is so limited. We have no idea why they exist and no good way to predict when one may erupt."

His frank admission surprised her, carrying as it did the recognition of the inadequacy of his own ability. Helping as best she could, she had been struck by his competency and his seriousness. The man might look as though he was best suited to hacking things to bits, but there was far more to him. Which made him all the more troubling to her.

"But we do know that the volcano here has erupted," she said, "even if it was more than three thousand years ago."

"That's true and it may be accurate to say that it will erupt again, but when will that be? Three thousand years from now or next week?"

She looked at him in alarm. "Next week? You think so soon?"

"I don't know and that's the problem. You don't tell three hundred-and-fifty thousand people that their world may be about to be blown apart unless you're damn sure you know what you're talking about."

"But if you wait too long to tell them—"

"Exactly. I need to be certain of what is happening, at least so far as that is possible. Is there anything else you can show me?"

She hesitated, caught between the urge to send him on his way as quickly as possible and the equally disturbing desire to continue in the company of the man who drew her so powerfully. She might prefer to be alone—she did still prefer that, didn't she?—but she could not forget that her own wishes were of small regard compared to the many lives that would be in danger, should the volcano really be about to explode.

"Yes, but it will be difficult to reach."

"Then we should not delay."

They crossed the island on foot, following the narrow paths Persephone had walked all her life. From the pleasant shade of the highland forest where she made her home, they climbed to a rocky plateau fragrant with the scents of wild grasses and flowers. Hawks soared above but did not trouble the herds of horned sheep that kept their distance yet showed no fear of the humans.

The day was warm and became warmer still. They stopped once to rest beside a small spring that bubbled up from the earth, then pressed on. By mid-afternoon, they stood on a ridge overlooking a black sand beach that gleamed like polished glass in the sun.

"I've never seen this much black sand in one place," Gavin said as he surveyed the beach. He raised a hand to shade his eyes. Persephone caught herself staring at him, yet again. A slight breeze blew up, flattening the back of his kilt. She swallowed hastily and started down the ridge toward the beach.

"What I want to show you is underwater," she said. "We will have to dive. Is that all right?"

Gavin followed her. She could not see him but she heard the amusement lacing his voice. "I'll manage."

She did not speak again until they reached the water's edge. It was her custom to swim naked, but that was out of the question now. She contented herself with removing her sandals and left her tunic on. "We will be going about fifty feet offshore, then about twenty feet down."

"How did you find this place?" he asked as he, too, removed his sandals and laid his sword on top of them. Contrary to his warning of the previous day, his kilt did not fall down.

Not disappointed—that would be absurd—she said, "I was looking for urchins. The sweetest among them are to be found here. They bring the best price in Ilius."

"I suppose there's no point telling you how dangerous it is to dive alone?"

She began wading into the water, but stopped to glance back at him. Standing in the surf, wearing only his kilt, he looked like the gods of old must have appeared in the imaginations of humans: supremely fit, noble and strong, possessed of a masculine beauty that delighted the eye and teased the heart. She was finding herself all too susceptible to his allure, thus sought refuge in gentle mockery.

"Don't worry, Atreides prince, I won't leave you."

The sea was almost flat, the water a deep shade of turquoise. She struck out, swimming steadily. Gavin caught up with her quickly. His strokes were smooth and strong. She sensed he was holding himself back to keep pace with her, but did not mind. They would be taxed soon enough when it came time to dive.

When she judged that they had reached the right spot, she stopped swimming and treaded water. "It is very important that you realize when you need to return to the surface for air. If you stay down too long, you will become light-headed and possibly disoriented."

"You know this from personal experience?"

"I know my limitations," she said pointedly. "I hope you do, too."

Without waiting for his response, she filled her lungs deeply and dove. The light faded behind her as she entered a twilight world. The water cooled rapidly, a further reminder that she could not tarry long. Beside her, Gavin nodded as she gestured downward. They passed a ledge of white stone before reaching the urchin beds. Though she was tempted to snatch a few of the spiny-shelled treasures, she refrained, and instead drew Gavin's attention to the thin swirls of smoke eddying from a fracture in the sea floor.

With her lungs rapidly emptying, she was about to return to the surface when she realized Gavin was heading farther down toward the fracture. Quickly she went after him and tried to grab hold of his leg to stop him, but he moved too swiftly. Well aware that her air was almost exhausted, but fearing that his was as well, she went after him.

To her great relief he did not go very far but did take a careful—and, she thought, far too long—look at the vents of steam rising from the floor of the Inland Sea. Only then did he somersault in the water and prepare to rise. Seeing her, he was clearly startled. With a quick, commanding gesture, he pointed upward, then waited until she rose ahead of him.

Scarcely did they break through to the surface than Gavin demanded, "What the hell were you doing?"

Gasping for air even as she flung water out of her eyes, she exclaimed, "What was *I* doing? What about you? I told you to be sure not to stay down too long."

"Then stayed too long yourself. I swear, Persephone, you try a man's patience!"

They were both treading water, glaring at each other. She opened her mouth, intending to berate him, but no words came out. She who had often secretly wished for someone to talk to was left speechless.

Not so Gavin. He wrapped a steely arm around her waist and struck out for shore, all the while keeping up a steady litany of purely masculine exasperation. "You think you can do everything for yourself, don't you? You don't need anyone or anything. You take appalling chances with your life and don't even seem to realize you're doing it. You've cut yourself off for reasons I can't begin to fathom and—"

His breathing, close against her, was smooth and even. He did not slow, but swam swiftly and steadily. She felt the coolness of his skin, the power rippling through his muscles, the brush of his legs against her own.

This was too much. She was not some helpless creature to be handled as he wished, lacking her own will. Angrily, she tried to twist away from him. "I don't need your help!"

"You think not? Fine!" Abruptly he released her.

Caught off guard, Persephone sank under the water. She came up sputtering, found him about to dive after her, and snarled, "Stay away from me."

Moments later, she stumbled onto the beach, her breathing labored, her heart pounding wildly. Panic ate at the edges of her mind. She had to escape, had to regain her solitude, had to . . .

. . . calm down and think with some semblance of reason instead of the treacherous mix of fear and desire that threatened to suffocate her.

He had only meant to help her.

In his own high-handed way, of course, but still . . . she could not hold him guilty of more than good intentions.

"Persephone . . ." He stood near her, rivulets of water running down his magnificent body, and spoke gently, with concern.

"I'm sorry—" She took a breath, fighting to steady her voice. "I was . . . unfair. I know you were only concerned. I'm just not used to that."

"Used to anyone being concerned about you?"

She nodded. "Despite what you think, I manage well enough by myself. I intend to keep right on doing so. Whether you understand that or not, it would be best if you accepted it."

"I understand more than you may realize."

"No, you do not. I have good and ample reason for living as I do."

"What reason?"

"I'm not going to explain it. It's not your affair."

Squeezing the hem of her tunic between her hands, she glanced at the sky. "We'd better start back. It will be dark before long."

They did so in silence, until they reached the place where they had rested on the way out. "I need to stop," Persephone said reluctantly. She sank down on the mossy ground and cupped her hands to drink.

Gavin followed. He stretched out, propped on his elbows, and looked at her. When she finished drinking, he asked, "How long have those vents we saw been there?"

Glad of something to speak of that did not involve her treacherous feelings, she said, "They first appeared a month ago. From what I saw today, they are growing larger."

"In the reading I've done, I came across mention of such vents in the vicinity of volcanoes. They are also associated with black sand beaches."

"Then an explosion, if it happens, could occur nearest to Deimatos?" she asked.

"That's possible. In such a case, it likely would trigger massive waves that would smash against the coasts."

Quietly she said, "Most people live along the coasts."

"They would have to be evacuated."

She turned her head, meeting his gaze. "Evacuate three hundred-and-fifty thousand people?"

A shadow moved across his face. She realized just then that he fully comprehended the enormity of what they might be facing. Even so, he responded calmly.

"A daunting task, I admit." Gavin stood and held out a hand to Persephone. Without thinking, she took it. His long, strong fingers wrapped around hers. His touch came without warning and sent a current of pleasure through her that almost made her gasp.

"Come back to Ilius with me, Persephone. Help me find out what's happening and, if necessary, convince others."

He couldn't be serious. She couldn't possibly do that. She had to pull away, get free of him, and she would the moment her brain convinced her body to move. Just then, the two didn't seem to be entirely connected. "You don't need me—"

"You're the only other person who's realized the danger we may be facing. I've been dealing alone with this for four months, living with it night and day. I need help."

"There are scientists . . . scholars . . ."

"Who know no more about volcanoes than I do. In all modesty, I've read everything in the palace libraries on the subject. I've put all I've learned into practical efforts, trying to make the theories fit what I see in front of me. There are times when I think it is coming together, but more times it seems as though the harder I try, the more confused everything becomes."

"Perhaps you are trying too hard."

"It has to be reasoned through."

"Certainly, but it also has to be—" She hesitated, unsure of how much she should say. If she were completely frank and open with him, he truly would think her mad and perhaps he would not be entirely wrong. She lived so differently from other people . . . thought so differently.

"It can be felt," she said finally. "If you let it."

"What do you mean, 'felt'?"

"Do you truly not know?" Perhaps he did not; perhaps she was the only one who did. Solitude heaped upon solitude, yet never truly alone precisely because of what she could feel.

Quietly she asked, "When you think of Akora, what do you feel?"

"Longing," he said promptly, "a yearning to be here. Or if I am here, then gladness, a sense of rightness."

She nodded, liking him suddenly, as opposed to just finding him all too alluring. "You belong on Akora."

"For the moment. Eventually my life must be in England."

"Why?"

His eyes—green shot through with gold, and fascinating in their own right—shuttered, concealing emotion she suspected he did not wish to share or perhaps even fully acknowledge. "Because I am my father's heir. The earldom of Hawkforte is very old and respected. We are called the Shield of England. One day I will have to take up that responsibility."

"Whether you wish it or not?" And he did not. She saw that clearly, felt it as though the power of his yearning communicated itself to her through his touch.

"Yes, whether I wish it or not. But for the moment, I am here, and I must try to do the best I can." His hand tightened on hers, not in the least painfully, but reminding her of his strength. "Persephone, if you don't come with me, what will you do, simply stay here and wait for whatever is going to happen? You know I can't allow that."

"Allow it?" She did try to pull free then, but he would not let her. Indeed, he prevented it in the most unfair way, drawing her closer until the warmth of his big, hard body enveloped her, his arm like steel at her back even as his eyes crinkled with humor.

"Best you know, I was raised to lead and to protect, bred for that as well, truth be told. I could no more stop doing that than I could stop breathing."

"And everyone else is just supposed to follow?" She spoke a good deal more tartly than she felt. Indeed, so close to him, held by him, she was in very real danger of melting.

Sun had kissed the thick lashes of his eyes, spiking them with gold. He had the look of a man who saw far and keenly, a hunter. A man who would not be denied.

"Not you," he said. "Walk beside me, not behind. Help me."

Somewhere on this earth there probably was a

woman who could resist this Atreides prince. All right, maybe not probably, maybe only *possibly*.

In any case, Persephone was not that woman.

She knew in the back of her mind what was happening. After all, she had read of such things. She was being seduced . . . by his smile, his voice, his touch, by the sense of being wanted, even needed. It was all very enticing.

And, as it happened, irresistible.

To be fair, she tried. She reminded herself that she had an acceptable life, one she herself controlled insofar as that was possible for anyone. She was—not happy—but surely she was content?

No, she was not, and in all honesty never had been. She existed uneasily with the past that had driven her to seek such isolation. Never had it occurred to her that she might hope for more. But now that hope beckoned, reached out and took her hand, summoned her to do good.

To just possibly wash away some measure of the shame and guilt that haunted all her days.

The man who stood before her, radiant and confident in the sun, could have been a troll and she would have had trouble refusing the chance he offered. But Gavin Hawkforte was a man to set a woman's blood racing. A dangerous man. She would do well to remember that.

"I will go with you," she said, even as she carefully and deliberately drew away from him.

CHAPTER IV

FROM THE MOMENT SHE MADE THE DECISION to go, impatience seized Persephone. She wanted to be away at once, but circumstances did not favor so swift a departure. They were still miles from her camp and night was coming on quickly. Morning would have to do, but it could not come soon enough.

A small sigh of relief escaped her when they finally reached the cluster of buildings near the shore. Left to her own devices, she would have gnawed a crust of bread, wrapped herself in a blanket, and drifted off to sleep staring at the stars.

But the presence of a guest—and a prince at that— summoned her to do better.

"Don't go to any trouble," Gavin said when she poked the cook fire back to life. "We're both tired."

She certainly was, but a glance over her shoulder

confirmed that he looked as though he could keep on hiking, swimming, diving, rescuing maidens, and all the rest for hours yet. Somewhere in all the many, many books she had read over the years, she had come across a description of the warrior training undergone by virtually all the men of Akora. Begun at about the age of nine, the training stressed fighting skills, of course, but it also built strength and stamina. Grudgingly, she had to acknowledge—if only to herself—that he surpassed her in both.

"I sleep better on a full stomach," she said, and continued poking up the fire until he came over, took the green stick she was using from her, and assumed the task himself.

With muttered thanks, Persephone went off to the small pond where she kept fish. The pond had begun as a natural feature of the landscape, but she had worked all of one spring to clean and deepen it, as well as to add a conduit to bring fresh water to it from the sea. Having fish stored meant she didn't have to depend on a daily catch in times of bad weather or on those rare occasions when she didn't feel entirely well.

She returned with a string of fat carp and proceeded to clean them, tossing the guts into the fire so that they would not tempt scavengers. Aware of Gavin watching her silently, she kept her attention on dinner. While the fish cooked, she blanched long beans picked the day before and quickly mixed dough for the flat bread that she then baked crisp and lightly browned on hot stones around the fire.

"The last thing I expected," Gavin said a little while later, "when I came here was to be so thoroughly spoiled." He was stretched out on his side near her, finishing off the remaining bits of the fish that, she had to admit, had turned out well. Why that should matter as much as it did she could not imagine. Still, she would not have been happy to make a poor meal.

The rounded curves of his shoulders and heavily muscled arms gleamed in the firelight. She tried not to look at him too much but found her eyes drawn back again and again. Too clearly she remembered what he had felt like against her in the water, his body hard and slick, at once alarming her and drawing her powerfully.

That would not do. She would be a fool to forget that he was one of *them,* an Atreides to the bone for all that he tried to be an Englishman. Why wasn't he in England then, doing English things? Drinking tea, perhaps? Riding to hounds, an appalling custom to be sure. What else did they do? Oh, yes, play cricket, a game she had tried to understand from yet another book but had ended up bewildered between balls, bats, bowlers, bouncers, and wickets.

"I cannot begin to imagine what you are thinking," he said with a bemused smile.

"Do you play cricket?"

"Good lord, no. I don't even understand cricket."

Before she could catch herself, Persephone laughed. "You're not being serious."

"I most certainly am. Now, my brother, he plays cricket and he's tried to explain it to me but I'm hopeless. All I can think the whole time he's talking about it is 'why?' "

Still smiling, she shook her head. "Why what?"

"Why would grown men do that? Spend hours—hell, days sometimes—knocking a ball around a field. I'm told it has to do with discipline, strategy, concentration, and I have no reason not to believe that is true. I just can't . . . *see* it."

She was caught despite herself, wanting to know more of this man. No, wanting to know everything. "What can you see?"

"The land . . . the water . . . how they interact with each other. How air moves over a field of grass and, given enough time, how it shapes the earth beneath." He leaned forward slightly, his face intent. "I think time has a great role to play. There are people who believe the world is only a few thousand years old—"

"Why do they believe that?"

"It has to do with the Bible. Have you read any of that?"

"Some, there are marvelous stories in it."

"Which is your favorite?"

Without hesitation, she said, "Samson and Delilah."

He winced. "I should have known, the hero unmanned through the wiles of a woman."

"Through her courage, she was defending her people."

"I suppose that's one way to look at it. At any rate, apparently if you work backward, adding up the ages of people mentioned in the Bible and the generations between them, it's possible to come up with a date for the age of the earth."

"A date you don't believe?"

"Well . . . it's only a few thousand years before our own history here on Akora begins. I find it hard to believe that people came out of the Garden of Eden, spread all over the world, and learned to sail ships, forge iron, and do all sorts of other things in so short a time."

"How old do you think the earth is, then?"

"Old . . . very old, at least compared to us. Every time I come back here, I feel that again." He sat up, resting both his palms against the earth as though anchoring himself. The fire was dying down, but she could still see him clearly. He was . . . perfect, in her eyes.

She closed them, shutting out the sight of him.

A moment passed before he said, "You're tired."

Persephone looked away, staring into the darkness that surrounded them. "It has been a long day."

"Go to bed, I'll take care of what's here."

She could have argued, insisted on doing it herself, but she was suddenly almost unbearably weary. Slowly, she stood. "The tide turns at midday."

He rose, looking at her. Sparks rose from the dying fire. "We'll talk in the morning."

She nodded and went, climbing slowly to her perch. It was only later, staring through the slates of her tree house at the sliver of the moon, that she wondered what there was left to talk about.

Y OU MAY NOT BE ABLE TO RETURN HERE," Gavin said. It was the hour after dawn. She had awakened to find him gone, and had known a small moment of panic before discovering the note he left scrawled on a bit of paper and pinned to the trunk of her tree.

"Taking a few more measurements," the note said.

He came back while she was still frowning over why he had not awakened her to go with him. Before she could ask, he set the bag with his tools and the poles aside, and came over to her.

He spoke gently, and as he did, his hand brushed her arm lightly in a gesture she supposed was meant to be soothing, but was anything but. Little prickles of energy danced along her arm everywhere he touched and made it very hard to listen to what he said.

"May not—" she repeated.

"Return here. If our concerns about what may happen prove correct, it is possible that this place will be greatly changed, perhaps even destroyed."

"I don't think that is likely." In fact, she had not thought of it at all, yet surely it should have occurred to her. The volcano was active in and around Deimatos. If it exploded, the island would take the full fury of the blast and everything that followed.

"Persephone, I understand this has been your home—"

"All my life or at least almost all. I cannot remember anywhere else."

"Then you must think about what you want to take from here."

How could she? Where would she begin? Her gaze darted around the clearing and the half dozen little buildings in it. So very little really, but her own. "I cannot—"

"You wish to take only memories?"

"I wish for none of this to be happening." Stark truth, for all that it sounded like the yearning of a child.

"I'm sorry." He looked as though he meant it.

She shrugged, struggling for dignity. "It is hardly your fault. I suppose I should make some preparations."

But what preparations, exactly, or how even to begin eluded her. While Gavin went off again to continue his measurements, she walked around the encampment, trying to decide what to do.

Her books, of course, she had to take those, as well as what clothes she possessed. She wasn't about to leave her bow and arrows, or her tools, her precious stock of nails, her pots. It would be foolish to risk losing them when surely she would be returning, if only to start over.

Or would she? The damage done by a volcano would take years, perhaps decades to lessen. She might have to make a new life for herself elsewhere.

Or she might have to do so under any circumstances. There was nothing to say that, having discovered her presence on Deimatos, the Atreides would allow her to remain.

So many possibilities and problems crowded into her mind, demanding attention. She pushed them aside, well aware that doing otherwise would waste precious time. What would be, would be, and she would just have to manage. Quickly, she began to gather up her belongings, collecting them in a small heap at the center of the camp. Despite her best resolve, she did pause here and there, struck by the memories contained within even the simplest things.

The ax she had traded for in Ilius was the third such she had owned. Its metal head was badly nicked from the tough work of cutting down trees to build her shelters. She ran a thumb over the edge pensively, thinking there were only so many times the same metal could be sharpened. Eventually, it was ground down to nothing. Everything had its end.

Here was a book of poems her mother had read to her over and over. A favorite of theirs, which Persephone had not opened in years. She did so now and breathed in deeply, smelling the fragrance of the pages that seemed, for just a moment, to intermingle with the lavender her mother had so favored.

Tears blurred her eyes. She shut the book and put it down, but an instant later she took it up again and opened it once more.

Rangle, dangle, fangle
So do sly words mangle
That which we would say
All the livelong day.

A silly poem, but it had made her mother laugh, all too rare an occurrence. Carefully, she put the small volume aside and took another, glancing at its spine, where the words were carefully embossed: *A Treatise on the Nature of Geography.* The maps inside it were decent enough but very small. Her mother had remedied the problem by drawing maps in the sand, then helping her outline rivers, mountains, and coasts with bits of shells and small stones. They worked on the maps for weeks until Persephone could find Paris as easily as Deimatos, the latter no more than a tiny white pebble set in the Inland Sea of Akora, which itself seemed absurdly small compared to the vast world.

Especially considering that it was the whole world in so many ways, or at least so much of the world as she had ever known.

She had no wish to know more. The thought of leaving Akora was utterly beyond her. Leaving Deimatos, with the possibility of never returning, was difficult enough.

It became more so when, beneath a folded cloak, she found the small wooden box that had belonged to her mother. Decorated with carved flowers and still bearing the vestiges of the paint that had covered it, the box held the remnants of a vanished life.

Cautiously, Persephone glanced round for any sign that Gavin might be returning. She neither saw nor heard anything that would indicate that. Reassured, she sat down cross-legged on the sun-warmed sand and slowly opened the box.

Its contents were well known to her but, as with the book, she had not looked at them in a very long time. Sunlight fell on the delicate bracelet, formed by strands of gold filigree laced through tiny seed pearls. The wire was so thin that from certain angles the pearls would appear suspended in air around the wearer's wrist.

On one of the very rare occasions when her mother spoke of her life before Deimatos, she told Persephone that the bracelet had been a gift to her on her sixteenth birthday. A gift given to a valued daughter with the promise of her life still before her, not to the shamed woman who brought dishonor to her house. She had never seen her mother wear the bracelet and had never done more than lightly touch it herself. Reluctant to do even that, she closed the box and added it to the pile.

What else . . . ? Slowly, she turned, looking in all directions. The cook shed . . . she had labored so long to construct the sturdy clay oven, but it could not be moved. The snug little hut where she slept on the few chilly days that swept over Akora in the winter. She had decorated the walls fancifully with carvings and paintings that amused her. Again, none of that could be taken. The racks where she dried fish—too large and cumbersome to save. The loom where she experimented with weaving, something she was convinced she would never be any good at. There definitely was no point trying to save that.

The fish! She couldn't leave them in the pond, where they would be trapped. The wooden sluice gate she had fitted into place was hard to move. She had to straddle both sides of the conduit and tug with all her strength before it finally began to inch up. Thinking of how much effort it had taken to construct the pond and conduit, as well as fill it, she had almost reconsidered. But while she thought it acceptable to eat fish, she was not about to let any of them die needlessly. Better they return to the sea.

And so they could, once the sluice gate was out. Nothing remained to impede their escape . . . except the tide itself, which had not yet turned. The fish, swimming contentedly in circles, showed no inclination to go anywhere. Fine, let them wait. The tide would change and eventually their tiny little fish brains would realize it.

Tiny little brains reminded her of the chickens she kept. Her shoulders sagged. The birds could fly, after a fashion, but not very well and certainly not enough to get clear of an island that might be about to explode. They would have to be rounded up and transported. The crates she used to take sea urchins to market in Ilius would do, but first she had to catch the chickens.

Half an hour later, sweating and panting, Persephone came to a stark conclusion: a chicken destined to be butchered, plucked, and cooked for dinner would walk along pecking at the ground, cheerfully oblivious of the fate about to befall it, whereas a chicken who was the object of a rescue effort would run around frantically, zigzagging in every direction and doing its level best to avoid its would-be protector.

A speckled hen, riffling her brown-and-red plumage, darted right between Persephone's hands and raced off, squawking fiercely. Three white-and-brown pullets dashed around her feet. Trying to avoid them, she lost her balance and fell, landing ignominiously on her bottom.

"Damn it!"

The sound of robust male laughter coming from far too near didn't help matters at all.

"Something wrong?" Gavin inquired pleasantly as he strode into the clearing.

She stood, resisting the urge to rub the offended portion of her anatomy, and swallowed a snarl. "What could possibly be wrong? I love running after incredibly dumb animals who don't have enough sense to be rescued."

"Is that what you're trying to do, rescue them?"

"I can't leave them here. They won't be able to get away."

Now that she said it out loud, her plan sounded foolish. After all, she had intended to eat most of the chickens eventually. To her relief, not to say surprise, Gavin merely nodded. "Do you have a net?"

She did and mentally kicked herself for not thinking of it. Once fetched, the net proved useful. They had rounded up half the chickens, when Persephone froze suddenly. Off to the side of the clearing, among the underbrush beneath the trees, she saw movement. Looking more closely, she sucked her breath in hard.

Staying very still and keeping her voice low, she said, "Gavin . . ."

"What?"

"Don't move. There's a boar."

She hated boars, especially the males. The females were only trouble if they were disturbed with a litter, but the males were always threatening. Equipped with razor-sharp tusks and nasty temperaments, they were far and away the most dangerous animals on Deimatos. She had tangled with them a time or two and didn't relish doing it again. Nor did it escape her notice that no such animal had ever come so close to her encampment. This one, with a vicious gleam in his eyes, must be especially bold, or perhaps events on the island were beginning to disturb the natural habitats of animals. Whatever the cause, the boar had to be dealt with quickly.

Her bow and arrows were on the other side of the clearing, far out of reach. She didn't even have a knife at her waist and the spears she used on occasion were stacked neatly near the cooking shed.

The boar's thick, bristly coat was raised in a ridge down its spine, signaling its intent to attack. To confirm matters, it pawed the ground with hooves capable of smashing a grown man's—or woman's—skull.

The chickens redoubled their frantic squawking. Persephone gauged the distance to the spears. She had a strong arm and a good aim—if she could get to one in time.

"Stay where you are."

She turned her head slightly, startled to realize that Gavin had moved closer without her, or apparently the boar, being aware of it. "Get behind me," he ordered.

That it was an order was beyond doubt. He spoke with the authority of a man long accustomed to being obeyed. The boar wasn't the only one bristling.

She was not a fool; the situation was perilous and she would be glad of help dealing with it. But she wasn't about to hide behind him and let him face the danger alone.

"If I can get to a spear—" she began.

"You're twenty feet from them across this clearing. He'll be on you before you get halfway."

"Look at his back. He's going to attack, whatever we do."

Gavin nodded. His hand went to the hilt of his

sword. Quietly, never taking his eyes from the boar, he said, "I'm counting on it. Now do as I say and get behind me." She might have argued further—she really didn't know at that point—but he added, "The longer you delay, the more danger you put us both in."

Certain she would regret it, Persephone stepped behind him.

The moment she did so, Gavin drew his sword. Before her startled eyes, he pulled his arm back, took aim, and hurled the sword point-first directly at the boar. He was thirty feet from his target, a difficult hit with a spear or knife. With a sword, it was almost unimaginable.

The animal turned an instant before the blade struck, taking the blow not in the throat where it had been aimed but in the side. Even so, it was an astonishing feat. An enraged shriek split the air as the boar charged directly at Gavin, launching itself at him. All four hooves lashed out, landing blows on his chest as the tusks snapped inches from his face. Fully expecting the assault, he was prepared for it. Grasping the animal's neck in one hand, he took hold of the sword with the other in order to pull it out. But the blade was buried deep and the boar fought with fury.

Persephone did not wait. She dashed across the clearing, grabbed a spear, and raced back. Gavin and the boar were locked in combat. Between man and animal there was no space at all. The slightest miscalculation would mean disaster. Without hesitation, she balanced the shaft in her hand, took aim, and plunged the spear directly into the heart of the boar. It gave one last piercing scream and went limp, falling onto the ground.

A moment passed, long enough for Persephone to realize that she was splattered with blood, as was Gavin. But the boar was dead and they were both blessedly, amazingly alive.

Her heart still pounding, she took a deep breath and then another. The light in the clearing seemed brighter somehow, and she was vividly aware of the scents of sea and land mingling on the light breeze. While the nearness of death yet lingered, the most commonplace aspects of life were revealed for what they truly were, small and perfect miracles.

"I never saw anyone use a sword like that," she said, unable to conceal her admiration. It had been a daring move and deserved praise.

"With hindsight, I should have let him get closer before striking."

That had occurred to her, and since he had brought it up . . . "Why didn't you?"

He shot her a quizzical look. "Closer to me meant closer to you."

"Oh . . ." He had put himself at even greater risk to try to afford her maximum protection. It was many years since anyone had taken care of her like that. She was not entirely sure how to respond and felt awkward doing so. Surely, anything she said would be inadequate. ". . . thank you."

"You're welcome." And that, it seemed, was that. He drew his sword from the boar, then bent down and wiped it clean on the grass.

She did the same with the spear, watching him as she did so out of the corner of her eye. He moved with such grace, every part of his body in harmony with the rest, his chest and back bare, gleaming in the sunlight, his legs beneath the short tunic powerfully muscled. When he rose, returning the sword to its scabbard, she forgot herself and stared at him openly.

"Something wrong?" he asked. "You're not hurt, are you?"

"No, of course not."

"Good. Where did you learn to handle a spear like that?" Before she could answer, he said, "And don't tell me you learned it from a book."

"Actually, I did, or at least I picked up the basics that way. The rest was trial and error." Much trial and much error, but she saw no reason to dwell on it. It had occurred to her that perhaps he was uncomfortable that she, not he, had finished off the boar.

But instead of voicing any hint of that, he said, "I'm beginning to understand how you have managed so well here. You have both sense and courage."

Had he told her she was the most breathtakingly beautiful woman on earth, Persephone would not have been more pleased.

All right, maybe just a little more.

As it was, her cheeks flushed. "You were right, though; I wouldn't have reached the spears in time without what you did."

He nodded. "We work well together."

She was mulling that over when Gavin glanced down at the boar. "It's a shame we have to leave here."

"Why is that?"

"Roast boar is excellent."

"You know how to prepare roast boar?"

He grinned. "I know how to *eat* roast boar." And with that, he scooped up a chicken, tucked it under his arm, and went after another.

CHAPTER V

I T WAS FINE THAT HER BOAT WAS BIGGER THAN his. That his had to be towed behind hers. In the overall scheme of things, it made no difference. Only a small-minded man would think otherwise. What mattered was that they got where they were going, not how. Even so—

"Where did you get this boat?" Gavin asked. He estimated it to be twenty feet stern to bow, single-masted, not Akoran but still well rigged, with tight, fluid lines that suggested the keel was laid in an Irish or possibly American shipyard. A good vessel, trustworthy in most seas.

Persephone checked the sail with practiced skill and glanced at him over her shoulder. The wind was picking up, and the water skimmed beneath them. Soon Deimatos would fade from sight.

"I found it about two years ago, run aground after a bad blow."

He nodded, unsurprised. Such was a common occurrence on Akora, where powerful storms racing across the Atlantic frequently caught hapless sailors, splintering them against the sheer cliffs that faced the ocean or, for those who still had a chance at life, hurtling them through the narrow straits that led to the Inland Sea.

"Do you know if there were survivors?"

"There were two men dead on board. They had lashed themselves to the mast but drowned all the same, probably as the boat was swamped. There was no sign of anyone else, although I did find books with the name of their owner written in them. They belonged to a man named Liam Campbell. Perhaps he was one of those who died." She spoke matter-of-factly, but the trauma of those deaths showed in the sudden bleakness in her eyes.

"Ironically enough," she added, "the boat itself was only a little damaged. I was able to repair it, and since I'd been sailing almost all my life, learning to handle it wasn't a problem."

So she had recovered a grounded vessel, buried the dead on board, repaired the damage, refloated the boat, and then learned to sail it quite competently.

And she had done all that alone. Moreover, she didn't seem to think anything particular of it.

"Your accomplishments are impressive," Gavin said.

She looked at him questioningly, as though suspecting that he was mocking her.

"I mean it, Persephone. I don't know anyone who's managed under the conditions you have, much less done so well."

After a moment, she murmured something that could have been "thank you" and gave her attention to the rudder.

Gavin took his turn at the sails and later at the rudder as she went below to fix a meal. They ate toward twilight and lingered on deck, watching the moonrise. The last of the clouds were gone, leaving an unimpeded view of the heavens.

He watched a meteorite flash across the sky, followed shortly by another. "Do you remember," he asked, "about eight years ago, there was an extraordinary meteor shower visible from Akora?"

"I do remember that. It was magnificent."

"Did you watch it with your mother?"

Persephone was silent for a long moment before she replied. "My mother died about six months before then."

Stretched out on his back on the deck, he turned slightly to look at her. She was seated on the bench beside the rudder, her knees drawn up to her chest and her free hand wrapped around them.

Her pensive mood matched his own and caused him to ask, "Why did your mother go to Deimatos? What made her pick that of all places to live?"

"She did not wish the company of others."

The night wind riffled the stray wisps of hair that

had blown free of her tight braids. She did not look at him, but kept her chin resting on her knees.

"That much is obvious, but why not?"

"She had reasons . . . personal reasons."

By which he concluded they would not be discussed. Prickly Persephone was not about to reveal her secrets.

But later still, when she slept, wrapped in a blanket in the bow while he steered them through the moon-bright night, he wondered what lay behind the strange course of her life.

And resolved that before very long, he would know what she was so determined to conceal.

THE ROYAL CITY OF ILIUS APPEARED IN THE MORN-ing, rising above the harbor, its tiers of houses in vibrant colors climbing ever higher until they reached the vast plateau of the sheared-off hill where the palace stood, so immense as to seem almost a city in its own right.

Persephone stood at the railing as Gavin brought the boat in. She tensed a little, anticipating the small surge of panic she always felt at coming from her isolation into the bustling capital of Akora, but, oddly, this time the panic was not there. Or perhaps not so oddly. She was well and thoroughly distracted, watching the man at the helm who moved with such strength and grace.

The muscles of his broad back rippled as he lowered

the sail. Sunlight gleamed off the thick mane of his hair, turning the dark blond strands to shards of gold. He turned suddenly and, catching her watching him, grinned.

She looked away, but not in time to stop a blush from staining her cheeks. The tide brought them the rest of the way in. Soon she felt the slight jolt of the boat settling beside the dock.

Without waiting for Gavin, she scrambled up and tied the line, securing the boat. He followed after drawing his own boat closer and fastening it next to hers. When she did not move, he asked, "Ready to go?"

She wasn't, but that made no difference. Picking up the small bag of belongings she had brought along, she walked with him into the city.

It was mid-morning and the streets were crowded. Young boys pushed handcarts while men and women maneuvered wagons along the busy roads. The occasional chariot passed, pulled by sleek, taut-muscled horses who tossed their manes and whinnied with impatience at their necessarily slow pace.

Tantalizing aromas wafted from the shops offering fruits, cheeses, breads, spices, meats, fish, and all the plentiful produce of Akora's fields, orchards, and pastures. Busy as they were, the city dwellers had time to stop at the roadside cafes for a cup of strong black coffee, a honey-dipped pastry, and, most popular of all, conversation.

Gavin was recognized and greeted all along the way.

He responded cordially when invited to refresh himself, but kept going. Vividly aware of the curious looks coming her way, Persephone was grateful for that. Always before, on her infrequent visits to Ilius, she had walked its streets anonymously. Only a tiny handful of people there knew her at all, and they had no particular reason to take notice of her. Or at least they hadn't. In the company of the Atreides prince, everything was different.

She was relieved when they came at last to the top of the hill and the palace straddling it. But that relief faded fast as they passed between the two immense stone lionesses, each easily the height of a half dozen men standing foot to shoulder, that guarded the entrance to the palace. Beyond was the vast courtyard, so large it was said the entire population of Akora could gather there.

The courtyard was framed on three sides by the palace. Columns in brilliant red, yellow, and orange rose three stories to a blue-tiled roof. The outer walls were a bright white except where they were decorated with geometric patterns. Beneath the eaves of the roof, carved stone horns jutted out. Broad stairs led upward to immense double doors that stood open.

"This way," Gavin said and led her away from the main entrance, down the broad colonnade to a stone staircase leading to a separate wing.

"Where are we going?" she asked.

"To the family quarters. You'll be comfortable there."

She would be comfortable? In the private apartments of the Atreides royals? Oh, certainly, she could see herself fitting right in.

"I can sleep on the boat."

He glanced at her but kept right on walking. She thought he gave a little shake of his head but couldn't be sure.

They came to a long hallway lined with carved doors set at broad intervals. One of them was thrown open. A slender woman who appeared to be in her sixties emerged. She wore an elegant tunic dyed the hue of goldenrod. Her white hair was arranged in a single braid down her back.

"Sida," Gavin said with a smile. "Not tidying up again, I hope."

The woman laughed, threw her arms around him, and gave him a warm hug. She was tiny compared to Gavin, but that didn't stop her from admonishing him.

"Your quarters are a mess, Prince, papers strewn here and there. I thought perhaps a wind devil had blown in through the window and upturned everything, but then I realized it was just the way you had left it."

"I can find everything in that 'mess,' Sida. The last time you tidied, I was lost for a week." He spoke gently and with good humor.

"Hmm, as to that, I merely brought in some clean laundry." Her razor-keen gaze shifted. "And who would this be, lord?"

"Persephone, who will be staying with us for a while. Persephone, this is Sida, who actually runs the palace. There are others here who think they do, but that's only because she lets them."

Cautiously, Persephone inclined her head. "I am pleased to meet you, lady."

"And you." Glancing at the small bag Persephone held, Sida asked, "Is that all you've brought with you?"

"Yes, it is."

"Very well, I'll put it inside."

She was reaching for the bag when Gavin said, "Persephone will be in the guest quarters, Sida."

The older woman's eyebrows rose but she said only, "As you wish, lord." Her look said far more.

"I'm afraid we've disappointed her," Gavin said as he opened the door to his own apartments and stood aside for Persephone to enter.

"My cousin, Amelia, got married a few weeks ago."

"I see . . ." Though she did not, not truly. Unless he really meant that Sida thought he should be married and that she, Persephone, ought to be a likely candidate. But surely that was impossible. "Who did she marry?"

"An American named Niels Wolfson. I like him; he seems to be a good man. They're in America now on their honeymoon."

She heard him, but only just, for most of her attention was taken up scanning the room. It was elegantly if sparsely furnished, with wide windows that looked out toward the harbor. There were a great many papers and books scattered over a broad table. What looked like scientific instruments were also in evidence, on the table and on shelves nearby. At the far end of the room was a large bed, and through an open door she could see a bathing chamber.

"This is what I wanted to show you," Gavin said, going over to the table. He drew out a small leather-bound volume. "It's a copy of the survey done in the last century. The person who did the survey, a woman named Amarensis—"

"A woman?"

"Did you presume it was a man? You shouldn't do that, you know. It is right and just that men use their greater strength to protect women, but that aside, women can do most anything a man can do."

A long moment passed. Finally, she said, "You are . . . teasing me?"

"No, I'm not. I meant exactly what I said. At any rate, Amarensis refers in her survey to a much earlier work. She used it as I'm using the survey she did, for comparison. The problem is, I haven't been able to find the work to which she refers."

"But surely it is in the palace library?"

"It should be, but there's no sign of it. Perhaps you could help me look for it again tomorrow. I'd also like to show you the lava flows beneath the palace."

"Yes, all right—"

"Good. Have dinner with me."

The sudden invitation—or directive—startled her. "What?"

"Dinner. You have to eat and I thought you might enjoy someone else's cooking. Not mine, of course, but we do have excellent cooks here."

"I'm sure you do." She answered without thought, her mind whirling. They had eaten together on Deimatos and on the boat. What difference here? Yet there was a difference in his own world, where he commanded such affection and respect. Where the stark reality of all that separated them could not be avoided.

"Let me show you to your quarters," he said gently, as though he had some inkling of her thoughts.

The room he took her to was at the far end of the family wing. He opened the door to a bright and spacious chamber, bathed in the late-afternoon light streaming through the windows. The walls were painted with murals depicting undersea gardens and the creatures inhabiting them. The furniture was simple but elegant—a bench and table along one wall, a bed almost as large as Gavin's own on the other side of the room, with several chairs and a couch in between. The floor was wood parquet, light and dark wood laid in geometric patterns similar to those on the walls of the palace. Everywhere she looked was grace and ease.

"I hope you will be comfortable," Gavin said.

She assured him that she would be, then waited, tense and poised as though for flight, until he left, striding away with a quick, flashing smile. "Dinner at eight."

"There is no clock." She knew of such things though she had never had need of one.

"Sida will tell you."

And he was gone, leaving her to wonder what he meant. She found out quickly enough when the door opened again to admit the woman she had met earlier, only this time bearing an armload of garments and a no-nonsense air.

They greeted each other warily before Sida got down to business.

"What sort of name is Persephone?" she asked with deceptive mildness.

"My own."

So curt an answer drew a frown in response and another question. "Who are your people?"

"Did Prince Gavin tell you to ask me that?"

"Of course not. The prince asks his own questions, as you should know." She set the garments down on a nearby bench and surveyed Persephone. "Let me see your hair."

"It is here on my head."

"I meant, let it down that I may see what is needed."

"Nothing is needed. It is hair, attached to my scalp."

"You cannot be so ignorant." When this brought no response, Sida appeared to reconsider that possibility. She looked Persephone up and down. "Why do you dress as a man?"

"This tunic is easier to move about in, and more comfortable."

"Take it off."

"*What?*"

"Take it off. For pity's sake, do not tell me you refuse to bathe?"

"Of course I will bathe. I do not require your assistance."

"As you wish, but make a good job of it. There are soaps and lotions by the tub."

"I will manage, thank you."

"When you have done, I will see to that hair."

"I told you—"

"And I tell you that you will be pleased with the results."

Persephone thought that the far side of unlikely, but she was glad to escape to the bath. The room was large, outfitted with a tub in the shape of a scalloped shell, a matching sink, and a tiled recess with a drain at the bottom and a gilded dolphin spout at the top. She chose the tub, turning the valves carefully to fill it. On Deimatos, she had to make do with the mineral spring not far from her camp. This was . . . not necessarily better . . . but different. And pleasant, as she discovered after she stripped off her tunic and stepped into the steaming water. On impulse, she took up one of the glass vials beside the tub, unstoppered it, and sniffed.

Jasmine, but more potent than any she had ever smelled, as though the very essence of the plant had been captured in a bottle. She poured a little into the water, watching as the iridescent oil spread out all around her. Lying back against the rim of the tub, she closed her eyes and let her thoughts drift.

Perhaps this was more than just different. Perhaps it was more than merely pleasant. The truth was that she had never known such luxury, had never even dreamt of it. Such things simply were not for her. Until now.

She opened one eye, then the other, and peered at the array of bottles within arm's reach. Removing one stopper after another, she discovered other scented oils and something else—a liquid soap, she thought.

Soap was among the very few things she had to acquire, trading for it with the sea urchins she dove deep to find. In her experience, soap was plain and serviceable. This felt like liquid silk, a fabric she had felt only once at a stall in Ilius, the sensation lingering in memory.

Quickly, before she could think better of it, she unbound her hair, dunked under the water, and rubbed the soap into the wet strands. When that was done, she washed her whole body, reveling in the sensation.

The water was beginning to cool before she rinsed off and emerged, toweling herself dry with a wide sheet of linen she found on a rack. Returning to the main room, she discovered Sida waiting for her.

"You were in there long enough. I hope you made good use of it."

"Well enough. Where is the bag I brought?"

"In the chest over there. But if you're thinking of wearing another of those atrocious tunics, I have something better." With a flourish, she stood and spread a garment over her arm.

It was another tunic, Persephone saw, but intended for a woman, being much longer and of far thinner material than her own serviceable garments. It was white, but a white such as she had never seen, seeming to glow from within. A sudden rush of yearning swept through her. To wear such a thing. To dine with the man who fascinated her. To pretend just for some little time that she was an ordinary woman, free to laugh and—dare she even think it?—to love.

Sida smiled gently. "Now let us see what we can do with that hair of yours."

CHAPTER VI

AN HOUR LATER, GAVIN PACED IN THE HALL
outside his apartment. He had bathed,
shaved, and donned a forest-green tunic embroidered
at the hem with gold. The day was waning, and softly
slanted light filled the hall. Off in the distance, he
could hear the faint sounds of people preparing for
evening. Shops were being closed, horses stabled, children rounded up.

These days even the most ordinary places or events
had the sharp, keen edge of impermanence. Gavin
knew too well that here, where the past was so carefully
nurtured and protected, everything he saw, everything
he touched, might be on the verge of slipping away
into mere memory.

It did not do for a man to think such thoughts too
long or too deeply. He let them go, turning his attention

to the door at the far end of the hall. He was staring at it, willing it to open, when a woman stepped out.

Persephone . . . yet not. This was not the huntress who winged an arrow past him and took him into the depths of a fiery hell. Who cooked like a dream, looked at him with longing, and prickled with pride.

This was an Akoran woman, lovely to behold. She wore a white tunic that shimmered and floated around her as she came toward him. She walked with her head high, not flinching from his gaze, but her shoulders were stiff and her hands were curled so tightly that her nails must be digging into her skin.

Her hair was released from its customary tight coil of braids, to flow down her back like a ribbon of gleaming silk. The tunic emphasized the high fullness of her breasts and her small waist before skimming over tantalizingly rounded hips and sleek thighs. As she came closer, he saw that her cheeks were flushed.

He strode down the hall with quick strides and met her more than halfway. "You look lovely."

When she did not respond at once but only continued to look at him, he took both her hands in his, gently uncurling her fingers. "Truly, Persephone, you do."

She took a long, shuddering breath. "I feel ridiculous."

His surprise was genuine. "Why?"

"I have never worn garments like this. They feel as though they aren't even there."

Gavin fought a smile. "I assure you they are. Your modesty is well protected."

"That's what Sida said, or words to that effect. She did something to my hair." She fingered a strand uneasily.

"It, too, looks lovely."

"Yes . . . well, thank you. You mentioned dinner?"

Understanding that she wished to change the subject, he nodded and moved toward the stairs. "How well do you know the palace?"

"Scarcely at all. I have been to the library here but really nowhere else."

"Then there is much for you to discover, starting with the roof." With a hand on her elbow, he guided her outside and around a corner, to an exterior staircase. As they emerged onto the vast expanse covering the many acres of the palace, Persephone looked around in amazement.

"I had no idea all this was up here."

"Most visitors don't." Gavin gestured to the paths that cut between fragrant gardens of herbs and flowers, many set with benches and fountains that splashed softly in the waning sun. "The palace itself can be difficult to navigate, with its thousands of rooms and corridors, so people started using the roof as a shortcut. That was centuries ago and over time they also found it a pleasant place to get away from the crowds."

Persephone nodded. "It's another world up here."

"One with many surprises. See there?" He indicated

a round white stone building with a roof that looked as though it had been cleaved in two.

"What is that?"

"The observatory. Akora's astronomers have charted the stars from this roof as long as there has been a palace. Our first telescope arrived two hundred years ago, brought from England. In short order, we learned to grind lenses and we've been making our own telescopes ever since. The latest one was finished about a decade ago and is in use now."

Even as they watched, a group of men and women garbed in dark blue robes appeared on the roof and walked toward the observatory.

Night was gathering, the first faint stars visible toward the east. The moon was a pale crescent brightening steadily as the last glory of the setting sun slowly vanished.

In a distant corner of the roof, well away from the observatory, torches flared. Gavin and Persephone walked toward them, coming at length to a garden framed in fragrant bushes heavy with small white bayberries. Within were beds of night-blooming white jasmine and the tall white lilies for which Akora was renowned.

"One of my many times great-grandmothers designed this garden," Gavin said. "She intended for it to be seen best in moonlight."

" 'Ill met by moonlight,' " Persephone said softly, the words coming from her without thought. There was nothing ill about the garden or being in it with Gavin, but the circumstances that had brought them together might prove dire indeed.

Gavin raised a brow. "Shakespeare?"

"His *A Midsummer Night's Dream*."

"You said something about always having books?"

"My mother brought sackfuls of them to Deimatos when she decided to live there. They were her great consolation. When I exhausted them, I found the library here."

"You borrow books?"

"Many, but I always bring them back . . . mostly." She caught a bloom of jasmine in her palm, holding it tenderly before releasing it. "I keep them for months, but I take very good care of them and I never borrow anything that does not have many, many copies."

"Did you know there are more than half-a-million books missing from the library?"

"What? That's terrible!"

"No, it's good. I'm sure the vast majority of them are safe within Akoran homes, and besides, the more copies of any book disappear, the more copies of it are made."

"Is that how it works? And to think how I've agonized."

"Over what?"

She cast him a quick, abashed glance. "Keeping certain books so long."

"Months?"

"Longer than that."

He laughed at her admission. "I'd be interested to know what you found so worthy of keeping."

"Some are practical—books about sailing, for instance, and carpentry." She did not mention that the others were works of poetry, plays, novels, and the sort. The stuff of fantasy.

They walked deeper into the moon garden. Persephone saw what appeared to be a stone table and beside it two padded benches facing each other across the table. Beyond the fragrances of the flowers she smelled the tantalizing aromas of—

"We're having dinner up here?"

"I thought you'd enjoy it," Gavin said. He pulled out one of the benches for her and waited until she was settled before taking his own seat. The table was set for two. An array of covered dishes were close at hand, several set over small, low-burning flames to keep their contents warm.

"This is lovely," she murmured, trying to hide her surprise. She had assumed they would be dining with others, not alone, and had been uneasy about meeting more people. Now she wondered if the alternative wasn't more unnerving.

"I made a few suggestions to the cooks," he said as he lifted the covers and peered into the dishes. With a grin, he added, "It looks as though they've outdone themselves."

"What is that?" she asked as he placed a plate before her.

"Steak with a red wine and peppercorn sauce."

She took a bite, closed her eyes and sighed deeply. "Heaven."

"You raise chickens—I saw them—and you catch fish."

Persephone nodded. "And on rare occasions when I have been in Ilius, I have bought small amounts of beef. But never have I prepared it so well."

He poured a ruby claret into two goblets and handed her one. "Did you ever think of leaving Deimatos?"

"I do leave from time to time."

"I mean permanently, to live somewhere else."

"Among people. That's what you mean, isn't it? You still think my life is unnatural."

"I do," he admitted without hesitation. "I also think it is unsafe and lonely."

"I am twenty-four years old, hale and hearty. How unsafe is that?"

"You have been fortunate. What about the loneliness?"

"You might be shocked by how little I feel that." Or had, before he came to disrupt the smooth order of her days.

Like a pond without ripples—placid, motionless, hanging suspended as though waiting for a breath of air. Or better yet, a good strong wind.

"Have you never thought of a husband . . . children?"

"No, never." She spoke emphatically and with truth. Longing for something she knew was beyond her reach was not the same thing as foolishly imagining it was actually attainable. Never had she misled herself about that. Always she had understood what was—and was not—possible.

"Someone to come after and benefit from everything you have done?"

"A few huts, a tree house, a boat, that's all I have done."

"Is that enough?"

The steak no longer tasted quite so good. She pushed her plate a little away and took a sip of wine. "What is enough in the final measure of anyone's days?" Looking at him, and seeing behind him the sea of stars emerging from the velvety night, she was emboldened. "What is enough for you, Atreides prince? When all is said and done, what will make you believe that your life was well spent?"

"Duty," he said without hesitation. "I must do my duty. I cannot do less."

"Your duty to your country?" He nodded and she struck unerringly, this time with no intention of missing. "Which country? You are heir to Hawkforte, Shield of England, as you have said, yet here you are on Akora."

"Because there is an unusual situation that requires investigating."

"But you want to make your life here."

He did not, she noted, attempt to deny it, but said only, "A man cannot always have what he wants."

They lingered over plump raspberries sprinkled with the candied rinds of sweet oranges. Off in the distance, the astronomers scanned the heavens. The moon rose, spilling a ribbon of silver light over the Inland Sea.

"This should endure forever," Persephone said, so softly that she hardly knew she spoke.

"I have thought the same, but what we wish is of no consequence compared to the forces that are present here."

The air felt suddenly chill. She looked at him in surprise. "You cannot mean that."

"Why not? Because I am supposed to believe there is something called the spirit of Akora that protects us?" He spoke with frank skepticism that shocked her. He could have doubted there were stars in the sky or wondered if the sun was real and she would not have been more startled. What she felt with every beat of her heart, what she knew to the very core of her being now was being questioned by an Atreides prince whose family supposedly had a unique relationship with the very spirit he did not believe existed.

"But there is. We have always known that."

"I know the evidence of my eyes, of reason and science."

"What of faith?"

"That, too, but I don't expect the God who created the Universe to do everything precisely as we would like. He seems to have ways we cannot fathom."

"There is also more to His creation than you may realize. The evidence of that is right here on Akora."

"I love Akora, too, Persephone but—"

"I don't mean anything so simple as love of one's native land. Can't you *feel* it?"

He reached out, taking her hand before she could think to withdraw it. "I feel the warmth of your skin." He rubbed his thumb lightly over the inside of her wrist. "The pulse of your life moving through you. All that is real. As for the rest—"

"You are afraid," she said. The revelation shocked her, yet it made perfect sense. He had, after all, told her enough about himself to make her understand.

Abruptly, he set her hand down. "It is well you are a woman." He leaned back, his eyes glittering dangerously. "I would not tolerate such an insult from a man."

His anger shimmered through her, terrifying in its force for all that he kept it in strict check. Even so, she faced him bravely. "I am as responsible for what I say or do as is any man, but that is a subject for another time. There is no insult in truth, Atreides prince."

"That I am afraid, a coward. That truth?"

"One does not mean the other, as you well know. Fear can stalk the bravest man and make him all the keener for it. You are torn in your loyalties, riven by conflict about your future."

"All this you know and on such short acquaintance? Your assumptions are in error. My future is in England, regardless of what happens here."

She caught the last raspberry in a silver spoon, lifted it to her tongue. It tasted of sunlight and summer, a rich and riotous flavor, and beneath all that, the sultry, complex flavor of the earth from which it had sprung.

Akora.

"You feel gravely tempted in a way you believe you should not."

He smiled reluctantly. "I am tempted, that much is true."

He was looking at her, his gaze lingering on her mouth, her throat, the curve of her breasts . . . Heat swept through her.

She knew suddenly what tempted him in the starlit night, beneath the moon.

How naïve he must think her. While she prattled on about reason and faith, he was contemplating matters of a far more basic nature.

With her.

"I think I should retire now," she said, and stood while her legs still held her.

Gavin escorted her back to her quarters. They did not speak as they traversed the roof and made their way to the family wing. Her door was in front of them before he said, "You see more than I would like, Persephone of Deimatos, but that doesn't mean your vision is less than clear."

It was, she knew, a concession, and a huge one given the insult she had dealt him. Her resolve, weak and poor thing that it was, began to crack.

"I have little experience with conversation. I am not very good at it."

"You manage well enough."

The door was at her back. She could feel the carved wood pressing against her skin. Where was the handle? . . . Open the door, say goodnight, go inside, shut the door.

He was close, so very close. A jolt of alarm tore through her, yet she was strangely rooted in place. His fingers curled around the back of her neck, holding her. How had they gotten there? She smelled sandalwood and the wine they had shared, the sun-kissed heat of his skin . . .

"Persephone—"

"What?" Her lips parted and were taken by his. She who had scarcely been touched, and not at all in so very long, was flooded by intimacy. His taste and touch, his mouth taking and giving all at once sent a surge of panic through her. Her hands closed on his shoulders. To push him away? If that was her intent, it proved no sturdier than the thin crust of ice on a water bucket on a rare winter morning.

And beneath it, revealed by that cracking ice, hot, surging passion that burned through her with dazzling speed.

Every inch of her body seemed in contact with his.

Her nipples ached against his rock-hard chest. His thighs were steel, his arms the same. Yet he held her so gently that she felt not forced or constrained, but strangely, seductively protected . . . even cherished.

It was too much. She could not bear this.

With a soft cry, she wrenched her mouth from his and twisted away. In an instant, she was free, but only, she knew, because he allowed it. That, in particular, rankled. She had taken care of herself for a very long time and never, since her tender years with her mother, had she let anyone have control over her.

"You presume too much, Atreides prince," she said and deliberately wiped the back of her hand across her mouth.

He stared at her for so long a moment that she wondered if she had well and truly gone too far.

And then he laughed.

Grinning at her, he said, "Prickly Persephone, you know nothing of men, do you?"

She dropped her hand, straightened her shoulders and glared at him. "I know how to gut one, should I ever need to."

This failed to have the intended effect. Indeed, his smile broadened. He looked suddenly much less the proud prince and far more a well-pleased boy.

"If you'd had a proper Akoran education, you'd know how to do a good deal more than that."

He reached out, a long, hard finger stroking softly down her cheek. "You can sail a boat, build a hut, gut a fish"—his gaze lingered on her mouth—"or a man, but you're without wiles. I've never known a woman like that."

She held herself very still despite the tremors of pleasure that flowed from his touch. "Is that what women learn on Akora? How to manipulate men?" She did not hide her contempt for any such notion.

"They learn how to please us. They are *very* good at it."

A traitor was stirring in her. An unknown creature who found the thought of pleasing this Atreides prince almost painfully enticing. She could not allow that.

"Because women serve while men rule?" she demanded.

He bent closer, and for a moment she thought he meant to kiss her again. She was steeling herself when instead he merely said, "Because women know what you have yet to learn. Pleasure, given and received, is the intimacy of equals. No one rules in the bedchamber, Persephone, and what happens in there shapes what happens everywhere."

A moment longer he lingered. She felt his breath on her cheek, his warmth against her skin. The traitor in her leaned a little toward him.

And he was gone, striding away from her down the hall toward his own quarters.

Perhaps not all that surprisingly, Persephone did not sleep well her first night in the ancient palace high on the hill above the Inland Sea.

CHAPTER VII

THE TUNIC PERSEPHONE WORE COMING OVER from Deimatos was not to be found. Neither was the extra one she brought along. When asked about them, Sida merely shrugged and said something about laundry.

Then provided another of the lovely white, shimmering garments favored by young Akoran women.

"I would like my own clothes," Persephone said as she sat at the bench before the mirror, suffering the older woman to dress her hair again.

"These clothes are yours."

"They are not."

"Yes, they are by Prince Gavin's order."

"I do not wish gifts from him."

"Why not? How has he harmed you that you would not accept his generosity?"

"You are twisting this around. I simply do not wish or need charity— *Ouch!*"

"You slept with your hair unbraided." Sida glanced toward the bed, turned down only on one side, only one pillow bearing the imprint of a head. "And for no good reason, so far as I can see. Moreover, you take offense where there is none."

Their eyes met in the mirror. Old to young. Wise to willing to learn, however grudgingly. "Your prince calls me prickly."

Sida laughed. "That boy always had a way with words."

"You knew him as a boy?" The thought of Gavin as a child was oddly enticing.

"I knew him from a newborn infant. He was born here, you know, just down the hall, in his parents' quarters. Princess Kassandra insisted on it."

"Her husband did not object?"

"The Hawk Lord adores her and would deny her nothing unless it was a danger to her, and nothing of that sort has occurred for a long time."

"Since the time of Deilos?"

"You know about that?" Sida shook her head. "A terrible time, never have I seen worse. The Vanax Atreus hovering near death after the attempt on his life, the Princess Kassandra stepping in to lead us. And what a good job she did—with the help of the Hawk Lord. We all rejoiced when they wed."

"Surely the Hawk Lord wanted his eldest son born in England, in the lands he will one day rule?"

"Perhaps he did, but he still agreed with the Princess Kassandra when she chose to be here instead. The first light that boy saw was Akoran light. The first air he breathed bore the perfume of his native land."

"Yet for all that, he fights his love of this place."

Sida stopped brushing. Quietly she asked, "Why do you say that?"

How to answer? How not to? There was so much she did not want to reveal . . . so many secrets that set her apart from others.

"It's just an impression I have."

"You do not know him well." This said with a shadow of doubt, as though perhaps Persephone did know something the older woman feared might be true.

"No, I don't."

Sida relaxed a little and resumed brushing. Soon enough, Persephone was as ready as she could be.

"Prince Gavin awaits you in the library," Sida informed her. "Do you know where that is?"

Persephone nodded. "I have been there before." Even so, she would have trouble finding it if she tried to negotiate the maze of corridors that led through the palace. Instead, she took the stairs to the outside and crossed the courtyard. At this hour, that vast space was already filling with the many visitors drawn to the palace. By midday there would be several thousand, come for all manner of reasons or none at all, save amusement.

She hurried along, heedless of the admiring glances that came her way from many of the men. Her mind was on Gavin and how she would feel seeing him after what had happened the previous evening. She was mulling that over as she came round a corner and walked straight into—

—a wall? No, not a wall, a man. A very tall, very muscular man with startlingly blue eyes, black hair, and a bold grin.

"Well, now, lassie," he said, speaking Akoran with an accent so thick she had some difficulty understanding him. "What's got you in such a hurry?"

His hands were on her shoulders, steadying her. She stepped back quickly, putting space between them, and stared at him.

This seemed to be her time for encountering very tall, supremely fit men with an air of blatant masculinity. First Gavin and now—

"Who are you?" she asked.

His grin was nothing short of dazzling. "Liam Campbell, sweetheart, late of Aberdeen, Scotland, but these days settling in right here on fair Akora. And you would be—?"

Liam Campbell? She knew that name. It was inscribed on the books she had found aboard the floundered vessel that was now her own.

"Mister Campbell . . . how long have you been on Akora?"

"Going on two years, lass, and a flash place it is but now would you like to tell me what's got you lookin' like someone just walked over your grave?"

Not her grave. The grave of his friends, or at least people he had known, whom she had buried.

"Mister Campbell . . . perhaps we could sit down for a moment?"

"Right enough, lass, just let me ask in passin', as it were, you don't happen to have a father, brothers, cousins, uncles or—Providence forbid—a husband likely to take offense at a friendly little chat, do you?"

Despite what she must tell him, the corners of her mouth twitched. "Do not be concerned." More seriously, she nodded to a bench set a little way apart from the bustle of the street. When they were seated, she took a quick breath and said, "You were shipwrecked here, were you not?"

"I was and right glad to discover those stories about strangers meetin' a bitter fate were untrue."

"You did not travel alone."

Stillness descended over him. He looked at her closely. "Out with it, lass. What is it I need to know?"

"I have books that belong to you. At least, I think I do. The name 'Liam Campbell' is inscribed in them."

"My books . . . how could you have come by them?"

"Your vessel washed ashore on one of the small islands in the Inland Sea. I recovered it." She looked down at her hands. There was no easy way to say what had to be said. "Mister Campbell, there were two bodies on board, both men. I have read that it is the custom of most *xenos* to bury their dead so that is what I did."

He exhaled deeply, shaking his head as though to ward off the sorrow that could not be denied. "They were my cousins. Good men."

"I am sorry."

He looked away but not before she saw the sheen of tears in his eyes. She waited, giving him time to come to grips with his emotions. At length, he said, "You took care of them and I'm grateful for it. I knew they couldn't have survived or they would have been found long ago but knowing they had a dignified end does help in some way."

"I'm glad and I will try to get your books back to you." Although how she would manage it under the present circumstances eluded her.

"Don't worry about that. You salvaged them fair and square. Besides, I'm no stranger to that very fine library you've got here."

A little shyly, for she remained unaccustomed to sharing her thoughts with anyone, Persephone said, "That's my favorite place in all of Akora."

"Mine, as well. I was amazed when I found out ordinary people could go in there and read anything they liked. It opened the world for me."

"There are no such libraries in . . . where did you say . . . Aberdeen, Scotland?"

"A small one or two for the rich but no place for the rest of us. Growin' up, I was lucky enough just to learn to read."

"I cannot imagine life without books," she said truthfully.

"I've been readin' that Plato fellow lately. You know of him?"

"A little. Some of what he says seems sensible enough, but some of it seems foolish."

"Now that's just what I thought. Gettin' through him's not easy but he's got a kernel or two of wisdom to share."

They went on to speak of other books they had both read and were chatting happily when a shadow fell across the bench where they sat. Persephone looked up to find Gavin watching them.

Gavin . . . but a Gavin she had not seen before. Not the man who had stood stone-faced while she shot an arrow scant inches past him. Or calmly confronted her rudeness. Or complimented her cooking. Or kissed her with devastating effect.

He came toward them swiftly and steadily as though he intended to go right through Liam Campbell, for all that the two appeared well matched. Still, the Atreides prince did not hesitate.

"Step away from her."

The Scotsman, who had risen quickly, ignored that

and scowled. "I recognize you. You're one of those Atreides."

"I am Gavin Atreides. Do as I say."

"Why? Because you and your family run this place?"

"We do not 'run' it, Mister—"

"Campbell. Liam Campbell. Looks to me like you think you do."

"Then you have mistaken the situation, Scotsman. And you have delayed the woman who was coming to meet me, making me come in search of her."

Liam took his eyes from Gavin long enough to glance at Persephone. Swiftly enough, he returned his attention to the man who challenged him. "If she were your wife, I'd owe you an apology."

"She is not."

"Your betrothed?"

"No."

Campbell's smile returned. "Fair game, then."

That did it. Never mind the strange flutter of excitement building in her as the two men confronted each other. This had gone on long enough.

"Not game at all, Mister Campbell," Persephone said as she brushed past him and past Gavin as well. Over her shoulder, she glared at them both. "The pair of you may butt horns all you like. I have work to do."

By an exercise of the strictest self-discipline, she did not look back again. But she did hear two deep male voices mutter:

"Later, Atreides."

"Anytime, Scotsman."

"That was ridiculous," Persephone informed him when Gavin caught up with her. "It's amusing when rams do it, but grown men . . ."

She glanced at him sideways, confirming that he did not look in the least annoyed. Indeed, he appeared well pleased with himself. "You're too innocent," he said.

It was on the tip of her tongue to contradict him, but she really couldn't do so. After that kiss the previous evening, he knew exactly how "innocent" she really was—as in, unschooled by the standards of normal Akoran women and, no doubt, inept.

"I look after myself, Atreides prince. I do not need or welcome anyone's help."

"You forget, I saw how well you look after yourself on Deimatos. It took me all of two minutes to disarm you and—" He pushed open the double doors to the library and stood aside for her to enter. Right behind her, he said, "—there wasn't a damn thing you could do about it."

The truth hurt and put an edge on her voice. "What about your claim that a man cannot hurt a woman?"

"An Akoran man. Campbell's not Akoran. He may be eventually, and his children, if he lives long enough to have any"—Gavin sounded skeptical on that score—"will be. But he grew up with different rules. You'd do well to remember that."

"Thank you for the advice, but I have no interest in

Liam Campbell or"—she looked at him pointedly—"any other man. Now, if that's settled, I'd like to see about finding the older survey to which Amarensis refers."

They entered a long, gracefully proportioned room a hundred feet wide and several times that in length. The ceiling soared fifty feet over their heads, vividly painted with murals of Akoran life. Light flowed from broad windows ranged above a balcony that ran all the way around the room. The walls were lined with shelves for books and cupboards for scrolls. Long, polished tables were equipped with comfortable chairs, inkwells, and lamps. Dozens of scholars were at work, served by busy librarians coming and going with material for them.

Persephone did not hesitate but went directly to a door set between tall bookcases. Beyond it was a circular stone staircase that led down to the levels of the library beneath the palace.

"You do know your way around here," Gavin said when they emerged into a large chamber filled row upon row with shelves that seemed to have no end.

"I would not have come to Ilius so often if not for the library."

"My cousin Clio has been known to sleep here."

"Here? Really?"

"She is the scholar of the family, particularly given to the study of our most ancient history."

"Is she a red-haired woman?"

"That's Clio. She inherited her hair color from her mother."

"The consort of the Vanax, Lady Brianna. Yes, I know of her. I saw your cousin several times here and once, I believe she was asleep."

"My aunt and uncle used to worry about it, but they've learned to let her be."

It was odd, Persephone thought, to hear the ruler of Akora and his consort spoken of in such familiar terms, as though they were ordinary people. Odd, too, to be given a glimpse into the lives of those she had always thought of as set apart, the stuff of legends.

Beyond all that was the thought of what it meant to have two loving parents who wanted their daughter to fulfill her dreams. On that she would not dwell.

"Your cousin is very fortunate."

"That is true, also very knowledgeable about this library. Unfortunately, she is not on Akora right now or I would ask her to help us search."

"I also have some knowledge of this place," Persephone allowed, "but I know someone who has a great deal more. Perhaps we can find him."

"Who are we looking for?" Gavin asked as they walked past row after row of books, manuscripts, and scrolls, the millennia of Akora's accumulated knowledge. Alone in the world, Akora had never suffered a dark ages or other period of loss and destruction. All that had ever been learned was carefully maintained and built upon. That, as much as anything else, accounted for the Akorans' proud determination to maintain their way of life at all cost.

Their path was lit by stone lamps set in iron brackets driven deep into the wall so that there could be no risk of them ever falling.

"A friend. We should find him this way." They went on a quarter-mile through the stacks before coming to a small recess outfitted as an office. In it sat a very old man wreathed in long white hair and an equally impressive beard.

"Nestor?" Gavin asked on a note of wonder. "I thought you had retired."

"So did I, Prince, but the experience paled after a few months and I was happy to return."

"You two know each other?" Persephone asked.

"I had the privilege of being one of young Gavin's tutors," the old man said with a smile. "We spent many a pleasant hour discussing the ancient Greeks and Romans, which, as I recall, you found vastly more interesting than so mundane a topic as mathematics."

"I have since broadened my perspective. Clio will be delighted to know of your return."

"And I will look forward to hers. Now indulge an old man and tell me how the two of you come to be here together."

"We are looking for a survey done centuries ago and referred to by one called Amarensis," Gavin said.

"Ah, yes, Amarensis." He smiled fondly. "I met her as a youth."

"She died a century ago," Persephone said.

"Not quite. I have seen only ninety years. She was still alive when I was born and for a while after that. Our paths crossed when I was about eight. A remarkable woman. I remember her still."

"She refers in her work to a survey done about five hundred years ago," Gavin said. "It is clear she had a copy of it and that it must have come from this library, but I have not been able to find it."

"Odd. Any such document should be easy enough to find."

"I would think so, but I have searched these many months without success. Moreover, none of the librarians have been able to find it."

Nestor, who Gavin knew had always liked a challenge, grinned. The old man rose slowly but steadily and shook the wrinkles from his deep blue robe. "Come along, then, let's have a look. A survey, you said?"

"A land survey. It included measurements of the elevation of the ground all over Akora."

"And it is this information you want?"

"Yes, in greater detail than Amarensis provides it."

"In all honesty, such a work would probably draw little interest. It is possible that there were only two copies."

"Why two?" Persephone asked.

"Because there is never only one copy of any work. If Amarensis borrowed one of the copies and failed to return it—"

"Only a single copy would remain," Gavin said, "and it is that which is missing."

Nestor nodded and led them unerringly through the stacks. They searched in every place the survey might reside, but at the end of several hours, even the ancient librarian was ready to admit defeat.

"I do not understand this," Nestor said. "As the only remaining copy of that survey, it would never have been released before another copy was made."

"No one would have been allowed to remove it?" Persephone asked.

About to speak, the old man hesitated. "No one . . . except one."

"Who?" Gavin asked. "Who would be the exception to such a rule?"

"The Vanax," Nestor said promptly. "Only the Vanax Atreus could remove the last remaining copy of any work from the library. Moreover, only he could do so without informing anyone or leaving any record that he had done so."

"But why would he—?" Persephone began, only to break off. The reason for the Vanax to remove a work that supported the fear that Akora might soon experience a cataclysmic volcanic explosion was obvious. He would want to hold such knowledge very close indeed, if only to prevent panic.

"Thank you, Nestor," Gavin said as he took Persephone's arm. "I think we know where to look now."

"May Fortune favor you," the old man said gently. He looked from one to the other. "My life is coming to an end, as is right and fit. But Akora goes on forever. In that, we must have faith."

Persephone held fast to his words as they hurried from the library back to the palace. "Nestor is very wise," she said. "We should not lose sight of what he is telling us."

Gavin looked grim. "We will do better to listen to what the movement of the land says. On that our fate may rest."

"Where do you think to find the survey?" she asked when they had passed out of the library.

"If Atreus did take it, there is only one place it will be."

He led her through the labyrinth of corridors into one of the oldest parts of the palace. There they entered a large but simply furnished room that looked out over the city beyond. The floor beneath their feet was stone, but deeply slanted where generations had trod upon it. The walls were decorated with austere geometric patterns of the kind favored by their ancient ancestors. Shelves held a collection of small sculptures that even at quick glance appeared the work of a master artist. A large, plain table dominated the room. Its surface was completely bare.

"What is this place?" Persephone asked.

"Atreus's office."

She glanced around anxiously, thinking they should

not be there. Surely the Vanax would object. Her eyes fell on Gavin. He was at the desk, opening a drawer. "What are you doing?"

"Looking for answers." Quickly he removed a single scroll, glanced at it, and nodded. "The missing survey." Along with it was a letter, sealed with a daub of red wax that bore the imprint of the royal bull's horns of Akora. Gavin broke the seal and scanned the letter. After a moment, he sighed deeply.

Persephone came around the table to stand beside him. "What is it?"

"Atreus left me a letter."

"I do not understand."

"He says if I have come this far, I remain concerned about the volcano. He expresses his confidence in me and says he is certain I will be able to handle the situation well."

"Why does he not tell you this himself?"

He looked at her in surprise. "Did you not know? Atreus and Brianna are in England on a state visit to the new young queen, Victoria."

"The Vanax and his consort are absent from Akora?"

"Is that not what I just said?"

"But you also said you made some report of what was happening. That your family knows of it."

"They bid me continue my investigations."

"I see." She did not, but a terrible suspicion was forming in her. "Your cousin Clio is also in England?"

Gavin nodded. "With her parents."

"She has a brother, the Prince Andreas."

"He is in America, to which he is the newly appointed ambassador."

"And your other cousin, what is her name, Amelia? She who is newly married to an American."

"On their wedding trip."

"Your brother and sisters, those you told me of?"

"In England. What is the point of this, Persephone?"

"Your other cousins, uncles, aunts, your parents, grandparents, all of them. Where are they?"

"In England and America. What does it matter?"

"Matter? Akora may stand on the verge of destruction—*again*—and every member of the Atreides family, save for you, is absent? Is that what you are telling me?"

"Obviously they are not all that concerned."

"Or they are very concerned, indeed."

The words—and the stark accusation they implied—hung heavy in the quiet of the room. Gavin dropped the letter and closed the small space between them. Taking hard hold of her, he demanded, "Just what are you saying?"

A spark of fear ran through her. In her clumsiness and inexperience, had she pushed him too far? What matter if she had? There were still truths that needed speaking.

"That the Atreides will survive, even if Akora and all the rest of us do not. The question is, will that be a happy accident or the result of deliberate design?"

His hands tightened on her, almost but not quite enough to inflict pain. "Atreus would never leave Akora if he believed it was in danger."

"And as Chosen, bound to Akora in ways the rest of us can only imagine, he would know, wouldn't he?"

Gavin hesitated. "I don't know."

"You have never spoken with him about it?"

"I know what everyone knows—the candidate for selection goes into the caverns beneath the palace. He undergoes the trial. If he is meant to be Vanax, he survives. If he is not, he dies."

"What do you make of all that?"

"Nothing," he said emphatically. "There has never been any reason for me to think about it."

"Liar." Pain shot through her arm. An instant later, she was free, even as Gavin looked horrified by what he had done.

"Damn you, Persephone!"

Rubbing her arm, she said, "Truth hurts, Atreides prince. I do not believe you have never thought of it, never wondered."

"I am not free to follow wherever my imagination might lead."

"Wherever your heart might, that's what you mean. You said as much yourself. Then let me tell you what every Akoran—including you—is supposed to know. The Vanax is chosen by the living spirit of Akora, that which sustains and protects us. That which has always been present in these islands from the beginning. That which is Creation itself, by whatever name you wish to call it. It is real, it is alive, and it is *here*. Why do you deny this? Why do you hide from it?"

"It is legend, nothing more."

A harsh laugh broke from her. "You are wrong, so wrong, and I cannot begin to understand why. You have every reason to know this."

"Because I am Atreides? I am Hawkforte first, Persephone. My life, my duty are there."

"No, they are not, Atreides prince, born of Akora. Sida told me the first light you saw, the first air you breathed were Akoran. And why? Because your mother—your seeress mother who could *see the future*—made sure of it. Did you never ask her why?"

"There was never any reason to ask!" He shouted the words even as he reached for her again. His eyes were hard, glittering with rage, and beyond that the struggle to deny. But his touch was controlled, firm yet gentle.

Persephone faced him unflinchingly. "*If* Akora is truly in danger, then there are only two possibilities: either your family is absent from Akora in order to assure their own survival, or the Vanax, the Chosen, has reason to know that you will see Akora safely through this crisis, exactly as he says in that letter."

"Atreus is incapable of dishonor and he would never trust another to take his rightful place here."

"You are certain of all that?"

"Absolutely certain."

"Then there is no danger. Is that what you believe?"

"No . . . perhaps . . . I don't know. There are signs of an impending explosion."

"As I have seen for myself." She took a breath, willed herself to put aside her own fears.

Her hand cupped his face. "You mentioned lava flows beneath the palace."

He nodded, covering her hand with his. They stood very close together.

"Show me," Persephone said.

CHAPTER VIII

"HOW FAR DOWN ARE WE GOING?" PERSE-
phone asked. They were descending a stone
staircase set into a wall near the family quarters. Her
voice sounded hollow against the walls streaked with
lichen.

"The caves are about sixty feet below the lowest
level of the palace," Gavin replied.

"It's getting cooler. Wouldn't lava flows make the
air warmer, as they do on Deimatos?"

"We have a way to go, to get to them."

He fell silent as they reached the bottom of the stairs.
The glow from the lantern illuminated a large chamber
that, for an instant, appeared to be filled with people. A
gasp escaped Persephone before she realized that she
was seeing life-sized statues, hundreds of them, set into
niches all around the chamber. So detailed were the

carvings, that she had the sense she was looking into the faces of individuals who had truly lived.

Beyond the statue room was a vast arch, the top of which faded away into darkness. When they stepped through it, the flagstone floor gave way to cool, damp earth. Slender cones, glittering as though studded with gems, hung from the ceiling high above and sprouted from the floor of the cave. The latter formed aisles leading to a deep rock ledge at the far end of the chamber. Something red gleamed there, but Persephone had scant time to wonder what it might be before Gavin guided her toward a tunnel branching off from the main chamber.

They had gone a little distance when she realized she could see beyond the circle of light cast by the lantern. The darkness in front of them was thinning, replaced by a pale glow.

"What is that?" she asked.

"There is water ahead that holds tiny life forms capable of producing light. They exist in other parts of Akora as well. Have you never seen them?"

Persephone shook her head. "If they are on Deimatos, it must be in parts of the caves that are sealed off from—" She broke off as they came out of the passageway onto what appeared to be . . . a beach? How was that possible? Yet water clearly lapped against damp sand. Lichens and moss grew in abundance, adding to the impression of an otherworldly grotto. There was even a small building, little more than a row of columns holding up a peaked roof that resembled a temple.

"What is this place?" she asked.

"We think it used to be on the surface. Incredible as it sounds, it seems to have been folded into the earth when the volcano exploded. People who managed to make their way here survived."

"Astonishing. I had no idea this existed."

"It's worth exploring, but later."

They continued on along another narrow passage, the entrance to which was scarcely more than a cleft in the cave wall. The living light faded behind them as the temperature began to rise.

After several minutes during which they moved steadily downward, following the slope of the passage, Persephone saw a red glow up ahead. At the same time, she smelled the acrid scent of sulfur.

"We are near a lava flow?" she asked.

Gavin nodded over his shoulder. "According to our records, lava has been seen here since shortly after the Cataclysm. The flow has waxed and waned but has never presented any danger."

That was hard to believe when they reached a ledge and Persephone saw the bubbling cauldron of fire and smoke lying before them. Plumes of sparks shot upward through the thin crust that formed and dissolved before their eyes. The walls glowed red where they were not seared black by fire. The heat was almost unbearable; it caused her to take a quick step backward.

"Up until a few months ago," Gavin said, "it was possible to cross the flow. Enough rock remained clear to form pathways. It was dangerous, but it could be done."

"Why would anyone want to take such a chance?"

"Atreus has come here regularly to check the lava flow, as has every Vanax before him. Aside from my uncle, very few people have any idea this flow exists."

"It is kept secret?"

He nodded. "To avoid alarming people unnecessarily." Gavin set the lantern down on the ledge where they stood and looked out over the inferno. "The traitor Deilos discovered this place. He used it to delude his followers into believing that Akora was on the verge of catastrophe and only he could save it. Given that, there is some irony in the fact that he died in these fires."

"Did he? How did that happen?" In the hot, sulfur-tinged air, Persephone's voice sounded high and thin.

"There was a battle here between him and Atreus. Deilos lost. If he'd been taken alive, he would have been held to account for his crimes. To avoid that, he leaped into the lava."

"He must have been mad."

"I've heard some say that, but I don't think it's necessarily true. Who knows what really drives a man to become evil."

"Is that what you think he was—evil?"

"His actions don't really leave any doubt. Have you seen enough?"

"Yes, more than enough." Her skin felt uncomfortably hot and her heart was heavy.

They returned to the grotto. Persephone was lost in thought, but not so much as to be unaware of her growing thirst. She glanced at the glowing water. "Is that drinkable?"

Gavin nodded. "The life forms within it do no harm." He hesitated, studying her. His gaze lingered, gentle yet compelling. She could not look away. "But there is better water here." With a nod of his head, he indicated the small temple. "If you are brave enough to risk it."

"I don't understand; what risk is there?"

"It is the water of joining." When she merely frowned, he asked, "Have you not wondered where it comes from?"

"Where what comes from? I have never heard of any such thing."

"In all your reading? But of course, it wouldn't be mentioned in books of carpentry and the like."

"You are mocking me." She was bruised enough with what she had just seen. More was not needed.

He looked at her gently. "No, Persephone, I am not. It's fine that you don't know certain things, just a little unusual. The water of joining is part of the ritual of marriage. Couples share it on their wedding night."

"Why?"

"It is said to give a certain . . . enhancement to love-making."

Never mind the heat of the lava. Her face flamed well enough without it. "Do you believe that?"

"I've never tried it."

"Water is water."

"Then let us quench our thirst."

He stepped into the small temple and turned, waiting for her to join him. It was very still inside, as though the air itself hung suspended. Persephone took a breath, let it out slowly.

"What is that?" A face gazed out of the ancient stone. So worn was it by time, that she could not tell if it was meant to be a man or a woman. Perhaps it did not matter.

"I thought you would know, since you are a believer. It is said to be the spirit of Akora."

"That is nonsense. Akora is Akora and far more. No statue, no carving can encompass it."

Yet even as she spoke, she wondered. Could the image have represented that in the minds of the first-comers to what had been one island, those who knew it before the Cataclysm? The carving looked ancient enough to date from that time.

Water flowed over the visage and the moss grew in every crevice of the stone. Eyes . . . nose . . . mouth . . . the face seemed to fade in and out of the earth itself.

Gavin bent, caught a handful of the water, and drank. "Sweet," he said after a moment. "And cool."

"Pure water, then, with nothing to taint it."

"Or explain its reputation."

She shrugged, held out her own hand, and drank. "People will believe all manner of things." They were so close her arm brushed against his. The touch resonated through her. "This I do know, though not from books of carpentry."

"I suppose I deserved that. Why did you come down here with me?"

"I wanted to see what you saw. See what convinced you there could be danger. I do understand now. It is very bad."

"You didn't expect what you saw?"

"No, not even what I've seen on Deimatos prepared me for this. I think until now I have clung to the belief that nothing so terrible as the Cataclysm could happen again. But seeing what is here, I must think otherwise."

Gavin took another drink, sat down on the ground, and stretched his long legs out in front of him. He had very muscular legs, including what she could see of his thighs below the short tunic he wore. She supposed he rode quite a lot, and trained, as warriors did, pressing himself to the limit with swordplay and wrestling. He was a very fit man; she would give him that.

He patted the earth beside him. "There might be another explanation."

She hesitated but did as he had silently bid and sat next to him, near enough to feel the warmth of his body. Her awareness of him took a further leap forward.

"What would that be?" she asked.

"What I said before. That we know little of the earth

and how it functions. We have steeped ourselves in superstition and myth for so long that we wouldn't know truth if we tripped over it."

"Your tongue has a bitter edge, Atreides prince, especially for one who has just drunk sweet water."

He laughed. "You see, that's exactly what I mean. There are people who seriously believe the water from here is an aphrodisiac, as though believing it would make it so."

"It just tastes like water to me." To confirm it, she had another drink.

"That's because you're intelligent and have a logical mind."

She spared a quick glance at him, to see if he was mocking her again, but he looked entirely serious. "Thank you. . . ."

"Does my saying that surprise you?"

"Well . . . yes, it does."

He leaned closer, brushing aside a stray wisp of hair that had fallen across her forehead. His touch was extremely . . . pleasant. She didn't mind at all when his finger trailed down her cheek.

"It shouldn't," he said. "Any man with half a brain can see that you're a lot more than merely beautiful."

"Merely beautiful?" There was an outside chance she might be dreaming. If so, she'd very much like to go on doing so. The Atreides prince thought her beautiful, intelligent, and—what else had he said? Oh, yes, logical. That part, at least, was true. She was a very logical person.

In fact, right then it seemed logical to have a bit more water.

Gavin did the same, then said, "It's a lot more pleasant in here."

Persephone nodded. "Much cooler. We probably didn't realize how hot we were becoming near the lava. That must be why we're so thirsty."

"That makes sense. You have an exquisite mouth."

"I—what?"

"Your mouth, it's exquisite."

"Oh . . . well, the truth is, I like you mouth, too."

He looked startled. "Do you?"

"Yes, at least I did when you kissed me." Had she said that? It was hard to believe, but then, she wasn't quite herself. She had felt overwhelmed by old pain and tragedy as she stared into the pit of hell where the traitor Deilos—so he was always called, as though he never had any other identity—died. Now, such a short time later, she felt almost . . . giddy? That couldn't be. She wasn't a giddy sort of person.

Yet she did feel distinctly different. The hope she had clung to, that her fears for Akora would prove unfounded, was gone. Time was fleeting and soon enough, possibly very soon, they might have to face a new Cataclysm. But just then, she drifted inside a bubble, suspended between one moment and the next, where nothing was completely real.

Or forbidden.

She who had been so long alone, looked to the man

who had drawn her from her solitude. The living light threw his features into high relief. He was a handsome man, that was undeniable, but she could see beyond the strength and symmetry of his features and the masculine beauty of his powerful body. What dwelled within was easily as compelling.

She caught a handful of the sparkling water and held it out to him. He bent, drank. She felt his tongue lapping at the center of her palm.

"Persephone." His voice was deep and slightly rough as he drew her to him.

In an instant she was under him. She ought to mind . . . and did try to . . . "Let go of me, oaf." She spoke mildly.

He laughed and pressed her against the cool, damp ground. "You say 'oaf' with more affection than you do 'Atreides prince.' That always sounds as though you're damning me."

Her hands pressed against his shoulders . . . curled round them . . . held onto him . . .

"But that's who you are."

"Oaf or prince?"

"Man . . . you are a man and I—I am a woman. But not like Akoran women. You said there were things I would know if I had been educated as they are. I don't."

"It's all right," he said gently and took her mouth with his.

Sweet, so sweet. Sweet water, sweet air, the touch of this man was sweet.

His kiss deepened and her body arched in response, hunger for him driving out all else. Their tongues met, played. She savored the taste of him, sought more. Her hands pulled at his tunic.

He moved away a little. Her soft cry of protest turned to a gasp of pleasure when he returned to her without his only garment.

Skin stretched taut over muscle and sinew . . . warm and alive . . . compelling . . . So different from herself, so amazing and fascinating. The need to be closer to him overwhelmed her. She ached, a heaviness between her thighs, unbearable . . . She had to—

"Don't be afraid," he said as he gathered the fabric of her gown in his big hands, raising it slowly, baring her thighs, her hips, her breasts, raising it over her head.

Cool air touched her, bringing brief relief to the heat from within. She shook, not from the coolness, but with self-consciousness, sudden shyness, and most powerfully of all, the fierce passion gripping her.

So many years alone, so much solitude, guilt and shame, anger and fear . . . Unbearable . . . Her face was wet, tears trickling down her cheeks. She tasted salt when his mouth left hers, moving down her throat, lingering where her life pulsed.

A power coursed through her unlike anything she had ever known. She could not stay still, could not restrain herself. Instinct drove her to touch him, experience him, know him—

"Slowly," he rasped, and cupped her breasts, his

thumbs rubbing over nipples so taut they were almost painful. His tongue followed and she cried out when he suckled her, pleasure drawing tight as a bow within her. Her entire body tensed.

"I can't bear this!"

He raised his head, looking down at her in the pale light of the temple. His features were thrown into sharp relief as he held fiercely to control.

"You can . . . you will." He moved down the length of her body, leaving a trail of fire everywhere he touched. His hands slipped beneath her buttocks, raising her even as his thigh thrust between hers.

Astonishment tore through her when she felt the long, hard strength of him. For just an instant, fear threatened to swamp all else. It vanished, dissolving under the onslaught of his caresses. Distantly, she was aware of hurtling from shock to shock. He drove her relentlessly, sparing her nothing, bringing her to wave after wave of pleasure so intense that she cried out.

On the crest of that shattering release, he entered her, slowly, so slowly, holding himself in strict check. He rose above her, the muscles of his powerful arms working. Seeing him like that—so intense, so determined—Persephone could not hold back. Her body tightened around him, drawing him deeper, even as hot, sweet pleasure began to mount again. She saw the start of surprise in his eyes and felt laughter bubble up in her. It turned to a gasp when he drove deeper, past the barrier of her innocence. For a moment pain seared her, but it was gone swiftly, as though it had never been.

Hard on it came ecstasy even more intense than before, lifting her higher and higher until finally, helpless, she cried out his name as the world dissolved.

LYING ON HIS SIDE, WITH PERSEPHONE CRAdled against him, Gavin stared at the stone face wreathed in moss. It looked for all the world as though it were smiling.

A trick of the light, no doubt, and of his own befuddled brain. But that brain was clearing rapidly now and in it was a single thought: What the hell had he done?

What he had wanted to do from the first moment he saw Persephone, standing so bold and defiant in her man's tunic, just before she winged an arrow past him. Right then, he'd wanted to lay her down on the sand and have her.

Well enough, that much was true, but even so, *what the hell had he done?*

A man didn't give into his baser urges, not if he had a shred of decency and sense. He had always presumed himself amply endowed with both, but now he had to wonder.

She felt so good in his arms, warm and supple as she slept. The woman of passion and fire, who had stunned him with her responsiveness, was a rare delight. But so was this aspect of her, bringing a quiet joy and a sense of rightness.

Yet it wasn't right, not remotely. She had been a virgin; he was an experienced man. He should have taken all that into account and kept his distance.

Moreover, his future was in England, whereas Persephone, for all her avowed preference for solitude, seemed intertwined with Akora itself. It was difficult, if not impossible, to imagine her anywhere else.

Carefully, he moved away from her and stood with his feet digging into the soft earth. Naked, he stretched, vividly aware of the bone-deep contentment he felt.

And just as determined to ignore it.

She slept on her side, with her back to him. He could see the sleekness of her flank, the narrow indentation of her waist, and the high curve of her breast. She was perfectly formed, exquisite, and there was some part deep within his very soul that cried out for her.

With a groan he could not entirely suppress, Gavin found her gown and laid it over her. His own tunic in hand, he went from the temple. He was still naked, standing in the grotto, when he happened to glance down and see her blood.

A low curse broke from him at the reminder of the full enormity of his lapse from sense and honor. He dove into the water and swam vigorously for several minutes while trying to decide what to do.

First things first. Emerging from the pool, he picked up his tunic, tore a piece from it, then donned what was left, tying it around his lean waist. It was sufficient for the bare requirements of modesty. Returning to the temple, he found Persephone still asleep. With a sharp glance at the face in the stone, which still seemed to be smiling, he soaked the torn cloth in the water. Gently, hoping not to wake her, he turned Persephone onto her back and removed the gown he had laid over her. She murmured but remained deeply asleep as he parted her thighs and gently wiped the wet cloth over her tender skin.

He had almost finished when he felt her watching him.

"What are you doing?" she asked as she lay unmoving. Her voice was faint, the words slightly slurred, as though sleep softened their edges.

"Taking care of you."

"I can—"

"I know, you can take care of yourself."

"Let me up." She reached for her tunic as she spoke, and dragged it over herself.

He moved a little away and turned his back, giving her a small degree of privacy while she dressed. Swiftly enough she was done, and moved past him.

His hand lashed out, closing around her arm. "Where are you going?"

She looked down at where he held her, then looked up at him deliberately. The British gentleman he had been raised to be knew he should release her. The Akoran prince saw no reason to do so.

"Back to the palace," she said.

"As though nothing has happened here?"

"Nothing has, at least nothing of importance."

He wasn't a vain man, he truly wasn't, but that stung. Moreover, it shocked him. "Persephone—"

"I mean it, Gavin. I don't know what came over us—perhaps there really is something in that water or perhaps we just—"

Us. At least she admitted they were both involved. His manner gentled. "Just what?"

"Just did what we wanted to do." Honesty heaped on honesty. He couldn't help but admire that.

"It doesn't matter," she insisted. "It can't. There is a volcano under Akora that may be about to explode again, endangering hundreds of thousands of people. That matters."

She was right, of course. She also was so lovely it almost hurt to look at her.

"What are you smiling at?" she asked.

"You." He slid his hand down her arm and clasped her fingers.

Their bodies swayed together, skin to skin, heat to heat, hunger surging . . .

A long, wavelike tremor undulated through the ground. The deep, rending sound of rock filled the air, followed swiftly by clouds of debris raining down on them.

CHAPTER IX

I N THE MIDST OF SWEEPING THE HALLWAY,
the boy stopped. He stared openmouthed at the
pair emerging from the stairway set in the wall.

"Prince? . . ."

"Is everything all right here?" Gavin asked.

"Yes . . . yes, sir, I believe so."

"No injuries?"

"Injuries? No . . . sir . . . Not that I know."

It was quiet in the hall. There was no sound of
alarm, no people rushing about, no one crying out for
help.

Holding Persephone close against him, as he had
done the entire time they were making their way from
the caves, Gavin asked the boy, "Did you feel it?"

"It . . . sir?"

The boy stared at him in genuine bewilderment. He

was perhaps thirteen, not much older, doing his required service. He appeared . . . not afraid, just puzzled, as though suddenly awakened from boredom for no evident reason.

"Never mind." Gavin gave him a quick, flashing smile of the sort he had mastered long ago. It had the desired effect. The boy looked at once reassured and relieved.

"He felt nothing," Persephone marveled as they continued down the hall.

"So it seems. The tremor must have been very deep."

"Perhaps that is good. Perhaps tremors like that have been happening all the time and we just haven't noticed."

"I don't think so." He opened the door to his quarters and ushered her in. Sida paused in the midst of straightening a row of books.

"There you are," the older woman said. "I was worried." Staring at them, she frowned. "What's that you've got all over yourselves?"

Only then did Gavin realize that both he and Persephone were covered with a fine white powder that clung to their hair, skin, and clothing. It must have been shaken loose from the ceiling of the cave when the tremor struck.

"Dust," he said, and did not elaborate further but instead glanced around the room. Although he might appear disorganized to some—to Sida in particular— he really did know where things were supposed to be.

His books, papers, instruments, even the furniture itself all appeared to be slightly off-kilter. The effect wasn't dramatic and would have been missed by almost anyone, but not by him.

"What's happened here?" he asked.

"I've no idea," Sida said. "I came by with fresh grapes"—she indicated the bowl on the table—"and found everything just a bit out of place, not your usual mess by any means, but . . . odd."

"You didn't feel anything, either?" Persephone asked.

Sida raised a brow. "Feel what?"

"Never mind," Gavin said hastily. "Thank you for the grapes, and for straightening up."

"I'm going," Sida said when it was obvious that was what he wanted. She had already opened the door when she added, "Nestor was looking for you."

"Do you know why?" Gavin asked.

"He didn't say."

"If you see him, tell him I am here."

Sida nodded and left. Persephone hesitated a moment, then she also turned to go.

"Don't," Gavin said. It was an order and a request all at the same time. He hoped she would concentrate on the latter, but he was fully prepared to enforce the former should that prove necessary.

"I need to bathe."

"So do I. We can do that here."

"I don't think—"

"Good, don't," he teased as he closed the distance between them. Beyond the windows, the life of the city went on as usual. Whatever had happened in the caves, for the moment there was nothing he could do.

Except follow his own desires.

"Have you tried the shower yet?" he asked.

Watching him with the same wariness he suspected she would give to anything new and dangerous, Persephone shook her head. "I'm sure I can manage it fine in my own quarters."

"I'm sure you can." He just wasn't going to give her the chance. Not with his blood running high and the need to touch her proving irresistible.

Swiftly cutting her off from escape, he backed her toward the bathing chamber. She moved a few feet, then stopped and faced him squarely. "Gavin . . ." This said with a note of warning, which he ignored.

"That's much better than 'Atreides prince' or 'oaf.' "

She had the grace to flush, if just a little. Even so, she said, "I mean it, I'm going to my own quarters."

He caught her at the waist, drawing her to him. Her cheek was smooth and warm against his lips as he murmured, "Indulge me, Persephone, and while you're doing that, let me indulge you."

WHEN EXACTLY HAD SHE STOPPED BEING an independent and self-sufficient person content to live alone and take care of herself?

All right, perhaps she'd never been truly content, but she had done well enough.

Until now. Now everything was changed.

Her head fell back, her hair loosened from its braid, tumbling almost to her bottom as she moaned softly. Standing under the rush of warm water, naked in the grasp of the man who held her so effortlessly, she could not seem to do anything except feel.

And feel and feel . . .

The powdery white dust of the cave swirled down the drain at their feet. Gavin's hands, slick with sandalwood-scented soap, cupped her breasts, his thumbs rubbing over her hardened nipples.

"Exquisite," he murmured, and turned her so that she was facing away from him. He washed her back, her buttocks, even her legs, bending to attend to each so thoroughly that before he was done she had to lean against the wall of the shower to remain upright.

He laughed as he straightened, turning her again to face him. Lightly, he ran a finger up along her inner thigh, stroking her where she was most sensitive.

Her hands braced to either side, the water pouring over her, she struggled against the tight coiling of passion that she thought should have been exhausted.

"Let it happen," Gavin murmured and slipped down her body, shocking her when he knelt before her.

This could not be . . . he could not . . . But he did, and the effect was immediate.

He caught her, holding her safe until she returned to

herself, but even then he did not relent. "My turn," he said, and when her face flamed at what she thought he meant, he laughed and handed her the soap.

"Easy, Persephone. Just do what you want to do."

Such encouragement—and permission—was heady, indeed. Her hesitation fell away as she gave into urges that would not be denied. He was a very large man. She had known that, but hadn't really had an opportunity to entirely appreciate it. His skin beneath her soapy hands was warm, smooth, and taut. An arrow of soft brown hair ran down his torso. Her fingers drifted over it until they encountered the thin but unmistakable line of a scar below his rib cage.

"What happened to you?" she asked softly.

"A mistake on the training field." When still she looked at him questioningly, he admitted, "I tripped."

She frowned to think of him in such danger. "It looks as though it could have been serious."

"Only to my pride."

"You are quite astonishingly beautiful."

He looked surprised. Indeed, more than that. She could have sworn he blushed.

Blushed? Her Atreides prince? What a delicious thought.

"You are beautiful," he corrected, and raised his hands as though to take hold of her. Beneath her challenging gaze, he stopped, tempered himself, and let his hands drop. "I am a man."

Her mouth twitched at the corners. "I have noticed that."

"I meant, men are not beautiful."

"Is that written in the books I have not read? Fie on them. You are beautiful, far more than I can be. I am ordinary. You are . . ." No need to give him *too* inflated a head. "You are otherwise."

"I think perhaps we perceive this differently,"

"Hmmmm." The conversation no longer interested her. She was lost in her exploration of his body. Entranced by his response to her touch. Fascinated by the transformation that came so visibly upon him.

How vulnerable it was to be a man. Desire and need so visible, not hidden as in a woman. How tempting to think that she could provoke him thusly—

"Persephone—"

His hands were tangled in her hair. She had slipped so naturally down his length, absorbed in her fascination, eager to touch him as he had touched her.

To know the scent and taste of him. To learn him with her eyes closed and all her other senses vividly alive.

To find within herself the power that found its source within him.

He let her, and to his credit, bore it well. But in the end, when he could stand no more, he drew her upright.

"We cannot," he said. "You are too new to this."

Already she was learning. "Do we not, I will be harmed."

"Unfair—"

She covered his mouth with hers, drawing from him his life's breath as she drew from him life itself, there as the water poured over them both and Akora spun away one more precious day.

T HEY EMERGED FROM THE BATHING CHAM-ber some time later, wrapped in thick robes Gavin had fetched for them. Persephone's hung down past her feet, its sleeves entirely covering her hands. Since growing to her full height, she could not recall feeling small, much less delicate. But of late she had come to feel both. It was one more unsettling discovery heaped upon so many others.

Yet another was that the world could not be held at bay any longer. Responding to a knock, Gavin opened the door. On the other side, Nestor smiled gently as he observed them both. "I hope I'm not interrupting—?"

"Not at all," Gavin assured him. "Come in."

Persephone fought the wave of self-consciousness that threatened to swamp her and found beneath it some morsel of poise. She clung to that as the elderly librarian drew from beneath his robe a small scroll and handed it to Gavin. "After you left," Nestor explained, "I had the thought that this might be of interest to you. It's shelved on one of the lower levels of the library. I was down there looking for it when the oddest thing happened."

"You felt the ground shake," Gavin said as he unrolled the scroll and scanned it quickly.

"Exactly, but how did you know? No one else seems to have noticed."

"We were in the caves," Persephone said. "The tremor was much stronger there."

Nestor frowned. "I see . . . then perhaps it really is just as well I found that." He indicated the scroll.

Coming to stand at Gavin's elbow, Persephone looked at what he was now reading in earnest. It was in a language she did not know. "What is this?"

"A letter," the librarian explained. "It is, of course, a copy—in the original Latin—dating from the first century A.D. The writer was a young man named Pliny, a Roman. He was an eyewitness to the explosion of a volcano that destroyed the town of Pompeii."

Gavin looked up from the scroll. His eyes were shuttered, his expression carefully blank. "Pliny writes that there were tremors in the days leading up to the explosion. Nestor, with all respect, how is it that you happened to bring this to me?"

"It is my nature to ask questions," the older man said quietly, "and to seek answers. For instance, I wondered why you sought a centuries-old report on the elevation of points of land in various parts of Akora. I wondered why such a report would be of interest to the

Vanax. Why he would remove it from the library, leaving no record that he had done so?"

"Where did this wondering lead you?" Persephone asked.

"To another question." With an apologetic shrug, Nestor explained, "Unlike the Vanax, you, Prince Gavin, cannot remove books without a record being kept. It was a simple matter for me to discover that you apparently have developed a consuming interest in the subject of volcanoes."

Gavin rolled up the scroll and returned it to the old man. "I hope you have not shared your discovery with anyone else."

"No, I have not, nor do I intend to do so. However, I would like to help you. From what I saw, you've read a vast amount on the subject, but I noticed you'd missed Pliny. That's why I went looking for him. After experiencing that tremor, I must ask you—your interest in volcanoes is not merely academic, is it?"

Gavin did not answer at once. He walked a little distance away and stood with his back to them, looking out over the city.

Behind him, Persephone pulled a chair away from the table and offered it to Nestor, who took it with a grateful smile. "I'm just going to get dressed," she said, hoping her cheeks were not as warm as they felt. Quickly, while Gavin was sufficiently preoccupied, she slipped from the room.

He turned, thinking to stop her, but then reconsidered. She had been through so much in so short a time. He understood her instinct to seek solitude, if only to regain her self-possession. That he would allow, though not for overly long. Soon enough she would have to accept that she now shared herself with him.

In the meantime—

"Thank you for bringing me this, Nestor," he said, indicating the scroll.

The old man nodded. "Pliny reminded me that our very oldest records contain recollections of the survivors of the Cataclysm. They might be worth looking at."

"I did look at them. They're very scant."

"I suppose people had all they could do building a new world. Still, I believe I'll dig a bit." He stood to go. "May I ask how you intend to proceed?"

Gavin recognized the question for what it was, acknowledgment that the situation was both delicate and urgent. He thought again of what it would mean to tell hundreds of thousands of people that their world might be about to end. Even the considerable courage and discipline he had always found among the Akorans would be taxed to its limits.

"To begin with, I am going to speak with Polonus."

Nestor nodded. "A good choice, Prince. Your uncle knows the pulse of the Council."

"I'm counting on that."

He saw the librarian out, then quickly dressed in a simple unbleached tunic and sandals. Leaving his own quarters, he glanced in the direction of Persephone's rooms, but kept going.

He found his uncle exactly where he expected to at that late afternoon hour. The palace school was quiet and almost empty. Only a few students still lingered. Walking past the rooms where he had studied during his stays on Akora, Gavin was caught between fond memory and concern for what might be coming. It still seemed inconceivable that a way of life built up over thousands of years could be destroyed, yet increasingly that reality was becoming inescapable.

It was uppermost in his mind when he entered his uncle's office. Polonus was just finishing a meeting with a young man who looked as though he would be more at ease on the training field than in the classroom.

"Your last effort shows genuine improvement," Polonus said kindly. "It's clear you've thought about the subject on a deeper level."

"I tried," the young man said. "Once I began to think about it more, it grew more interesting."

"You may find that generally happens when you use your mind."

The young man nodded, inclined his head courteously to Gavin, and took his leave. When they were alone, Polonus said, "And there you have it, the reason I teach."

"That moment of awakening?" Gavin asked with a smile.

"Precisely. Six months ago, Jason gave every evidence of having a block of wood where his brain was supposed to be."

"Your perseverance pays off, and not for the first time, as I can attest."

"Oh, you were never that bad." Straightening his papers, Polonus added, "So what brings you here?"

Gavin hesitated. Only Persephone and Nestor knew of his fears. Once he told Polonus, who was himself a member of the Council, there would be no going back.

But there was also no standing still.

"I need to talk with you," he said quietly.

Polonus raised a brow. He was a slender man of medium height, in his early fifties. Pleasant enough in appearance, he might have passed unremarked were it not for his gentle brown eyes, which reflected a caring, compassionate spirit.

"Not here," Gavin said. "Let's take a walk."

They left the school and crossed the courtyard in front of the palace. A little-trod path led down to a beach. Polonus said nothing until they reached the water. As Gavin stood, staring out at the sea, his uncle asked, "What requires such privacy?"

"A personal matter. And another that is not so personal."

"Which would you rather begin with?"

"The first. Polonus . . ." This required some delicacy. "You knew the traitor Deilos."

The older man frowned slightly. With a touch of wryness, he replied, "That is a kind way to put it. As you are aware, for a time I was one of his deluded followers."

"For which you long ago made recompense. I have no wish to revive unpleasant memories, but I would like to know——" He broke off, suddenly unsure that he wanted to continue. Such irresolution was foreign to him. He would not indulge it.

"I would like to know more about Deilos. For instance, did he ever marry?"

"Marry?" The question clearly surprised Polonus. "Why no, he wanted to marry your mother. When he was thwarted in that, he tried to kill her."

"It's not possible that he ever had a wife?"

Polonus looked at him closely. "Anything is possible, but I never heard of it and I think I would have." He grimaced. "We were fascinated by him, you see, as only the naïve can be by one who offers very simplistic answers to life's complexities. At any rate, everything to do with him was grist for gossip—what he ate, drank, what he said about the most ordinary things, how he looked at any moment. If he'd had a wife, we would have gone on and on about her."

"Then he had no children?"

"Children? Now that is a different matter. The getting of children hardly requires marriage."

"True enough, but it is rare for an Akoran child to be born outside of marriage."

"Deilos visited England. Do you mean to ask if he fathered a child there?"

Gavin shook his head curtly. "No, I don't."

"An Akoran child, then. A child no longer, of course, not if Deilos was the father. A grown man . . ." Polonus's gaze turned shrewd. "Or is it a woman?"

Rather than reply directly, Gavin asked, "Did you ever hear of anyone like that?"

"No, I didn't, but Deilos presented himself as a man of great morality. I know it's hard to believe such a thing, given his murderous actions, but it happened all the same. Had he fathered a child, especially out of wedlock, I think he would have gone to great lengths to keep it secret."

"He would have needed help doing that, wouldn't he?"

"Yes, I suppose he would have."

"Deilos had family: a mother and a sister."

"Two sisters. The mother is long dead, but the sisters are still alive."

"Do you know anything about them?"

Polonus thought for a moment. "I know they were not blamed in any way for his crimes. Deilos left a sizable fortune, as I recall. They were judged to be his heirs and the estate was divided between them."

"But they never took possession of Deimatos?"

"That's true. The island had been in Deilos's family for generations, but in light of the rather horrific events that occurred there, I believe the sisters agreed to deed it to the public trust. My impression is that they were glad enough to be rid of it."

Grimly, Gavin said, "I'm sure they were eager to put it all behind them."

"I suppose so. Now, you mentioned another matter."

Wrenching his thoughts back in the direction he knew they must go, Gavin explained. He spoke slowly and calmly, taking Polonus step-by-step through everything he had discovered.

The older man listened intently. He asked good questions, just as Gavin expected of a man who trained others to do the same.

Halfway through their conversation, much of the color was gone from Polonus's face. When Gavin finished, his uncle was silent for several minutes. Finally, he asked, "Does anyone else know?"

"Nestor does, but he won't speak of it to anyone. There is also one other."

"Who?"

"Her name is Persephone, and I think it's time you met her."

CHAPTER X

GOOD SENSE, WHICH SHE USED TO HAVE aplenty, told her she would be wise to rest. And she did try. But the bed, even the idea of a bed, was too new and her eyes would not stay closed. After tossing and turning for the better part of an hour, she gave up and sought some other occupation.

It was not difficult to find. Scarcely had she risen and straightened her clothing than she knew where she wanted to go.

Not that she should, she was quite well aware of that. It would be foolish in the extreme, courting trouble. That didn't stop her. She hurried down the hall, keeping a careful eye out for anyone who might seek to stop her. No one appeared. She reached the staircase in the wall without hindrance, and started down it.

At the ground level, she did as Gavin had and set

spark to tinder, to light a lamp. With it in hand, she proceeded. The statue room looked even vaster and more strangely fascinating than it had before. She paused long enough to wonder who might be represented there and what each person had done to merit what must surely be an honor.

Moving on, she hurried through the first cave and took the passage Gavin had shown her. When she reached the buried beach, she set the lamp aside carefully. The light cast by the tiny life forms in the water revealed the small temple. She approached it cautiously, all too mindful of what had occurred within it.

Was she mad to return here? What need drove her? In Gavin's company, she had been far too distracted to take more than distant note of her surroundings. Now she focused much more clearly. The face in the moss looked slightly different from what she remembered, as though it was more in repose now than it had been.

That wasn't possible. A carving did not change, except with the wear of time.

She bent down, staring at the face. Water continued to trickle past it, but she was not so foolish as to drink. This time her mind would remain clear.

"Who are you?" she murmured as she reached out, brushing a finger over the stone.

The warm stone.

Warm? How could that be? The water must surely cool it.

Perhaps the lava flows were closer than they seemed.

Yet she saw no evidence of them. Moreover, the ground when she touched it held no hint of heat.

Yet the stone felt warm; that much was undeniable. She sighed, sitting back on her knees, and continued looking at the face.

The feeling came slowly, creeping over her so gradually that she scarcely noticed until it fully encompassed her. Even so, she was not alarmed. She had felt this most of her life, this sense of unity with something vastly beyond herself, something that lived, that felt, that watched, and, above all, that cared.

Something that was, beyond any question, real.

Gavin believed she had dwelled in solitude, especially since her mother's death, but the truth was that she had never truly been alone.

Akora was always there.

The spirit of Akora, people called it, and for them it was a matter of faith. For her it was certain knowledge. The awareness of something alive in the world, vastly beyond herself, yet as intimate as a grain of sand in her palm. It was the spark of every dream and the comfort of every fear.

"You . . ." she said softly and felt just a little foolish. But she was alone, there was no one to hear her, and she had no reason to temper her response. "Are you here, truly?"

Beneath her hand, the warmth seemed to stir.

Persephone leaned against the moss-covered wall. She closed her eyes, breathing deeply. Softly, she said,

"Help me. Help me to understand what is happening . . ."

Behind her eyes, fire leaped. Great flares of flame ripped from the earth, hurtling toward the sky. The ground shook as crevices opened into a hellish landscape. Black clouds covered the sun. Lava poured forth in immense, slowly rippling waves. Where it touched the sea, vast plumes of steam rose as the ocean itself seemed to boil away.

Yet it did not. The lava cooled. The sea lapped against it gently. The sky cleared and seabirds returned. Where the lava had glowed red, there was black ground. New earth, born of fire, in time bearing life.

She snatched her hand away from the stone face. The water gurgled softly, sparkling over the moss, falling gently to the ground, sinking away into the earth.

It was going to happen. Any hope she had entertained that the Cataclysm was not about to return was gone. Yet hope remained, for life would endure . . . or at least such life as could survive the explosion itself.

She had to tell Gavin.

Gavin, who did not believe.

No, who would not let himself believe. There was a difference. Duty-bound to a life in England. Shield of England. It sounded like something a man of honor could not walk away from, and he was that, her Atreides prince, for all that he was also mistaken.

He belonged to Akora, as he belonged to her.

The first was true, but the second surely was not. He could never belong to her, could never be more than a stolen moment kept wrapped in precious memory.

Convince him. Show him the way. Guide him to feel what you feel, know what you know.

She stood, pushing aside her own longings, steeling herself for what must be, and went from the temple, her pace quickening as she reached the stairs and climbed out of the twilight of the caves and into the light of a fading day. She was hurrying when she reached the corridor, confronted there by Gavin, who stood glaring at her, hands on his lean hips.

"Where the hell have you been?" Gavin demanded.

His manner took her aback. This was not the passionate and giving lover she had come to know, or even the noble prince whose patience and self-control seemed nearly endless. Engulfed as she was in deep and serious purpose, his blunt masculine challenge surprised her. Yet she would have answered him, probably with equal bluntness, were it not for the other man standing behind him, regarding her quizzically.

"I went for a walk." And then, sweetly, she added, "Is something wrong?"

"I didn't know where you were."

She who was utterly unaccustomed to anyone thinking about her for any reason was struck by this. It shouldn't have touched her so deeply, so she told herself, yet it did all the same.

"Well . . . as you can see, I'm fine."

"Yes, well . . . good." Gavin turned to the older man, who continued to regard them with friendly interest. "This is my uncle, Polonus. Polonus, this is Persephone."

"A pleasure to meet you, my dear," Polonus said. "Are you from Ilius?"

"No, I am not." Nor did she volunteer her origins. On that subject, she preferred to remain entirely silent.

"Ah . . . I see."

"Persephone is aware of what is happening," Gavin said. "She has been helping me."

"Then we three should speak together," Polonus said.

At the far end of the family wing was a pleasant area with large windows overlooking the sea and arranged with comfortable couches and chairs. Gavin sat beside Persephone as the two of them faced Polonus, the older man watching them both closely. Whatever he saw must have pleased him, for he smiled gently.

"Have you considered what your next move should be?" he asked Gavin.

"We must go to the Council."

"To what end?" Persephone asked. She was not disputing him, but wished to understand what he intended.

"Their cooperation will be needed in any effort to prepare the people for what may be coming," Gavin explained.

For what *was* coming, but she would not blurt that out in front of Polonus. Rather she would wait until she and Gavin were alone. "They *must* believe you. But is that likely?"

"I believe him," Polonus interjected. "At least to the point of regarding this as a matter requiring close attention, and I am a member of the Council. Another of Gavin's uncles, Prince Alexandros, is also a member, but Alex is not on Akora at the moment. That leaves three others—the healer, Elena, who is the eldest among us; Marcellus, who previously served with distinction as chief magistrate; and Goran, who until the death of his father several years ago was called Goran the Younger. Now he is just Goran and he may be the hardest to convince."

Persephone leaned back against the couch. She was close to being exhausted, yet still she struggled to understand. "Why is that?"

"He is from Leios," Gavin said, naming the island on the opposite side of the Inland Sea from Ilius. Persephone had sailed there several times and been impressed by the beauty of the place renowned for its magnificent horses. When she said as much, Gavin grinned. He looked younger suddenly, a glimpse of the man he would be, were it not for the responsibilities he carried.

"The horses of Leios are a marvel," he agreed, "but Leios is also justly known for the plainspoken stubbornness of its people. They are slow to rouse and slower still to act, but when they do, I doubt any are stronger or steadier."

"Then this Goran would be an important ally."

Polonus agreed. He and Gavin went on to talk about how the counselor from Leios might best be approached. Or at least that was what Persephone thought they were talking about. Her eyelids were growing heavier by the moment, as she struggled to stay awake.

It was a struggle she had to win. She had to talk with Gavin, to convince him— But the day that had begun with Sida brushing her hair, and had continued so tumultuously, had taken an insurmountable toll. She was not aware when her head settled against Gavin's shoulder or when he glanced down and, seeing her asleep, drew her close against him.

At length, the Atreides prince said, "I thank you for your help, Uncle. Persephone has anticipated us, but I think we should all get some rest." He stood, lifting her gently in his arms. She did not wake, but nestled against him as naturally as though she really did understand that she belonged there.

Polonus also rose. "Since Goran is in the city now, there is nothing to prevent you from addressing the Council tomorrow. Would you like me to arrange it?"

"I would. There is no point in delay."

He bid his uncle goodnight and was turning to go when Polonus said quietly, "I see no hint of Deilos in her."

Gavin stopped. His arms tightened around Persephone as though to protect her, but that was foolish. She slept and heard nothing. More to the point, Polonus meant her no harm. He had, sensibly enough, discerned the reason for Gavin's earlier questions about Deilos and come to his own conclusions.

"She does not resemble him either in her appearance or her manner," his uncle continued. "However, she does remind me of someone."

"Who?"

"I don't know. I cannot place it. Perhaps with time, it will come to me. Or perhaps she will simply choose to tell you herself who she is."

Polonus departed by the stairs leading down from the family wing. Alone in the corridor, except for sleeping Persephone, Gavin did not hesitate. The guest quarters were a short distance from where he stood. He walked right past them and continued on down the hall to his own apartments. Without disturbing the woman in his arms, he pushed open the door, kicked it shut behind him, and carried her over to the bed. His bed.

Moonlight flowed through the windows as he laid her down. He removed her sandals, then followed them quickly with her gown. In England, the women wore clothing of astounding complexity, intricate with buttons, loops, and clasps. There was also a great deal more of it, most particularly given the growing prudishness of fashion. Dressing—and undressing—were time-consuming and elaborate rituals. Not so on Akora. Persephone's gown was genuinely modest, and it came off with ease.

The sight of her body gleaming pale in the silver light had the predictable effect and then some. He hardened so quickly he had to suck in his breath and remind himself that she was both new to passion and exhausted. He was not—*not*—a churlish oaf, although the temptation to forget that was all but irresistible.

He could find another bed or he could toss a blanket on the floor and sleep there. The latter had no appeal and the former was out of the question. He would not leave her. Instead, he steeled himself and lay down beside Persephone. She stirred slightly but did not wake.

With a heartfelt sigh, Gavin turned on his side and gathered her close against him. Sheltering her in the arc of his big, powerful body, he resigned himself to a long night.

Eventually, he fell into a light sleep filled with trails of thought that seemed to go nowhere in particular.

Persephone . . . who was she? What was she hiding?

Hawkforte . . . duty . . .

Evacuation? How? So many people . . .

Persephone . . . so soft, so . . . right . . .

The face in the cave. He had known it all his life, seen it more times than he could recall.

He had never touched it.

He would someday, and then . . .

Hawforte. Duty. He could not follow his heart, no matter how strong the need. He could not . . .

Persephone.

"Persephone."

A cool hand touched his shoulder. A soft voice drew him from the sleep that offered no respite.

"Gavin, wake up, you're dreaming."

He lay on his back, caught in the momentary paralysis that sometimes accompanies sudden waking. Persephone was beside him, one hand holding the sheet over her breasts and the other touching him. In addition to the sheet, she wore a beguiling blush. Damn, she was good to wake up to.

"I was wondering how to evacuate three hundred-and-fifty thousand people," he murmured. "That is, if it has to be done."

She looked away from him for a moment. When she looked back, her eyes were deeply shadowed. "It will have to be done."

"We don't know that yet."

"I know it. Gavin, you must listen to me."

What he wanted to do was draw her down into his arms and kiss her thoroughly. But she looked so earnest, so determined, that he held back.

"I never meant to fall asleep last night," she told him. "I was just waiting until I could speak to you without Polonus being present."

"You can do that now," Gavin said. He sat up, tossed back the covers, and stood. Behind him, he heard a soft gasp. Amusement laced his voice. "It's not unusual for a man to awaken aroused, and your being here guarantees it."

"I shouldn't be here. Why didn't you take me to my own room, or better yet, wake me?"

He rubbed a hand over his jaw, recalling that he needed to shower and shave. Polonus wouldn't waste any time summoning the Council. "I didn't want to," he said.

His bluntness surprised her. "You didn't want to?"

"No, I wanted you here with me."

"To sleep?"

His mouth twitched. "Yes, to sleep. It's odd though. I have a marked preference for sleeping alone, or at least I used to."

"So did—do—I."

Facing her, unabashed, he said, "Which is it? Does your solitude still hold such appeal?"

She sat up in the bed without losing her grip on the sheet, and faced him squarely. "You know it does not."

"You have not said so—until now."

"Be satisfied that I have—now. We have far more serious matters to discuss."

"It can wait until I've showered."

"Gavin . . . this is urgent."

"You could shower with me."

Her blush deepened. "I do not think that is a good idea."

He shrugged. "As you wish. I won't be long."

When he returned, still damp from the quick shower and with a towel wrapped around his hips, Persephone was draped in a soft white caftan and seated at a table beside the windows.

Sida had brought breakfast and gone again. They were alone, save for the words that hung unspoken between them.

He took a seat across from her. She poured him coffee. There were circles of buttered toast, coddled eggs, and paper-thin slices of sweet ham. It was all very domestic, very pleasant. Indeed, he was surprised by how much he enjoyed it.

They ate in silence for several minutes before Persephone put down her fork, touched the napkin to her lips, and said, "You must listen to what I say."

Gavin took another swallow of his coffee and refilled the cup. Inwardly, he braced himself. "I always listen."

"And you must believe."

"That is another matter, but I am willing to give serious consideration to what you tell me."

She looked less than satisfied by that but prepared to continue. Slowly, she said, "Ever since I was old enough to know anything, I have known that Akora is alive."

This again. He had thought she would tell him who she was, but she was back to what they had already discussed. All the same, he said, "So it is believed."

"No, so it is. I think because I have lived so much alone, in the midst of such quiet . . . I don't mean just the quiet of no noise, but the quiet within, when there are few distractions. You speak of listening. I listened to the earth, the water, the wind. I heard Akora."

"Persephone . . ." He paused, wanting to tread carefully around what she was saying. He was only just beginning to suspect how much he cared about this woman. Even without the ancient prohibition against harm, he could not imagine knowingly hurting her. "You have been so much alone, as you yourself say. In those circumstances—"

"You think I am hallucinating?" She spoke mildly, as though she had anticipated that he would entertain such a notion. Perhaps she had considered it herself.

"No, nothing so harsh. I think it is only natural that you would imagine the presence of some other being—"

"Oh, Gavin, it isn't that. I'm not imagining anything. What we know of as Akora may be only a tiny fragment of something far vaster, but whatever it is, it is real. I've known all my life what it has been through, and I know now that it is changing." She paused and took a breath. He saw the pain in her. "The Cataclysm is going to happen again."

Her absolute certainty rang like steel against stone. That, more than anything else, struck him. He pushed away from the table and rose, needing a little distance. "We don't know that."

She, too, stood, straight and slim in the light of the new day. Her brow was creased, her gaze intent. "I

know it. You must hear me. Open your mind and your
heart—"

"It is my mind that has discovered what's been happening to Akora. What do you think I've been doing
all these months? Studying, exploring, discovering—"

"Yes, you're right, of course, your mind isn't the
problem. It's your heart."

"Emotion will not solve this."

"But reason will? How can you hope to find a true
answer through reason alone when you admit you lack
the knowledge to discover what is happening, simply
because such knowledge does not exist? But *listen* to
me, you are of Akora, you—"

"We have spoken of this. My duty lies in England."

"Wishing will not make it so."

"I do not wish it! Damn it, Persephone, I do not!"
His hands were hard on her. He had no memory of
crossing the small space between them, but he had
done so all the same. He had to touch her, hold her.
Had to make her understand somehow.

"I do not wish it," he said more calmly. Her nearness
soothed him, even as he entertained the thought that
she was an infuriating woman—opinionated, stubborn, lacking in tact, and determined to make him
confront unpleasant truths.

No wonder he loved her.

"What's wrong?" she asked, her eyes suddenly wide
with alarm.

"Wrong? Nothing's wrong."

"You looked very odd there for a moment."

He'd wager he had, considering that he'd felt as though all the blood in his body had decided to pool in his feet. This was ridiculous. He was a man bred to courage. The small matter of love wasn't going to undo him.

He gathered his thoughts, a task that probably would have proceeded more quickly if he had let go of her. He wasn't inclined to do that. But his touch did gentle as he said, "All right, let me understand. You believe you have some sort of special contact with the living Akora, that you can 'feel' it? And this has led you to be certain that the volcano is going to explode. Is that right?"

"Yes, and I know you don't believe me but—"

"I don't *not* believe you. Hell, if you were a member of my family, if we were actually related, I'd be inclined *to* believe you."

She frowned at what that seemed to imply. "You would find me more trustworthy?"

"No, it has nothing to do with that. The fact is, my family's history is littered with women who had unusual 'gifts,' for want of a better word, although they more often seem to have been burdens, if not outright curses. My own mother is a good example, but there have been many others."

"Your mother is said to see the future."

"*Used* to see the future. She hasn't in years, my whole life, really, and from what I understand she's damn glad

164

of it. But there was a time when she had that ability and it saved Akora."

"From the traitor Deilos?" Her gaze flicked away from him, then returned.

"Among other dangers. Then there's my Aunt Joanna, who finds things, or at least she used to." He smiled. "These days, she claims she can't find a hat pin, but there was a time when her ability was really needed and then it worked unerringly."

Persephone frowned in puzzlement. "But the Princess Joanna married into your family, did she not? She wasn't part of it originally."

"That's true, but the line of Hawkforte is entwined with Akora. A younger son of Hawkforte came here centuries ago and married into the Atreides family. It seems he brought this matter of the 'gifts' with him, although they never show up in men, only in women."

He looked down at her thoughtfully. "That was many generations ago. Perhaps there is a distant connection to my family in your lineage."

"I doubt that."

"We keep excellent records. All you have to do is tell me who you are."

Silence descended, punctuated by the song of finches nesting just outside the windows and the distant, muted sounds of the city beyond. The sun was well above the horizon and climbing.

Head high, she separated herself from him. "I am

Persephone." Pride underlay her words—and, he thought, a hint of sadness. "That is enough for me."

He let her go because there was no choice. The Council would assemble and grave matters had to be addressed. The march of events would not wait for any of them.

If Persephone was right—

The gifts had always appeared among the women of his family when they were needed most. In some cases they developed over years, before vanishing when a crisis was past.

Persephone might be continuing that pattern. In which case, the situation might be even more immediately dangerous than he realized. Time could be very short, indeed.

On the cusp of that thought, he dressed quickly and went from the room, out into the current of the day.

CHAPTER XI

ALL YOU HAVE TO DO IS TELL ME WHO YOU *are*. The words rang in Gavin's mind as he left Persephone and went quickly down the corridor toward the outside stairs. He had made it sound simple, deliberately so, but she had deflected him. *I am Persephone. That is enough for me.* Denied what he wanted to know, he still couldn't help but smile. She had courage and more, an innate sense of her own self that would have sat well on a woman—or a man—many decades her senior.

Perhaps that was the result of having been alone so much. Or perhaps it had to do with the demons she had confronted.

He was certain that there were demons. The only question so far as he was concerned was how to exorcise them.

Then there was the matter of her "gift." No doubt

his reaction had surprised her. It would have done so even more if she had known the full extent of his acquaintance with such "gifts." Persephone had heard something, at least, of his mother and aunts, but she knew nothing of the generations of other women stretching back through time in whom similar "gifts" had occurred.

Always in times of peril.

That much fit, for certain. As did the fact that she could be a distant member of his family. Somewhere in the library of Akora was a copy of his family tree. There was one volume for each century. At last count, there were thirty-five volumes. Some were very old, having been created from ancient scrolls. Others were much more recent, comparatively speaking. He had been present when the current volume was brought out of the library, rather ceremoniously, to be inscribed with the name of his cousin Amelia's husband, Niels Wolfson. In time, the names of their children would be added, along, one day, with those of the spouses of those children and the children they had in turn.

He had no idea how many names in all were inscribed in the many volumes, but the total had to be in the tens of thousands, at least. Almost all those people had lived out their lives on Akora. It was hardly a stretch of the imagination to believe that one or more of them had crossed paths with Persephone's own ancestors.

But the nature of her gift . . . He had never heard of such a thing, at least not concerning a woman. To be able to *feel* Akora? There was a widespread belief that the men who became Vanax had some sort of special relationship with the land they served. No one knew exactly what that might be, except the men themselves, of course, and they did not speak of it.

At least, Atreus did not. Atreus, his uncle and his friend, who had helped to guide him through every step in his life. Atreus said very little about what it was to be Vanax. He just went about doing the job extremely well. He was also a devoted husband and father, and a truly gifted artist.

At the bottom of the stairs, where they opened onto the palace courtyard, was one of the many fountains to be found throughout Ilius, and indeed all over Akora. This fountain was different in one respect, though likely very few people knew it. The stone carvings around and above the fountain were Atreus's work. So, too, were other carvings and statues around the palace and its grounds, very few of which were actually known to have been created by the Vanax. Atreus was, at heart, a modest man with no need to plaster his name hither and thither. He had told Gavin once that the work should speak for itself, with none of the expectations and preconceptions that would come from its being known as the creation of a particular man.

The fountain was wreathed in ivy that, though carved

from stone, looked as though it might begin to sway in the wind at any moment. The degree of detail was extraordinary, revealing even the veins that pumped life through each individual leaf. Half-concealed within the ivy was a face, or more correctly, the suggestion of a face. Odd that he hadn't noticed it before. He'd walked by the same fountain hundreds of times, at the very least.

Yet now, bending closer, he saw that the face really was there. It wasn't a trick of the light or his own mind. The face was muted, to be sure, barely emerging from the stone, as though Atreus meant only to hint at it. Carefully, Gavin reached out and touched a finger to where he judged the mouth of the face to be.

The stone was warm.

He straightened without taking his eyes from it. The sun was in the east, casting the fountain into shade. It would be hours yet before the warmth of day could heat the stone. And even then, cool water bubbled up against it, continually refreshed by an underground spring.

Yet there was no mistaking, the stone held warmth.

Quickly he pressed a hand to the side of the palace itself and was relieved to find it cool. For just a moment, he had wondered if the surging lava flows might not have advanced suddenly. But all was as it should be except for the face within the fountain.

On impulse, he dipped a hand into the water and drank. It was fresh, cool, and delicious. People could collect rainwater and sometimes did, but they were willing to do the hard labor of digging wells to acquire water they thought was far better.

He'd helped to dig several wells the spring he was . . . thirteen? No, fourteen. He'd gone over to the island of Leios with a crew of boys his age, under the supervision of men who knew about the digging of wells. Also about the rearing of boys.

The men had begun by asking the boys how they thought a well ought to be dug, then inviting them to implement their suggestions. They waited patiently while the boys dug . . . and dug . . . and dug, discovering in the process that it was a great deal harder than they'd expected. Dirt walls crumbled and collapsed, but never managed to trap anyone because the men always seemed to know when that was about to happen and ordered the boys out in time. Water did not appear when it was expected, requiring them to consider long and hard where they should dig. Simply removing dirt quickly became impossible, until they realized the gears and pulleys lying in the pile of supplies weren't there by accident and built a simple hoist.

In the first week, they dug one working well. And learned in the process lessons for a lifetime, including about each other—who wanted to plunge right in without thought, who saw the value of planning, who kept going even when exhausted, who summoned good cheer and humor to uplift spirits, who led and who followed, and in the end, who pushed forward to drink from the well first, who held back until the thirst of others was met.

Through it all, the men watched, listened, and took note. Later, after they all returned to Ilius, Gavin encountered several of them coming out of Atreus's office. They stopped when they saw him, nodding and smiling before going on their way. He'd had dinner alone with Atreus that night. He couldn't remember what they talked about, but he recalled it was pleasant.

He hadn't thought of any of that in years, but the memory was strong in him now as he stood on the verge of a task vastly beyond the digging of a well. He faced the need to save a people, to convince them to see what he saw, to recognize their danger and act to protect themselves from it.

His mind on that, he set out across the courtyard but didn't get very far before he was greeted by many among the crowd gathered there to conduct all manner of business. First one man and then another, many he knew personally but some he did not, drew him into conversation. Some sought his advice; many merely informed him of their news and asked for his own. Was he staying long on Akora this time? How were matters in England? Was it true a young girl was queen there now?

He made no mention of what was uppermost in his mind but responded cordially and managed, little by little, to make his way across the courtyard toward the lions' gate. He was almost there when Polonus caught sight of him.

His uncle sighed with relief when he finally reached Gavin's side. "I've been looking for you. I was wrong; Goran isn't in the city. That is, he is visiting here from Leios, but he left Ilius yesterday to inspect a mill twenty miles south of here. I've sent word for him to return, but it will be several hours yet."

"Have you told the others—Elena and Marcellus?"

"I have, and of course they wanted to know why the Council would be summoned with both Atreus and Alexandros away. I put them off as best I could, but they'll be looking for answers and quickly."

"Then I'd better have them. In the meantime—" Any delay was unwelcome, but he would put it to good use. It was in his mind that he wanted to buy a gift for Persephone. That was a simple enough thing for a man to do, but he knew she could not possibly have been given very many gifts in her life and none recently.

Having taken leave of Polonus, he headed down into the city. The day was bright, sun-washed and vibrant. Everywhere he looked, flowers bloomed in neat gardens, along walls, and in hanging baskets beside the houses painted in vivid hues of blue, yellow, green, and red. Farther into the city, shops were open and busy, with goods arranged in neat displays and awnings unfurled over them. Below in the harbor, several dozen ships rode at anchor. Others were visible out on the Inland Sea. Toward the west, haze concealed the three small islands that included Deimatos, and beyond them the large island of Leios.

He paused for a few minutes outside a store offering glass bottles of the sort ladies favored for their perfumes. Each was beautifully formed, the glass interlaced with swirling patterns of gold and silver, and fitted with matching stoppers. They were tempting, but somehow they didn't quite seem to fit what he was looking for.

A little farther on he came to the entrance to the scribes' quarter, an old name harkening back to the long-ago days when books had to be copied out by hand. Now the neighborhood rattled to the sounds of printing presses, but it still accommodated craftsmen who used the finest papers, printed with the greatest care, and bound the results in engraved leather. The choices there seemed endless—poetry or navigation, history or weapons making? He moved on.

If there was any place in the world a man should not have a problem buying a gift for a woman, it was Ilius. Shops abounded with lovely fabrics, exquisite jewelry, perfumes and lotions, little ornaments whose purpose he could only guess at, anything and everything likely to please the cherished ladies of Akora. But nothing quite struck his eye.

He had stopped by a shop of an entirely different sort: one selling weapons, and was pondering his difficulty finding a gift for Persephone when a shadow fell across his path. Turning, he saw the Scotsman from the day before.

"Atreides," Liam Campbell said, a slight curl of the

lip suggesting the encounter was not the high point of his morning.

Gavin inclined his head grudgingly. "Campbell."

"Seems like we got off on the wrong foot."

It was as much of an apology as any man was likely to give another he did not know well, and Gavin took it as such. In turn, he said, "Seems like. Persephone tells me you lost friends coming here."

"They were my cousins as well."

"You have my sympathies. How are you settling in?"

Campbell smiled slightly. "Can't complain. I've gone partners with an Akoran on a merchant ship. We've been doing well on cargoes brought in from the Continent but we're thinkin' of seein' what the Yanks might have to offer."

"You might want to talk with my cousin Andreas the next time he's here." This was, of course, assuming there would be a next time, but whatever danger the volcano presented, a man had a right to think of the future. "He's just been appointed ambassador to Washington."

"Has he? Does that mean Akora's goin' to be openin' up a bit more?"

"A bit. We've come quite a way in just the last few years, but we remain cautious."

Campbell nodded. "That's fair. You've got a good thing here. No sense wreckin' it." He glanced down at the display stall next to Gavin. "You're lookin' for a knife?"

"No, not really." But one caught his eye just then, a blade about eight inches long with a leather hilt and matching scabbard dyed a deep, rich blue and set with pearls.

He was turning it over in his hands when he became aware of Campbell's expression. "You like that?" the Scotsman asked.

"I'm not sure—"

"Wouldn't have thought it was to your taste."

Abruptly, Gavin realized the direction of the Scotsman's thoughts and grinned. "I'm looking for a gift for Persephone."

Campbell gave a relieved laugh. "Oh, well then, that's all right. Except . . . you're really thinkin' of givin' her a knife?"

"You don't think she'd like it?"

"Hard to say . . . I don't know the lass." Quickly he added, "Which isn't to say I wouldn't like to."

Gavin's gaze narrowed. "You're going to start that again?"

The Scotsman shrugged. "Probably not. She may not know it yet, but . . . let's just say, I saw the way she looked at you."

"She also tore a strip off me."

"They only do that when they like you."

"Is that a fact? Well, then, what do you think?" He indicated the knife. "Should I or shouldn't I?"

Campbell laughed again. "Depends. Would you call yourself a confident man?"

"Reasonably. Why do you ask?"

"If you knew you wouldn't be givin' the lady any cause for complaint . . ."

Recalling Persephone's passionate response to him, Gavin nodded. "The knife it is then."

He concluded the sale but lingered a little longer, joining Campbell in examining the selection of swords. The Scotsman had a good eye for steel. By mutual accord, they continued the discussion of Spanish versus Austrian steel and the relative merits of the short sword compared with the long, over cold meats and cheese washed down by ale at a nearby tavern. A man had to eat, after all, and it didn't hurt any to do it in good company.

PERSEPHONE CAME DOWN THE ROAD FROM THE palace, then stopped and stared. At first she thought she was seeing things, but a second glance clarified the matter. There the two of them were, bare-chested and basking in the sun, at their ease over mugs of ale, in the midst of what gave every evidence of being a jovial conversation.

Men. Never mind that she had, until very shortly, known next to nothing about them or that she knew perfectly well she still had a tremendous amount to learn. She was woman enough to be unsurprised. Not to mention smart enough to have no desire to step into that particular encounter.

Instead, she skirted around a side street that led down to the harbor. Her boat was at the quay where she had left it. She went below and took a quick look around the small cabin crowded with all the things she had brought from Deimatos. Among them were Liam Campbell's books. It was all well and good that he felt she had salvaged them fairly, but she suspected they were the only remnants of his former life. She thought it only right to return them to him. The books were mixed in among her own in several crates, which she hauled up onto the deck so that she didn't have to remain in the stifling cabin.

The day was warm and there was very little breeze. She worked quickly, sitting cross-legged with the books all around her until she had found the two dozen or so volumes with Liam's name in them. Returning the rest to the cabin, she jumped down onto the quay and called to a young boy passing with a handcart.

"Would you know where a man named Liam Campbell lives?"

"Campbell . . . let me think . . . big fellow from Scotia?"

She nodded. "That's him. I have some books of his. I'd like to return them." She would especially like to do that while the gentleman in question was occupied elsewhere.

The boy nodded toward a warehouse just beyond the quay. "That's his place."

She looked at it doubtfully. "You're sure?"

"Lives up above. Makes it easier to keep an eye on business."

Convinced, Persephone thanked him and went back on board to gather up the books. With them in her arms, she crossed the quay to the warehouse. It was a sturdy building of whitewashed stone, two-storied, and with a slate roof. Double wooden doors stood open. She went through them into the cool interior and found herself in a large room, easily fifty feet in one direction and thirty in the other. Part of the room was used for storage; she saw crates, boxes, and bales. The smaller portion served as an office. A woman of middle years, wearing a dark green ankle-length tunic, was standing by a worktable. She saw Persephone and smiled.

"May I help you?"

Indicating the books, Persephone said, "These belong to Mister Liam Campbell. May I leave them here for him?"

"Yes, of course." The woman cleared a stack of papers off a nearby table. "Put them there. Liam isn't here right now, but if he comes back before I leave I'll tell him about them, otherwise my husband will."

"That's very kind of you, lady . . ." The woman had a kind and friendly manner that matched her appearance. Her face was round, open, and appealing. Her dark brown hair was sprinkled with silver, braided and coiled around her head.

"Melissa, and you are . . . ?"

"Persephone." Curiosity and the woman's cordialness prompted her to ask, "Does Mister Campbell work here?"

"He's in partnership with my husband. Cato and Liam run several merchant ships bringing goods from the Continent to Akora."

"I see—"

"It was Cato who found Liam," the Lady Melissa said cheerfully. "When he was shipwrecked. So exciting to actually find a *xenos*."

"I suppose it would be—" She remembered reading that any who found a stranger washed up alive on Akora's shores regarded the discovery as a blessing and the beginning of a very special relationship. It was not uncommon for such *xenos* to be taken directly into the families of their discoverers and quickly made to feel at home.

"We haven't met before, have we?" Melissa asked.

"No, I don't believe so." She had met people on her trips to Ilius, but this lady was new to her.

"It's just that you look a little familiar—"

Persephone paled slightly. The last thing she wanted was to meet someone who could connect her to her own past. "Thank you for your help. I must be going."

She turned to leave but stopped when the older

woman stepped forward quickly and laid a gentle hand on her arm. "Wait . . . I'm sorry if I said something to distress you."

"No, of course you didn't. I just have to go."

Ignoring that, Melissa said, "You're not from Ilius, are you?"

"No, I'm not. If you'll just tell Mister Campbell about the books." As discreetly as she could manage, Persephone pulled away. The older woman did not try to detain her further. Glad of that and anxious to be gone, Persephone turned toward the door through which she had come. Her gaze fell on the stone lintel directly above it. Carved into the stone was a single word: "Deimeides." And beneath it a date several decades in the past.

Without thought, Persephone turned again and faced the woman. "Why is that written there?"

Melissa stood with her back straight, hands folded in front, and regarded her steadily. "It is my family name. My grandfather built this warehouse. My sister and I inherited it upon the death of our brother." She paused before saying quietly, "I have thought of taking the stone down, for, as all know, my brother covered our name with dishonor."

"Did he?" She heard her own voice coming from her own mouth and yet seemingly also from a great distance, as though she no longer entirely inhabited her body. *Her brother?*

" 'The traitor Deilos' all call him, and sadly it is

deserved. But there was a time when the Deimeides name stood for far better. In memory of that, I have left the stone where you see it."

Slowly, Persephone said, "I did not know he . . . Deilos had sisters."

"Is there any reason why you should? He who was my brother is spoken of rarely these days, I am happy to say."

"No reason . . ." And every reason. She was looking at a woman she had never suspected existed. That was astonishing enough, yet there was another? Melissa had spoken of a sister.

"Does your sister live in Ilius?"

"Electra and her husband have a vineyard several hours travel to the north." The older woman paused a moment, then asked, "Dear, are you all right? You're very pale. Perhaps you should sit down."

"I'm fine, really." She had to get out, away from the eyes that were both kindly and keen. In another moment, she would be at very real risk of blurting out far more than she should.

Quickly she murmured her thanks again and left, this time without stopping. But her gaze did brush the stone lintel again just before she stepped beneath it.

The light outside was bright compared with the dimness within the warehouse. She had to pause for a moment to let her eyes adjust. As she did, her mind raced.

There was a time when the Deimeides name stood for far better.

Could that possibly be true? Was there more to the legacy of Deilos than infamy and shame? She began walking, heedless of her direction, but stopped before she got very far and looked back toward the warehouse. Melissa was standing just beyond the open doors, talking with a middle-aged man who by his manner might be her husband. Both of them looked in Persephone's direction.

She left quickly, escaping into a shadowed lane that led up toward the palace. She had reached it and was crossing the courtyard when Gavin called her name.

"There you are," he said, coming up to her. His gaze sharpened. "Is everything all right?"

"All things considered, I suppose so. Do you know when the Council meeting will be?"

"Goran is out of the city but will be on his way back by now. It shouldn't be much longer." With a hand to her elbow, Gavin drew her aside, beneath a recessed arch that was one of many leading to the ground floor of the palace. "I have something for you." He released her and held out a small package wrapped in fabric.

She looked from it to him in bewilderment. "Something . . . ?"

"A gift," he explained gently and pressed the package on her. "Go on, open it."

She did so but hesitantly, uncertain of how to react. Her mother had given her gifts, simple things made by her own hands, but there had never been anyone else to give her anything.

The fabric parted to reveal a flash of blue and white. Blue leather, she saw as she looked more closely, decorated with pearls. It was breathtakingly beautiful, so much so that a moment passed before she realized the leather was shaped into a scabbard and within it . . .

A knife, hilted in the same leather but without the pearls that would have impeded its grip. The blade, engraved with swirling designs, curved to a lethal point.

Gavin was standing very close to her. She looked up at him, seeing to her astonishment that he appeared just a little uncertain. "You're giving me this knife?"

He nodded. "Do you like it?"

"It's the most beautiful thing I've ever seen."

He relaxed then and grinned. "I thought it would appeal to you. It's for slaying boars and . . . other things."

She wasn't going to cry, absolutely not. That would be shameful. A woman worthy of such a knife did not go about weeping. Even so, her eyes were damp when she tucked the knife into the belt of her tunic and, because she could do nothing less, put her arms around Gavin. "Thank you," she murmured, breathing in his warmth and strength.

His arms closed in turn around her. In the shadows beneath the arch, he held her tightly, willing the demons to be gone.

CHAPTER XII

THE COUNCIL OF ADVISORS TO THE VANAX of Akora met in a small, plainly furnished room that had nothing to distinguish it from numerous other such rooms in the vast palace.

It did have an oval table surrounded by chairs that did not look particularly comfortable. Seeing them, Persephone wondered if they were intended to discourage long-windedness.

There was also a large map of Akora hung on one wall, a scattering of copper braziers on tripods that remained unlit on a day that did not require their warmth, and a tray of goblets accompanied by a beaded pitcher of water.

The men and one woman gathered in the room looked no more exceptional than their surroundings, which was to say that they appeared to be a selection of entirely ordinary Akorans. Neither their manner nor their dress suggested they were anything else.

Which just went to show how deceptive appearance could be. Collectively, they wielded significant power and the responsibility that went with it.

Elena, the only woman present besides Persephone herself, was in her eighth decade. White-haired, somewhat stooped, the renowned healer needed the assistance of a cane, but otherwise appeared entirely engaged and capable.

She was chatting with a man Persephone guessed must be Marcellus. Slender, with closely trimmed dark hair and beard, and a muscular bearing, he looked younger than what she guessed to be his fifty or so years. The former magistrate was known to her through his excellent books on Akoran history, all of which she had read several times.

They were joined by Goran, who arrived last, nodded to Gavin, cast an inquiring glance at Persephone, and went over to join his fellow counselors. In his midthirties, the youngest counselor was almost as tall as Gavin and had the look of a warrior, not surprising since virtually all men on Akora were warrior-trained.

With all assembled, Polonus wasted no time. Speaking quietly, he said, "Thank you all for coming on such short notice. Please be seated. Prince Gavin has a matter of importance he must discuss with us."

When they had all settled round the table, Gavin began. First he introduced Persephone, saying only that she was assisting him. Then without further preamble, he said, "There is a possibility that the volcano that tore Akora apart more than three thousand years ago is going to erupt again soon."

The three counselors who had not already known reacted to this announcement in varying ways. Elena's head snapped up and her eyes glittered. She had the sudden look of a much younger and fiercer woman. Marcellus's big, capable hands clenched into fists. Of them all, Goran showed the least response. He picked up a stylus lying beside his tablet and twirled it idly between his fingers. Yet his gaze locked intensely on Gavin.

"Why do you say this?" he asked.

Calmly and concisely, Gavin described his actions of the past several months and what he had discovered. He concluded, saying, "The lava flows beneath the palace have never approached the levels they have now reached. Similarly, the lava flows in the caves of Deimatos are also greatly increased. Steam vents fueled by escaping lava have appeared off the coast of Deimatos. Yesterday, there was an earth tremor deep below the palace. There may be more such tremors coming, signals of an approaching explosion. We face a time of crisis . . . and decision."

Several minutes passed while those gathered around the table absorbed this. Finally, Elena spoke. "Prince Gavin, I must ask what I suspect is foremost in all our minds: Where is the Vanax in all this?"

"Atreus is aware of the situation. I prepared a preliminary report several months ago, which he has seen. He has expressed his confidence that the situation will be handled properly."

"Then he is not concerned?" Marcellus said.

"I would not say that," Gavin replied.

"But he is not here," Goran pointed out. "And surely if the Vanax had any reason to believe Akora was in danger, he would not have left."

That, Persephone thought, was the crux of it. Naturally enough, people who knew the Vanax well and placed their faith in him would believe his absence signaled there was no real danger.

This, more than anything else, was what she and Gavin had to overcome.

Quietly she said, "It does not seem useful to speculate about the motives of the Vanax." Especially not since she herself regretted having done so. There truly was no point. "What matters is what is actually happening. The volcano is about to explode."

"You are so certain?" Elena asked, eyeing her closely.

"Yes, I am. I can feel it."

The counselors glanced at one another around the table. Before any of them could speak, Gavin said, "We are all aware that there have been occasions in the past when women possessed of unusual abilities helped to save Akora from great danger."

Polonus raised a brow. "Are you suggesting this lady is another of these women?"

Very deliberately, Gavin reached across the table and took her hand. "Yes, I am."

Her breath caught. For a seemingly endless moment, she truly could not breathe or think or do anything except overwhelmingly feel. Never had she expected this. Gavin's faith in her and his willingness to express it before people whose opinions must count highly with him astonished her. She did not deserve this, could never hope to merit it. And when he knew why, he would realize just how undeserving she truly was.

But for the moment, how achingly bittersweet it was. To her dread, she feared she was about to cry.

"That would be extraordinary," Elena said, not unkindly. "It would suggest she has a connection to your family, for it is only among the women of your own line that such gifts are known to have occurred."

The stylus moving between Goran's fingers, stilled. Persephone felt the razor-keenness of his gaze. "Is there such a connection?" he asked.

"Not to my knowledge," she said as calmly as she could manage.

"Family lineages are complex matters," Polonus said smoothly. "No doubt it would be a fascinating subject for another time."

Persephone looked to him gratefully, but Goran was not to be diverted. "It seems to me it is a subject for *this* time," the youngest counselor said pointedly. "After all, we are being asked to give weight to what the lady says, based on the possibility that she possesses some special ability. Absent any reason to believe that, skepticism would seem the wiser course."

Gavin's hand tightened on hers. He looked about to respond when Persephone said quietly, "Believe me or not, as you will, Counselor Goran. But each day—each hour—you delay preparing the people of Akora for what is coming may mean deaths that might have been avoided."

To his credit, Goran winced. She thought him a decent man, just reluctant to believe that his world was about to be torn apart. "Prince Gavin presents facts," he said. "Honest men may disagree on what they mean, but they are there for all to see. You say only that you can 'feel' what is going to happen. What does that mean?"

It was a fair question, though she had no easy answer. Slowly, she said, "Everything has its own pattern—the shape of a leaf, the course of clouds across the sky, the movement of the stars in the heavens. When something changes, the pattern is disrupted. I think it's possible to feel that, to know on some level that the pattern is no longer the same. I felt it with Akora, so I went to see if I could find out what was wrong. That's how I found the lava flows on Deimatos and the steam vents as well."

"You found them?" Elena interjected. "How did you come to be on Deimatos?"

Again, Persephone hesitated, but there really was no

way around this. She had known that when she took her seat at the table. "I live there."

"No one lives there." Marcellus spoke with the authority of a man certain of what he is saying.

Elena looked at Persephone thoughtfully, but she addressed the former magistrate. "How can you be certain?"

"Because it is forbidden," he explained. "When the traitor Deilos died, Deimatos was deeded to the public trust. It cannot be occupied or, indeed, used in any way without authorization by this Council."

The aged healer smiled gently. "My dear Marcellus, you don't really believe that something cannot occur simply because it is judged to be illegal?"

"Of course not, but why would anyone take up occupancy in such a manner? To maintain it, they would have to cut themselves off from the rest of Akora."

"That is precisely what my mother wished to do when she went to Deimatos," Persephone said quietly.

Goran's gaze narrowed. "Your mother? Why would she choose such a thing? For that matter, who was she?"

"That's enough." Gavin spoke without emotion, his words all the more forceful for that, cutting off any response she might have made. "I did not ask Persephone to come here to be interrogated. You may consider what she says or not, as you will, but know that I will act with or without your support."

This visibly startled the counselors, but Marcellus

rallied quickly. "With all respect, Prince, you have no authority."

"Do I not?" Far from being offended or angered, Gavin looked amused. Persephone had no idea what to make of that except that it hinted at the unbreachable confidence of the man, as much a part of him as the power of his body and mind. "I am the only member of my family on Akora at the moment," he said. "That being the case, I must act as I believe they would, most particularly as Atreus would."

"You seek to act in place of the Vanax?" Goran inquired with mildness that barely concealed disparagement.

Gavin shook his head. "I would never presume to do that. But I will fulfill my responsibilities. What must be done, will be done."

"What is it you consider needs to be done?" asked Polonus.

Without hesitation, Gavin said, "The people must be informed and they must begin to prepare."

Elena shook her head. "Telling them could lead to panic, which in turn could cause injuries or even deaths."

"There will be no panic," Gavin said. "It will be up to all of us to see to that. Akorans are courageous and disciplined. Once they absorb the initial shock, they will respond well."

"Your confidence in our people is impressive," Goran said dryly. "And I don't disagree with it.

However, you are asking us to trust you"—he nodded toward Persephone—"and this lady on a matter of the gravest importance. We would be derelict in our duty if we did not insist on time to consider what you have said and weigh the consequences of whatever we may do before we act."

"We really can't just plunge in," Elena agreed. "There must be time to think first."

Marcellus nodded. "It would be different if the Vanax were here, but he is not, and whatever you say, Prince Gavin, you do not have his authority."

"He has his letter," Persephone said. She had kept silent as long as she could, and she would do so no longer. They did not understand or they did not believe; whichever it was, she could not blame them for it. But neither could she let precious time slip away.

"What letter?" Marcellus asked, looking from her to Gavin, who hesitated before he replied.

"A private letter from Atreus to me. You may see it if you wish, but I don't think—"

"Thank you," Goran interjected. "We would like to see it."

Gavin withdrew the letter from the small pile of papers he had brought with him to the meeting and handed it to Goran, who read it swiftly before handing it on. Each of the counselors read it—Polonus last of all, who returned it to Gavin with a small smile.

"So Atreus has confidence in you and is certain you

will be able to handle the situation well. Why did you hesitate to tell us of this?"

"As I said, the letter is private."

"The Vanax seems content to leave this matter to you," Goran admitted, making no effort to hide his surprise. "I cannot recall Atreus ever entirely delegating a matter of genuine importance to anyone, but he seems to have done that now."

How long, Persephone wondered, had these members of the Council been serving on it together? How long had they worked together? Years, she surmised, for they seemed to have mastered the art of communicating with one another without words. A look that went round the table, a quick series of nods. Goran was still frowning; Marcellus appeared thoughtful; Elena smiled. And Polonus . . . he looked quietly satisfied.

"Well, then," Polonus said, "I propose we all listen to how Prince Gavin thinks we should proceed on this matter."

"Yes, how do you think we should proceed?" Goran asked with just a hint of challenge.

Gavin rose and walked over to the map hanging on the wall. Pointing to the large island on the far western side of the Inland Sea, he said, "It is two days sail to Leios. Goran, you should leave immediately."

The youngest counselor leaned back in his chair with the air of a man not about to leap from it. "Should I?"

"Someone must go, and I can think of no one better suited to the task than you. The people of Leios must know of their peril. In every household, they must prepare themselves, their boats, and their animals—I presume you will want to take your horses?"

"You can be certain we would not leave them." Goran looked aghast at the mere thought. "But prepare how? If you are right, there will be no place of safety."

"There will be one," Gavin said. "And only one. The open sea."

"Not the Inland Sea?" Elena asked.

"No, the sea beyond Akora. It is fortunate that we are a seafaring nation. Even so, evacuating three hundred-and-fifty thousand people—and their animals—is a daunting task. Every ship we possess must be bent to it and quickly."

"You're talking about thousands of vessels," Goran said, but thoughtfully, as though he already calculated how it might be done. "The largest naval and merchant vessels should be able to carry several hundred people each, but will that be enough?"

"Don't forget all the fishing boats," Marcellus reminded him. "Many of them ply the open sea."

"Every vessel must be well supplied with food and water, for people and animals alike," Gavin said. "We have no way of telling how long we will have to remain at sea."

Persephone saw at once that the counselors had not thought of that. As the implication of Gavin's words sank in, they looked for the first time truly struck with dread at what lay before them.

Elena spoke little above a whisper. "You mean, we may not be able to return?"

"We will return," Persephone said quickly. "Akora will survive and so will we, provided we act in time. But Prince Gavin is right, we will have to be prepared to stay at sea until it is safe to return."

"What of everything else?" Marcellus asked. "Our art, our books, all our treasures. What is to be done with them?"

"The library must also be evacuated," Gavin said firmly. "It holds our collective memory, the knowledge of who and what we are. Polonus, I entrust this to you. Nestor will help, I am certain, and he will enlist anyone else you need. But make sure you disperse the contents of the library very well. Do not send every copy of any book on the same vessel."

"I must summon the healers," Elena said as she stood. "They, too, must be spread out among the ships, prepared to deal with such injuries or sickness as may occur."

"There is much yet to determine," Marcellus said. "What limits do we set upon what can be taken? When exactly do we know to embark? How do we keep the fleet together once we reach the open sea?"

Quietly Polonus said, "How do we convince people that the world they have always known may be about to end?"

Gavin took a breath. He looked at once relieved the meeting had gone as well as it had and steeled to the immense task ahead. "If Persephone and I are right, there will be ample signs."

Goran pushed back from the table. His face was grim. "So be it, then. Let us begin, that we may make a good ending to all this and may Fortune favor us."

The old Akoran blessing echoed in Persephone's mind as she followed Gavin quickly from the room.

"Find Sida," he told her as soon as they had left the Council members. "Tell her what is happening—"

"She will not believe me."

He touched his hand to her face gently. "Yes, she will. Tell her you speak for me, that she will believe. Every family in Ilius has ties of some kind to the palace. Sida will know how to reach out to them quickly."

She nodded, still struggling to absorb that it was truly happening. Looking up at him, she asked softly, "Where will you be?"

"With the garrison. Persephone, I must know you will be safe. Promise me, if we are separated, you will not delay. You will get away from here."

She lowered her eyes, suddenly afraid of what he would see in them. The thought of losing him was unbearable, yet how could she not?

"Gavin, it is you who must survive. Surely you realize that?"

"No one man's life is so important—"

"Yours is. When you first showed me that letter from Atreus, I reacted badly and I am sorry for it. I let ignorance overtake me. But I have had time to think, and most of all, to come to know you." Her cheeks warmed at the reminder of just how very well she had come to know him. "Have you not thought why you are here instead of Atreus?"

"He did not know how close we were to—"

"How could he not know? He is Vanax, chosen to rule by Akora itself. He is the one person who would know. But he left, and moreover, he left you in charge."

"I'm not following this and there is little time—"

She moved closer, her hands on his broad shoulders, her body pressed close to his, savoring the warmth and strength of him. For the last time? No, she could not think of that.

Standing on tiptoe, she touched her mouth to his, drawing his breath into her. Softly, so softly, she whispered, "Heir to Hawkforte, duty-sworn to England, yet here on Akora all the same. Here where all will look to you, not to Goran or Marcellus or any of the others, but to you. As they are meant to look, that they, too, may know you."

He stiffened against her. "You are putting too much on this. Atreus could not have known what would happen, or he would have stayed."

"He did know and so do you. Listen to your heart, Gavin. Listen to who you are."

Her voice broke. The tears that had threatened too long would not be denied. Before he could see them, she whirled away and ran down the long corridor, swift and fleet over the ancient stone. Running from him, from herself, from the craven temptation to cling to him, the world and all in it be damned.

Behind her, she heard him call her name, but she did not stop. He would want to come after her, of that she was sure, but he would not. He would go to the garrison, to the men who, like him, were trained to confront any danger, accept any challenge, and overcome any obstacle.

The men he would lead into the terrible time of testing about to descend on them all.

And she?

She would find Sida and together with her would do everything she could, to the very limit of her strength, to save as much of Akora as could be saved—its people and animals, its art and books, its dreams and memories, all the precious fabric of a life constructed over thousands of years.

That, at least, she could do.

She brushed her tears aside and hurried on.

CHAPTER XIII

GORAN, BOUND FOR LEIOS, WENT IN SEARCH of Gavin before departing the following morning on the turning of the tide. He found him with the garrison at the training fields outside Ilius. There, where the fighting force renowned throughout the world honed deadly skills, men were busy stacking weapons, rounding up horses, and dismantling tents, all for transport to the harbor.

The youngest of the counselors wasted no time getting to the point. "Marcellus wants to send magistrates to the farms outside the city to warn people of what is happening."

Wiping sweat from his brow, Gavin straightened. He was bare-chested in the sun, hot and preoccupied. In his mind was a list of all that needed to be done. It seemed endless. "Is that a problem?"

"The people here in Ilius know the magistrates. They respect them and they'll follow their direction. Not so the country folk." Goran paused a moment. "At least not if they're anything like the people I know on Leios. They tend to be . . . not distrustful of authority, exactly, just skeptical of it."

Gavin swatted a fly away. "What are you suggesting?"

"You should go yourself," Goran said promptly. "They'll be more inclined to listen to you."

"They don't know me," Gavin pointed out.

"They know *of* you. They know your parents and they trust them. They know one of your sisters, too— Atlanta. She came over to Leios to have a look at things and she's spent a lot of time on the farms and vineyards outside Ilius."

"She's fascinated by plants," Gavin said quietly, thinking of the older of his two sisters. Atlanta was nineteen, and if she wasn't as fond of Akora as he was, she came very close.

"At any rate, people will listen to you more readily than they will to others. You should be the one to go."

"You must have some idea of how much there is to be done here."

"And I can see it being done," Goran said bluntly. "Look, I've a tide to catch, so I'll make this quick. If you go, there won't be as much discussion or delay as there will be otherwise. With time of the essence, you ought to think of that."

Gavin did, after the counselor had gone. He had planned to stay in Ilius and help with all that needed to be accomplished, but Goran did have a point. As in England and elsewhere, city folk and country folk did not always see eye-to-eye. Atreus was a master at bringing them together, but the diplomatic skills of the Vanax were not necessarily equaled by his magistrates, who tended to be blunt-spoken men with very clear-cut notions of how things ought to be done and limited patience for discussion.

Perhaps he ought to go, and not alone. Much as he would have liked to credit his own eloquence for bringing the Council around to the urgency of the crisis they faced, he realized the key moment had come when Persephone insisted on revealing the letter from Atreus. She had gauged the mood of the counselors better than he had and realized what was needed to convince them.

She might be equally adept at swaying the country people. Besides, it would give them an excuse to be together.

A wry smile crossed his face as he reflected that, after just one night apart, he was looking for excuses to keep her close. All the same, he could make a solid case—to himself as well as to her—that they should both go.

Having finished his tasks on the training field, he paused just long enough to take a quick shower under the water tanks set up for that purpose and change into a fresh kilt before heading back into the city.

Barely had he regained Ilius than he was struck by

how much things had changed there already. Fires were cold, no smoke rising from them. In front of shops and houses, the walkways that would normally have been kept swept clean were showing accumulations of dust and sand blown up from the harbor. Laundry was not hung out to dry. Couples did not stroll hand in hand. Children did not dart about laughing. The normal life of the city was suspended.

It might never return.

A wave of grief unlike any he had ever known welled up in him. For just a moment, the sun-washed street and everything in it seemed to waiver in front of his eyes. He blinked and the world settled back into place, but the experience shook him. In the months since he first began to suspect that the volcano was awakening, Gavin had not allowed himself to truly think that the life of Akora might be coming to an end. At first, he thought what he suspected would turn out not to be true. Even when he had to acknowledge that the preponderance of evidence said otherwise, he didn't allow himself to contemplate what it would mean. Oh, he grappled with the practical aspects well enough but emotional considerations were pushed aside.

Until now. Standing in the bright sun-washed day looking at cold fires and somber children, he could no longer deny how completely he loved Akora. How integral it was to his being. And how terrifying was the thought that it might vanish forever.

He was a man bred to courage, trained to withstand

the terrors of death. But this threatened to undo him. He was struggling for breath, when a hand touched his arm lightly.

"Gavin . . . are you all right?"

He turned to find Persephone beside him, her lovely face wreathed with concern. At once, the fear nibbling at the edge of his soul subsided, at least a little.

"I'm fine," he said, and willed it to be true.

"You don't look fine. Is the sun too much?"

"No, of course not." He was fortunate in that, despite his close resemblance to his English father, even the summer sun of Akora did not trouble him.

He focused on her more clearly, covering her hand, still resting on his arm, with his own. "I was hoping to find you." They had parted the previous day amid such strong emotion that he was glad to see she appeared calm. "Goran has suggested I should bring word myself of what is happening to the settlements outside Ilius."

"But there must be dozens, if not more. How could you bring word to all of them?"

"I can't, but I can go to one of the largest and alert people there, and they can spread out to tell the rest. The challenge is to convince those first people, to make them take this seriously."

Without hesitation, she said, "Goran is right. You are the man to do that."

"Come with me."

She did not conceal her surprise, but he also saw the

quicksilver flash of pleasure that darted behind her eyes. Even so, she said, "Sida is keeping me very busy."

He stepped a little closer, taking her hand in his. "Come anyway. You helped to convince the Council."

"Atreus's letter did that. Take it with you."

"These are country people. They know Atreus and respect him but they won't give that letter the same significance that the Council did."

"I'm sure you'll have no trouble persuading them—"

"The men, perhaps; they've been through warrior training. They're used to accepting authority and taking orders. Women, however—" He bent his head, his breath warm against the curve of her cheek. "Women need more careful handling."

She stepped back just a little. Her smile was bold, challenging, and utterly feminine. Also, a bit chiding. "I think it likely you've been persuading women to see things your way since the very first moment you discovered women existed."

He had the grace to look a little sheepish. "That long?"

"At least; however, I will go with you."

Her swift accord surprised him. He had thought to have to work a little harder to convince her, but a sensible man did not question fortune's favor. Instead, he moved to solidify his advantage.

"I thought we'd go by chariot." He had decided on that because he had no idea if she could ride at all, much less well enough to cover the distance required without discomfort. There were no horses on Deimatos and he doubted her rare trips to Ilius had afforded her the opportunity to learn how to ride. Besides, he thought a chariot would appeal to her and saw instantly that he was right; her eyes lit up.

"A chariot? I've seen those but I've never ridden in one."

"You'll enjoy it," he assured her, and led her back toward the palace, keeping up a good pace to make sure she would not have time to change her mind.

WHAT WAS SHE THINKING OF TO GO OFF with him like this? His presence was a sweet torment that haunted her waking hours and followed her into her dreams. Worse yet, he unleashed a slew of emotions, all seemingly at war with each other. She was drawn to him and wanted to flee from him. She yearned to be with him and feared the terrible price she would have to pay when the inevitable parting came. She lived by reason, practicality, and the refusal to be defeated. He made her feel weak, filled with visions of an impossible future, wanting to cast aside all sense and risk everything on a wish.

So, of course, the best possible thing to do was spend yet more time in his company.

Her mother had loved unwisely and too well. She had paid with her pride, her future, and her hopes. Her daughter was of altogether sterner stuff.

Or was she?

He had only to ask and she agreed. That was the real shock of it. She didn't even try to refuse him, not really. Her hand in his, she was content to follow him up the road to the palace, through the courtyard, and around the back to the stables. It was a long, low building of white stone topped with red tiles, which stretched almost the entire length of the palace but was separate from it by several hundred yards. Behind it, trailing down the hillside in the opposite direction from the city, were vast stretches of paddocks. At that hour, they were filled with horses put out to graze.

Gavin fetched a bridle from a tack room. With it in hand, he went up to one of the nearest paddocks, let loose a long, low whistle, and stood back as a magnificent black mare, her coat gleaming with dark undertones of silver, lifted her head, looked in his direction, and broke into a gallop.

"Easy, Hippolyte." Gently, he patted the horse down the long white stripe between her eyes, crooning to her softly as she bent her head and pawed the ground.

"You named her for the Queen of the Amazons?" Persephone asked.

"She seemed to deserve nothing less. Do you know much about horses?"

She knew they were large, powerful, and best avoided. A stray swat from their hindquarters could knock a person down. A sudden kick from a hoof could do far worse. And then there were the odiferous piles they left everywhere. "A little . . ." she said, not taking her eyes from the mare who looked back with what Persephone couldn't help but think was a baleful glare.

"Hippolyte is a magnificent horse. I was there when she was born and I've raised her from a foal." As he spoke, he continued stroking the mare, who neighed softly and butted her head against him.

She was jealous of a horse. That was marvelous. To the swirl of her emotions, add envy of a dumb animal. "We should be going."

Gavin nodded and quickly drew the bridle onto Hippolyte, who suffered him to do so with grace. Leading the mare from the paddock, he said, "She's trained for riding but prefers the chariot."

Persephone's anticipation of the ride fell a notch. She gave the horse another skeptical glance and was rewarded with a swish of a well-combed tail. But to give credit where it was due, once harnessed to the chariot, Hippolyte behaved admirably. Stepping into the wicker frame, Persephone was surprised by how very light and fragile it felt. She gripped the side with one hand and mustered a smile as Gavin took his place in the front and lifted the reins.

Hippolyte took off with a lurch, causing Persephone immediately to hold on with her other hand as well. She made the mistake of glancing down just in time to see the ground passing in a blur. With a gasp, she raised her eyes and pinned them firmly on the horizon.

"W-where are we going?" Persephone hiccuped,

struggling to keep her balance as the chariot leaped over a bump before landing on the road leading north.

"Sanctuary," Gavin replied, naming a place she had heard of but had never visited. "It occurred to me that this is an offering day. Hundreds of country folk will be there. We can tell them what's happening and organize riders to take the word to every settlement."

As plans went, it was a good one. All they had to do was travel twenty or so miles to their destination without being flung out of the chariot and left for dead at the side of the road.

"Enjoying yourself?" Gavin asked over his shoulder. He stood with his feet planted firmly apart, the powerful muscles of his arms flexing as he handled the reins. The wind blew his hair back, revealing the hard lines of his face and throat. He looked relaxed and in good humor.

"Of course," Persephone muttered, and was surprised to discover not too long afterward that she actually was doing so. Whether Hippolyte had settled down somewhat or she herself had adjusted to the rhythm of the chariot, she couldn't really say. She knew only that she felt able to relax her grip slightly.

"I thought chariots were sturdier," she said to Gavin's broad back, directly in front of her. His skin was smooth and sun-burnished, the muscles beneath his shoulder blades powerfully articulated.

"Did you? They're built for speed, so they can't be heavy."

"That makes sense." She spoke absently, fighting the

urge to let go of the side entirely and wrap her arms around him instead.

Rather than do that, she concentrated on where they were going. The Sanctuary, as the grove of ancient olive trees outside Ilius had been known for thousands of years, was immortalized in story and legend. It was there, so it was said, that one of the great dramas in the life of Akora after the first Cataclysm had been played out.

One of the few survivors of the Cataclysm, a young priestess named Lyra, had fled there with a small group of other women in rebellion against the rule of the warriors who had come as conquerors to their shattered home. There they had taken their stand, refusing on pain of death to surrender to a life of subjugation.

And there, when hard men finally set aside their anger to reach for the hope of something better, the ancient agreement had been struck—the warriors would rule and the women would serve . . . but no man would ever harm a woman.

Ever since, the place where all this was said to have happened had been a favorite among Akorans, especially on the one day each month when offerings were brought to the priests and priestesses who maintained the grove.

The road along which they were traveling became busier. They passed other chariots, and wagons, riders, and people on foot. At length, they approached the stone wall that marked the entrance to the grove.

"Do you think what's said about this place is true?" Gavin asked as they passed beyond the wall.

"Some of it, perhaps, not all."

"Why not all?"

Drily, she said, "I don't think the women built a wall of fire to protect themselves from the men, or that the flames were taller than the tallest warrior, or that they burned without cease for ten days and nights."

Drawing the chariot to a halt, Gavin asked, "Or that Atreides leaped over the flames to claim his beloved?"

"That, too."

"But he did claim her, that much we do know, and the ancient scrolls say there were scorch marks seen here for years afterward." Stepping onto the ground, he quoted: " 'Year Fifteen after the Cataclysm—the last marks of the burning are faded from view and can no longer be seen.' "

Taking the hand he offered, Persephone stepped lightly down beside him. "You can't really quote like that from the Annals, can you?"

"A few passages. That one stuck in my mind in particular." A bit sheepishly, he said, "I came out here ten years ago and spent some time wandering around, hoping I might somehow discover evidence of what had happened."

"After more than three thousand years? Did you really expect to find anything?"

"No, but I couldn't resist the urge to try. I did notice something though." He pointed in the direction of the grove of olive trees they were approaching, their gnarled trunks and silver-gray leaves etched by sunlight. "The trees obscure the lay of the land, but the outer edge of the trees forms a circle and when you walk within it, the ground rises."

"What does that mean?" she asked, genuinely curious.

"There's a mound concealed under the grove. The trees must have been planted on top of it. Of course, none of the trees we see dates from Lyra and Atreides's time, although most are several centuries old. As far as I know, the mound has never been explored. My cousin Clio talks of doing so, but many people regard the place as, if not holy, close to it and wouldn't look kindly on its being disturbed."

As they spoke, they stepped within the grove. Olive trees needed a goodly amount of room in which to spread both their roots and branches, so the trees were spaced well part. Walking among them, Persephone's eye fell on the small plaques set at the base of many trunks.

"What are those?" she asked.

Gavin followed the direction of her gaze. "All the trees here are donated by various families. To be invited to plant a tree is a great honor. On the plaques are inscribed the names of the givers." He pointed to one of the largest and oldest trees near them. "See there, it says 'Atreides,' meaning it was planted by someone in my family, from the look of it a century or so ago."

"A pleasant custom."

"Also a practical one. The oil pressed from the olives

grown here is used to light the sacred lamps all over Akora."

"I had heard that—" She broke off, staring at the plaque of a tree she had just noticed. It was younger than the one Gavin had indicated but no less sturdy. The plaque at the bottom said "Deimeides."

Straightening slowly, she asked, "How old would you say this tree is?"

"I'm not an expert on olive trees but I'd say . . . fifty years or so."

Fifty years. Half a century ago, someone in the Deimeides family had been considered worthy of planting a tree in the sacred grove of Akora.

There was a time when the Deimeides name stood for far better.

Just then, standing in the sunlight filtering through the branches of the olive trees, Persephone felt the first faint stirrings of hope that it might be true.

A woman wearing the scarlet tunic of a priestess saw them and set down the basket in which she was placing the olives she was picking. With a smile of recognition for Gavin—and of kindly interest for Persephone—she came toward them.

Moments later, the priestess's smile was gone and she was hurrying to gather the other servants of the grove to hear what Gavin had to tell them.

CHAPTER XIV

"I REALIZE THIS IS VERY DIFFICULT," GAVIN said. He stood before the priests and priestesses, who had gathered to hear what he had to say. There were twenty of them in all, the usual number in service at the Sanctuary at any one time. Half were men, the other half women. The younger among them wore white, the older were garbed in scarlet.

Persephone was beside him. They had drawn apart from the visitors to the Sanctuary, not wishing to alarm them. They would have to be told soon enough, but first, Gavin wanted to inform those he hoped would respond quickly and effectively.

"All the evidence points to the likelihood that the volcano under Akora will explode soon," he continued. "We can't be absolutely sure, but if we ignore these warnings, we may be sealing our own fate."

The response was immediate and clamorous. To a man—and woman—no one was prepared simply to accept what he said. But then he had not expected them to do so.

"When did this begin?"

"How did you discover it?"

"Why would this happen?"

The questions came fast and furious. Gavin held up a hand. Quietly he said, "We will tell you everything we know, but unfortunately there can be little time for discussion. Several months ago, I became convinced that Akora was changing. The land was rising, not so quickly or dramatically that most people would notice, but enough so that I could confirm the matter when I took measurements. At about the same time, I discovered that lava flows that had been in existence for centuries, if not longer, were increasing beyond their highest recorded point."

"And you said nothing of this?" asked the woman who had first greeted them. Her name was Rhea, and she was the most senior of the guardians of the grove.

"I told the Vanax and a few others. They bade me continue to study the matter, which I did. Eventually, that led me to Persephone, who had been discovering some of the same phenomena for herself. We joined forces to work together."

"And now you are both convinced of this?"

"We are," Persephone said, "although, as Prince Gavin said, there is no way for most of us to be absolutely sure. Unfortunately, if we wait until we can be certain, it will be too late."

Rhea frowned, but she did not disagree. "You say this is already known in Ilius?"

Gavin nodded. "Preparations to evacuate have begun."

Despite the grimness of the situation, one of the younger men in the circle remarked, "I can just see all those merchants and shopkeepers running around trying to figure out what to do first. It would be funny . . . if it weren't—" He broke off, looking a little sheepish.

A few of the others smiled wanly, but most remained somber. A young woman drew reluctant nods when she said, "We have been wondering if something was wrong."

Surprised, Gavin and Persephone looked at each other. "What do you mean?" Persephone asked.

"There are fewer olives on the trees this year and several springs in the area have run dry. This despite the rains being good."

"The birds did not nest as long as usual," an older woman said. "Most raised one clutch of eggs but never laid another, as they often do." She glanced around the group. "Remember, we spoke of it?"

The others nodded. A man said, "Many birds are gone altogether, at least from these lowlands, and we've seen burrowing animals—moles, mice, even snakes—on the surface more often of late. They, too, seem to be leaving."

"And last week," yet another woman said, "all the fish in the pond near here died without any warning. We found out why when we felt the water. It was suddenly far too warm for them to live in."

"So there are other signs," Persephone murmured. She stepped a little closer to Gavin and slid her hand into his. "The land is being disrupted by the forces within it, but it will return to what it has been, assuming we are here to help it do so."

Rhea had been watching her closely. Now she came to Persephone and lightly touched her cheek.

"Who are you, Lady, that you come here with the prince? He is known to us, you are not, and yet there is something about you, something familiar—"

"Persephone has helped to determine what is happening," Gavin said quickly. "She understands the rhythms of Akora and sensed all was not as it should be."

"Did you?" Rhea asked. She removed her hand but did not back away. Instead, she continued staring at Persephone. What she saw seemed to confirm something in her mind. At length, she said, "I have been here at the Sanctuary for a long time, since I was younger than you are now. Many have come, completed their service, and gone, but I stayed through good times and bad."

"What kept you here?" Persephone asked.

"The sense that I belonged, that I could be useful. And after what I had seen happen, I knew how important it was for each and every one of us to work for the good of Akora."

"What you had seen . . . in the bad times?" The priestess's gaze was compelling; Persephone could not bring herself to break free of it. Nor did she truly try. She felt a connection to the older woman, though she could not begin to imagine why.

"When the traitor Deilos came," Rhea said quietly, "he found fertile ground among young people serving here. I was a young woman then myself and remember it all too well."

They weren't there to talk about Deilos; they were there to warn people about the volcano. Anything else was wasting time. And yet the temptation to know more was irresistible.

"I saw the name of his family—Deimeides—in the olive grove."

Rhea nodded. "Many Deimeideses served here as priests and priestesses over the centuries, and they always gave generously of their wealth in support of the Sanctuary. They were an old and honorable family, much respected."

"Yet Deilos came from them." She had never before thought of where he came from. Now it seemed she could think of little else.

"Who can fathom the mystery of evil?" Rhea asked. "It takes root among us and we can only ask why."

"Why did people listen to him? Why didn't they see what he really was?"

The questions had haunted her all her life, yet Persephone had always assumed there would never be any answers to them. Now, face-to-face with the woman who just might prove that wrong, she could not deny the cry of her heart.

"He pretended to care only about the well-being of Akora," Rhea said, "to honor our traditions and want to protect them. The Vanax Atreus was determined to bring us into the wider world. Many were afraid of what that would mean."

"Isn't it usually the old who are more conservative than the young?" Gavin asked. His hand tightened around Persephone's, silently reminding her of his nearness and his strength.

"In some ways," Rhea said. "But the young, who are just beginning to find their place in the world, may feel threatened by any change. They want to cling to what they know. Deilos was seductive. He understood exactly what to say and do. Some of our best minds fell to him."

She stepped back a little farther, looking at them both. Her gaze was gentle and wise but also filled with questions. "I had a dear friend, a priestess also in training here. We had known each other from childhood. She was a young woman of courage and honor, yet she was one of those who succumbed to Deilos."

"What happened to her?" Persephone asked softly.

"I don't know. I never saw her again after she left here with him." Rhea hesitated, then said, "I heard she went back to her family but did not stay there." Her voice fell a little, but her eyes remained on Persephone. "There was talk of a child."

"No doubt there is much to be learned from the past," Gavin interjected abruptly. "But just now it is the present—and the hope of the future—that require our attention. Counselor Goran is going to Leios to see to it that everyone there is notified. I need your help to do the same here."

"And we wish to help you, Prince," an older man said. "But what you are telling us, what you are asking us to believe, is such a . . . violation of the natural order. Birds lay or do not, animals come and go, and even fish may die sometimes for mysterious reasons. But none of that means the world is about to end."

"The world is not," Gavin said quietly, "and Persephone believes that neither is Akora. Something will remain here and we will be able to return, but only if we survive."

"What is it you wish us to do?" the man who had spoken mockingly of the townspeople asked. He was not mocking now but was intent and focused.

"Send riders to every homestead, farm, vineyard, and settlement on this island. Tell everyone what I have told you. The priests and priestesses of the Sanctuary will be listened to. People will realize that they must take this seriously and act."

"Act how?"

"All must assemble at Ilius in three days' time,

bringing with them only what goods they can carry, food to sustain themselves, and their animals."

"What about the crops that are still in the fields?" a young woman asked. "The harvest has been good, but it is not finished. What do we do about what remains?"

"Leave it," Gavin said flatly. "There is no time to spend trying to bring in every last bunch of grapes or grain of wheat."

"There are sheep in the high pastures," a young man pointed out. "They cannot be brought down in three days' time, much less transported to Ilius."

"Then they, too, must be left."

This sparked much comment, for most of those gathered in the grove were themselves country people. They would not readily leave any animal to die, even those intended for slaughter. Rhea let them run on a few minutes, then held up a hand.

She was still looking at Persephone as she said, "The spirit of Akora has always protected us, but we know that catastrophe came to this land once before. We have hints in our records—only hints, but not to be ignored—that Lyra had some warning and tried to save her people. But she was young and they were reluctant to listen to her. Only a handful survived, and there would have been no survivors at all without the arrival of Atreides and his warriors."

She turned to Gavin, looking directly at him even as she spoke also to the others. "Now another Atreides comes to tell us that we must save ourselves. It may be that there truly is no danger, but if we fail to act, there will be no second chance. Further, there is only so much we can do in so short a time. Our first priority must be to help preserve the lives of our people."

That seemed obvious to Persephone, but the others did not accept it so readily.

"What about the grove itself?" a young woman asked. "How can we just leave it?" Her voice broke. She looked truly dismayed.

"If you remain," Gavin told her gently, "you will not be able to do anything to save it. The grove will survive or perish with or without you. You must look to preserve your own life and those of others."

"You could take cuttings from the trees," Persephone suggested. The thought had just occurred to her, but she seized on it. "Perhaps the same can be done everywhere. That way, something can be saved."

"It would take generations for the trees to grow to what they are now," the young woman protested, but she looked hopeful despite herself.

"Then generations hence will praise our foresight," Gavin said. "Whatever happens here, at least some of you must take word to everyone else. People have little enough time to prepare themselves as it is. There cannot be any delay."

"I will go," a young man said as he stepped forward. "My family's farm is to the south. If I leave now and ride hard, I can be there by morning. I'll stop at every holding along the way."

"I'll go north," another said, and was quickly joined by a third man, who offered to ride with him.

More quickly than would have seemed possible, the priests and priestesses put aside their doubts and fears, and the natural desire of any people to believe in their own safety. Swiftly they organized themselves. Some would remain at the Sanctuary to gather what could be saved, including the cuttings Persephone had suggested. But the others would spread out over the whole of the island, carrying word of the crisis.

"Your faith in us is flattering, Prince," Rhea said as plans were being made. Maps were brought out and examined, the best routes debated. "But it would help if we could bring word from you directly." She indicated a small whitewashed building where the records of the Sanctuary were kept. Some of those they had spoken with were already in the building, beginning the task of packing up the records for transport to Ilius. "If each of those who go could carry a letter from you . . ."

Seeing the wisdom of that, Gavin quickly agreed. A table was brought out into the sun and he set to work. The first task was to decide what to say. He settled on a simple and direct message:

The bearer comes in my name. Heed the warning he brings. Come to Ilius without delay. Gavin Atreides, Prince of Akora.

At the bottom of each letter, he affixed a blob of hot wax and pressed into it the imprint of his ring bearing the bull's-head seal of the Atreideses.

By the time he was done, the riders were ready. They came to him singly, each receiving words of encouragement along with the letter. For the most part they were young, but there were among them several who were older. These cast the more wistful looks around the grove, as though seeing too clearly all that might be about to be lost. But their grip was unfailingly firm when they took Gavin's hand and pledged not to fail.

"I'll get them on the road, if I have to set fires under their sandals," one man promised as he swung up onto his horse.

A few of the others nearby heard that and laughed, but the laughter faded quickly as the moment to depart came upon them. Persephone watched as Gavin said a few more words.

"Do your best, that is all anyone can ask." He repeated the words every man among them had learned in warrior training and that the women, as well, had heard often enough. " 'Be calm, be confident, and do not waver.' "

"In short, be Akoran," one of the younger men summed up succinctly.

Gavin smiled. "Yes, exactly, be Akoran. We have only to do that—all of us—and we truly will survive. So will Akora."

It was a promise borne more of faith than of reason.

And yet, standing in the shadow of the grove where once he had searched for marks of ancient fire, he felt the truth of it to his bones.

Felt also the gentle touch of the woman who stood beside him, her hand in his. When the last of the riders had gone, and Rhea had returned to the little building, Gavin drew Persephone into his arms. His kiss was deep and tender, possessed of passion and so much more.

Behind them, wind whispered through the branches of the olive trees as the sun slanted westward, taking with it one more precious day.

CHAPTER XV

"CAREFUL!" THE VERY LARGE MAN DIRECT-
ing the loading of cattle onto one of the many
ships jostling for space in the harbor of Ilius bellowed
the command. When he was certain he had the attention of everyone within earshot, he added more pleasantly, "That cow's not going to do you much good,
boyos, if you get her on board with three legs instead of
the recommended four."

The young boys attempting to load the cow in question looked suitably abashed. They redoubled their efforts, but with significantly more care. Bleating her
own dissatisfaction, the cow slowly but steadily went
up the gangplank and onto the ship.

In the midst of wiping the sweat from his brow,
Liam Campbell caught sight of the woman who was
standing nearby, smiling despite herself.

"You think it's funny, lass?" he said with a grin of his own and no rancor in his voice.

"I think it's better to laugh than to cry, Scotsman," Persephone replied. She was tired, dirty, and approaching a state of blessed numbness, which meant, she presumed, that she was like everyone else in the streets of Ilius and beyond, through every part of Akora.

A controlled sort of near-chaos was visible everywhere she looked. In the three days since the people had been informed of their peril, reactions had followed what she supposed with hindsight was a predictable course. First came widespread shock and disbelief followed hard by denial. This could not possibly be happening. It was a mistake, a misunderstanding, there was some other explanation than the one that filled them all with gut-wrenching terror.

Hard on that came anger, which, mercifully, had passed quickly. Guided by Gavin, aided by the garrison, and encouraged by men and women who stepped forward as natural leaders and organizers, the people of Akora were rallying.

A steady stream of animals brought from farms near Ilius was being loaded onto vessels. Nearby, a human chain made up of clerks, soldiers, and ordinary citizens stretched from deep within the library beneath the palace, all the way to the docks and into the holds of the ships. Precious books and scrolls were being passed hand-to-hand with great care but all speed. Immense piles of bundles, baskets, crates, and trunks were spreading out over the docks, still growing faster than they could be loaded. Clay vessels as tall as a ten-year-old child were also collecting, filled with precious olive oil and wine. Barrels of water were being rolled up the gangplank and onto the decks, even as more arrived in wagons.

In the midst of all this, Liam Campbell walked over to Persephone. The Scotsman looked tired but determined. He also appeared in good humor. "I'll take laughter anytime, lass. And how are you on this fair day?"

"Well enough. How do you think all this is going?"

He shrugged. "I'd have expected worse. The longer I'm here, the more I think you Akorans have Scots blood in your veins."

"Possibly." She sat down on a pile of bundles and fanned herself. Liam joined her. They shared a few moments of silence, watching the activity all around them.

At length, Liam said, "Where's that Atreides fellow?"

"Gavin is with the garrison. They're bringing the vessels in and out of the harbor, organizing the outlying farms, and generally maintaining order."

In truth, she had seen almost nothing of Gavin and told herself that was for the best. The problem was believing it.

"Mind tellin' me something?" Liam asked.

"What's that?"

"Do you really think that volcano's going to explode?"

"Yes, unfortunately I do." No need to go into details with him. He was turning out to be surprisingly likable, but even so, there were things she would not say.

"I don't know," Liam said. He leaned forward, resting his forearms on his knees. "Before I washed up here, I spent some time bumpin' about the South Seas. They've a fair number of volcanoes there and they go off from time to time, but not without plenty of warnin'."

"What kind of warning?"

"Runs the gamut: earth tremors, steam plumes, sometimes mud flows before there's any sign of lava. Of course, all that can happen and lead to nothin'. Folks who live near volcanoes seem to be pretty much at ease with 'em."

"Perhaps it is a false ease, masking fear."

"You mean like whistlin' past a graveyard?"

She looked at him in surprise. "What does that mean?"

"It's an old expression. People don't much like walkin' past graveyards—makes 'em nervous. So they whistle, to pump up their spirits." He thought for a moment. "You don't have those here, do you?"

"Graveyards? They exist for those *xenos* who wish them. Even so, how are the dead to be feared?"

"Hell if I know, never made much sense to me. I just figure they're folks gone on ahead."

"That is a nice way to think of it, Liam Campbell."

"Thank you, Persephone. That's a pretty name, by the way."

"She was the daughter of Demeter, goddess of harvests. Hades took her down into the underworld, where she was condemned to remain several months each year."

He was silent for a moment, digesting this. "Your mother named you that?"

She couldn't help but smile; he sounded so aghast. "I think she meant well."

"How's that?"

"Persephone—the first one—was reprieved. Originally, Hades wanted her to stay in the underworld forever."

"But she didn't get free completely?"

"No, she didn't. She had to come to terms with that part of her life, to accept it, and even to find the good in it." Persephone's voice trailed off. She had never spoken of such matters with anyone and found it strange to be doing so with the Scotsman. Yet he had prompted her to a realization she had not grasped before.

What had her mother truly meant by naming her as she did? And more than that, by raising her as she had, in near-total isolation? Of necessity, she had learned to know and depend on herself. To have confidence in her ability to overcome virtually any obstacle. To not merely survive, but to find the beauty and pleasure in each day for herself.

So that when she did finally encounter the world—and most particularly the man who shattered all her notions about life and its limits—she was so much more than the legacy of the past. Could that possibly be?

"Something wrong, lass?" Liam asked gently.

"No . . . no, I'm sorry, my mind wandered."

"You're tired, you ought to get some rest."

He was right, but there was still so much to do. She was reminded of that when a line of blue-clad people suddenly came onto the dock. She recognized them as the astronomers she had seen the night she and Gavin dined on the palace roof. They were carrying between them several large, heavily wrapped objects, handling them with extreme care.

"The telescopes," she said softly. "They must have taken them apart."

Liam stood, preparing to return to work. "Hope they don't regret it. People won't be happy if all this turns out to be for naught."

"It won't, unfortunately."

"As you say, then. Do you know what boat you're goin' on?"

"My own," she said without hesitation. It had not occurred to her that she would take another's place when she could provide one for herself.

"Now why doesn't that surprise me?" Liam asked, a

touch wryly. "I'm tellin' you, lass, dig deep enough and you'll find out you're Scots."

"I take that as a compliment, Liam Campbell, and thank you for it. May Fortune favor you and keep you safe."

"She always has, lass," he said with a grin before, with a backward glance in her direction, he returned to the dock.

Persephone remained where she was for a while. The day, ironically, was magnificent: the sky a clear azure blue untouched by clouds, the air scented with the perfume of the lemon groves. It was a day for lovers to stroll arm in arm, for children to play unfettered, for poets to dream, and for the old to bask in the warmth of lives well-lived.

A day to store up in memory, with no telling when another would come.

She lingered a little longer, stealing a bit of rest, but soon enough she returned to making herself useful. Teams of women were cooking for the multitude at work on the docks and the city beyond. Persephone joined them, ladling out soup and stuffed breads to weary men, women, and children. With their food in hand, people clustered in small, largely silent groups, the children leaning close against their parents for comfort. They lacked energy for conversation and besides, what was there really to say?

She was filling a bowl for an old but still straight-backed man when she looked up and saw Gavin. He was surrounded by a group of warriors with whom he was speaking. How at home he looked among them, she thought. Bare-chested, the powerful muscles of his torso gleaming in the light of the torches set all around the dock as night fell, he wore only a creased white kilt and dusty sandals. His dark blond hair looked wind-blown and he could do with a shave. Nothing about him signified any special rank except the attention the other men gave to him. When he had finished speaking, he nodded toward the tables of food. The men lined up, and Gavin took his own place at the far end.

She knew he saw her, could feel him watching her, and dropped her eyes. Vividly aware of him, she nonetheless kept all her attention on each man, finding a smile and a few friendly words to go along with the food that was obviously appreciated.

Finally, after what seemed an interminable time, Gavin stood before her. Her hand shook slightly as she picked up a bowl and filled it for him. "The soup is good," she said softly.

"I'm sure it is. Have you eaten?"

She nodded. "A while ago. Everything seems to be going . . . as well as it can."

"So it does." He reached out, his hands cupping hers around the bowl. His touch was warm, tantalizing, banishing for the moment the fog of weariness that had settled over her.

Reluctantly, she drew her hands away, burying them in her apron.

"You should get to bed soon," Gavin said gently.

"Yes . . . I know, I will."

He accepted the spoon she offered him and the bread. His men had taken seats nearby. She could see several of them glancing in their direction. One elbowed the man next to him and grinned.

Gavin smiled. He bent a little closer, his breath warm against her cheek. "Sleep in my bed tonight, Persephone."

Her heart, already beating hard enough to make itself known, leaped. "Your bed—?"

"I'd just like to know you're there."

"Can you? . . . That is, you should sleep, too." If her face got any hotter, the men would be able to read her thoughts by its glow. Looking at him more closely, she saw how very tired he appeared. There were deep lines on either side of his mouth that were not present normally and his eyes were reddened by fatigue. She should not ask him for anything when so much clamored for his time and attention.

"I've been staying with the garrison," he said.

He would do that. She tried to understand and hide her disappointment. "Of course—"

"But I'd rather sleep in my own bed tonight." Very matter-of-factly, as though it was the most ordinary thing, he added, "I'll likely be late."

"Certainly . . . I don't expect—"

"Do expect, Persephone. You have every right to do so."

She managed, just barely, to finish emptying the kettle and put it away. Other women were arriving, those who had rested earlier, and who would work through the night to feed those who were doing the same.

For herself, she was going to bed. Gavin's bed.

Half an hour later, when there was absolutely nothing left for her to do, Persephone slipped away. She slowly climbed the road to the palace. The houses she passed were quiet and dark. She supposed people were trying to get a few hours of rest in the homes they would be torn from all too soon.

She was halfway up the road from the harbor when a gray cat crossed her path. She stopped suddenly, struck by sudden worry over what would happen to all the many beloved pets of Akorans. Since coming to Ilius, she had seen that every household kept cats, dogs, goats, pigeons, doves, and everything else imaginable.

Even as she was pondering it, a girl of perhaps fifteen darted from the shadows of a nearby house. "Mowmow, come here."

The cat did stop and glance back, but being a cat, it made no move to obey. Even so, the girl did not hesitate but swooped down on the animal, holding it close. "Silly Mowmow, I can't be chasing after you, not now. You're sleeping in your basket."

The cat, busy having its ear rubbed, did not appear to object.

Seeing Persephone, the girl smiled shyly. "I didn't realize anyone was here."

"I was just passing on my way to bed. I'm glad you found your cat."

"So am I. I couldn't bear it if anything happened to her." The girl paused, then asked, "Is your family ready?"

Disinclined to try explaining yet again that she had no family, Persephone merely nodded. "Just about. Yours?"

"As well as we can be. Mother can hardly bear to leave anything, but we understand there's limited space in the boats." With the candor of youth, she blurted out, "It's all so unbelievable, isn't it? Like some strange sort of dream. I keep expecting to wake up."

"I wish we could all do that. Unfortunately, we just have to get through this."

"I suppose . . ." Holding the cat close, the girl looked around. As though to herself, she said, "I've lived on this street all my life. I always thought if I moved away when I marry, it would probably be no farther than the next neighborhood over. The farthest I could ever think of going was Leios. To think that none of this may survive—"

"Don't think of that," Persephone said quickly. On impulse, she went to the girl and put an arm around her shoulders. The cat blinked at them both.

"What counts are the people—" She smiled down at

the cat. "Excuse me, Mowmow, what matters are all that live on Akora. We can rebuild everything else."

"Rheanne—?" An older woman emerged from the house, smiling when she saw the young girl. "There you are, dear." Looking to Persephone, she asked, "Is everything all right?"

"Fine," Persephone assured her, "just a wandering cat."

The older woman came closer. "Why, you are the Lady Persephone, are you not?"

"My name is Persephone but—"

"Sida has spoken of you. You are the . . . friend of Prince Gavin." The two women, mother and daughter most likely, exchanged a quick glance followed by knowing smiles.

"Prince Gavin is very handsome," Rheanne said. She giggled. "Half the girls I know have terrible crushes on him."

"Do they?" Persephone could not stop herself from asking. She had never been a girl like Rheanne and her friends, knew nothing of youthful infatuation. Love had come to her full-blown.

Love?

Love.

There really was no point denying it, even to herself. She was too tired even to try. "Prince Gavin is a very good man."

The older woman nodded. "We are fortunate he is among us, especially now."

The reminder, gentle as it was, recalled Persephone to the circumstances they all shared. She made her farewells to Rheanne and her mother—and to Mowmow—and continued the climb up to the palace. By the time she passed between the twin stone lionesses guarding the palace gates, the effort of putting one foot in front of the other seemed almost beyond her. She had to grip the stair rail and pull herself up the final steps to the family quarters. The corridor that loomed ahead seemed to go forever, but at length she reached the door to Gavin's room. Too exhausted even to hesitate, she pushed it open and went inside.

The room was wreathed in darkness broken only by the starlight streaming through the windows. The big bed beckoned, but so did the bathing chamber beyond. Dropping her clothes off as she crossed the inlaid stone floor, she reached the bathroom naked and quickly turned on the water valves in the shower to full force. The tub tempted her mightily, but she was too exhausted to risk sinking into it. Instead, she stood under the downward rush of water after soaping herself clean. Some unknown time later, she woke to the realization that her head rested against the wall of the shower and she was virtually asleep on her feet.

With a low groan, she turned off the shower, wrapped herself in a towel, and padded back into the bedroom. With the last tiny remnant of strength she possessed, she made a cursory effort to dry herself off before tumbling under the sheet.

Some time later—she had no notion how long—she woke briefly to the sound of rain. No, not rain, the shower. The shower was on again. For some reason that wasn't entirely clear, that made her smile. She sank back into unconsciousness only to wake again to the sensation of strong hands stroking her legs.

Her bare legs, unencumbered by any sheet, part of her bare self stretched out on her bare back on the bed that belonged to . . .

Gavin.

He loomed over her, a dark and formidable presence in the starlight. She could not see his face, but she knew the touch of his body, as naked as her own, and the deep rumble of his voice as he spoke her name.

"Tell me if I should let you sleep," he murmured.

Her answer surprised her and, she suspected, shocked him. Perhaps being roused from sleep so delightfully banished her inhibitions. Or perhaps it was the effect of standing on a precipice with everything in the world she knew about to change.

Whatever the case, she reached down boldly and cupped him in the palm of her hand, squeezing lightly. "That would not be a good idea."

His laughter shook the bed. "Apparently not. Release me, sweet Persephone, before my ardor is spent too quickly."

When she looked at him uncertainly, he said, "I have been without you too long."

That didn't seem like something she could object to,

so she did as he asked and was rewarded instantly when he slipped down the bed and—

Rubbed her feet, catching one in each hand, digging his thumbs into the supersensitive pads just below her toes, stroking deep and hard as bolts of pleasure shot straight up her spine.

"Oh, ooohhhh! Don't stop! That's incredible . . . *ooooohhhhh!*"

"You know, there's a theory," he said quite pleasantly, as he kept on doing exactly what he had been doing, to devastating effect. "That under certain circumstances, a woman can reach sexual release simply by having her feet rubbed in exactly the right way. It has something to do with nerve connections, I believe."

"It's a good theory," Persephone gasped as her back arched.

"The toes are supposed to be especially sensitive if—"

She shot up off the bed so suddenly that Gavin lost his balance and landed on the floor. A shocked moment of silence followed before they both burst out laughing.

He stood up—a huge, rumpled, thoroughly aroused male—and rubbed his backside before launching himself straight back onto the bed. In an instant, he was on top of her, holding her firmly beneath him as he grinned down at her.

"If your feet are that sensitive, I have to wonder about the backs of your knees."

"The backs of my knees are fine. Now let me up."

"No, I don't think so." Instead, he flipped her neatly over and straddling her, proceeded to satisfy his curiosity.

Long before he was done, her hands were digging into the pillows and she was moaning helplessly. His tongue stroked, teased, stroked again to devastating effect. Far in the back of her mind, she realized she was being exquisitely primed by a master, brought right up to the brink of release again and again, only to be left teetering.

It was sheer torture and she loved every moment of it, but the cost of lying passively beneath him, subject to his will, was becoming intolerable. She tried to turn over but he would not permit it, instead slipping an arm beneath her hips and raising her so that she was kneeling facedown on the bed. His hands cupped her breasts, squeezing lightly even as he moved between her thighs. She gasped when he entered her and again when he withdrew almost entirely before returning hard and fast, driving into her over and over.

She could not touch him, could not change the pace of his taking of her, could do nothing except experience the torrent of sensation he unleashed. That torrent took her in great, writhing waves that coursed through her body; long, rippling undulations that seemed to go on and on without end. On the crest of pleasure so intense that she balanced on the knife edge of unconsciousness, she heard him cry out her name.

Long, dazed moments later, she returned to herself enough to know she still lay beneath him, her face resting against the smooth damask pillow, her legs still spread wide to accommodate him. Gavin was a deadweight slumped on top of her, but she couldn't mind. The feel of him was strangely right and comforting. She did try to draw her legs together, but gave up when the effort proved futile.

Deep within, her body resonated to the slowly fading echoes of passion. She felt exquisitely sensitized. Every breath she took heightened her awareness of her wet, swollen sex. The air was musky with the scent of their lovemaking. Heat poured off his hard, unyielding body that seemed to surround and engulf her even in sleep.

To return to sleep in such a condition seemed impossible, yet she did. And when she next knew anything, the sun was shining brightly and she was alone.

CHAPTER XVI

THE KNIFE SLIPPED. PERSEPHONE STARED
down in surprise as a thin line of blood blossomed across the pad of her thumb. The small, stinging pain made itself known a moment later. She sighed, more with irritation than concern, and set the knife aside. Wrapping a corner of her heavy apron around her thumb, she pressed hard against the wound. As she waited for the bleeding to stop, she looked around the orchard.

The grove of olive trees was one of many that surrounded Ilius. Broad, gnarled trunks supported branches heavy with leathery green and silver leaves. Most of the olive harvest was already in, but the oil-pressing was barely under way. If it had to be interrupted for more than a few days, it was likely the entire crop would be lost.

If the very worst happened, the orchards themselves would perish. But they would live again if the work Persephone was helping with succeeded.

She took her apron away, saw that the bleeding had stopped, and picked up her knife. Carefully, she sliced through a young stem, wrapped the cutting in a moist cloth, and laid it in her basket, which was already half-filled with similar cuttings.

All around her, men and women were doing the same, taking cuttings from the strongest trees. Before they were done, there would be thousands of such cuttings laid carefully aside for the day when it might be necessary to plant new orchards.

She straightened after putting another cutting in the basket and stood for a moment, pressing her hand to the small of her back, where a dull ache was growing. Far off in the distance, beyond the olive groves, she could just make out a line of people moving along the road. Likely they were headed out to the lemon groves that lent their distinctive perfume to Akora through much of the year. Sida had told her that cuttings were being taken everywhere—from jasmine, roses, the wild lilac and thyme that grew on the hillsides, the poppies in the high fields, the citrus and apple trees in small family gardens—everything that could be preserved.

But so much would be lost. She could not bear to think of it, so she went on working, the steady rhythm of her task keeping her mind mercifully blank. When her basket was full, she brought it up to the road, where wagons waited to take the precious loads of cuttings down to the docks.

The man driving the wagon greeted her warmly. "Good day, Lady Persephone. Everything going all right?"

Lady Persephone. This was the second time someone had called her that. It sounded very strange. But the man looked as tired as everyone else and she saw no point in correcting him. "We've made a lot of progress. I wonder, could you give me a ride back into Ilius?" She had told Sida that she would find her again, to catch up on what still needed to be done.

The man's smile broadened. "I'd be honored. Here, let me help you up." She needed no help, but accepted it all the same, removing her heavy apron before stepping up into the seat beside the driver. When she was settled, her tunic smoothed around her, the wagon rolled on. It stopped several more times, to take on additional loads of cuttings from workers in the orchard. Many of them also greeted "Lady Persephone."

With the orchard behind them, they took the road to Ilius. The man—who introduced himself as Marcus—seemed inclined to chat.

"I don't mind saying, Lady, my dear wife is upset by all this. Not that she isn't holding up well, but it's a strain on her all the same."

In fact, Persephone had observed that the women of Akora were managing astonishingly well. She recalled that she had seriously believed they were downtrodden and subservient to the men, and now she wished she could apologize to each and every one. Even so, she also realized that the men were concealing their own concern, expressing it indirectly as more a matter for the women.

She said gently, "I'm sure your wife appreciates all you are doing."

He nodded gruffly. "She said that just last night after the children were in bed."

"How many children do you have?"

"Two daughters and a son." He chuckled. "They're a handful and then some." More somberly, he added, "I always thought they'd be safe here. Everytime I heard about trouble out in the world—war and the like—I felt sorry for the people out there, but I never worried about us. I figured if trouble came here, we could handle it, and it wasn't likely to come anyway."

But now it had—more trouble than any of them had ever imagined—and she understood his distress full well. Even so, she said, "We will survive this, you know. However bad it is, we will go on. Your children may know an Akora that is different from this one, but they will still be Akoran."

Several moments passed before he replied. "We might not have survived if we hadn't had warning. People are saying Prince Gavin has been concerned about this for months. It's why he's been going round doing what he has, taking measurements and the sort. And you—" He broke off, looking at her.

"What about me?"

"You've been helping him; everyone can see that. As for the rest—"

"What rest?" she asked quietly.

"People are wondering, that's all. There's no harm meant."

"What are they wondering about?"

"The two of you, I suppose. The women say you came out of nowhere." He smiled a little abashedly. "They think it's romantic."

She had no notion what to make of this. That she who had gone all her life unnoticed should be the object of such speculation was deeply disconcerting.

"It distracts them," Marcus explained with a shrug. "Gives them something happier to think about."

"I suppose—"

"Want me to take you up to the palace?"

In her distraction, she had not noticed how close they were to Ilius. The city lay before them, gleaming in the sun. Her throat tightened at the sight of it.

"No, thank you, I would not take you out of your way. The docks will be fine."

"As you wish," he said, and urged the patient horse forward.

Persephone took her leave amid the crush of wagons waiting to unload. She hurried up the road, weaving her way through the crowds of people weighted down with all manner of personal goods as well as treasures still being removed from the palace.

Just past the lions' gate, she found Sida giving directions to several dozen of the palace staff. When they dispersed to their tasks, the older woman nodded briskly to Persephone.

"Lady, work continues in the orchards?"

"I believe it is almost done. And here?"

The older woman looked weary and, of even more concern, discouraged. "Not so well. I believe the librarians have realized they cannot hope to save everything. They are trying to make choices now. It is very difficult. So much else will also have to be left behind—the beautiful murals on the walls, furnishings, glassware too fragile to be quickly packed, the works of the Vanax himself, only a few of the smaller of those can be taken."

"Does Prince Gavin know?"

Sida nodded. "He was on his way to the caves when I last saw him, but he knows."

The older woman hurried off. Persephone continued into the palace. The place she had known only a little on her visits to Ilius and had come to know much better in recent days already seemed irrevocably changed. The usual knots of people gathered for impromptu conversations were gone. Entire vast audience rooms were completely empty, as were long stretches of corridors. All activity was focused on the library and a few other areas.

A sense of hollowness opened up inside her, but she resisted it. This was no time to think of everything that stood to be lost. Instead, she found the staircase leading to the caves. She reached the statue room and saw that nothing had been taken from there. No doubt the statues were simply too large to be moved, but the thought that the memorials to the great men and women of Akora would be lost was especially daunting.

She found Gavin in the cave that held the small temple. He was just emerging from the passageway leading to the lava flows. His face was grim and his white kilt appeared blackened in places.

Hurrying to his side, she looked at him anxiously. "What is happening?"

His expression softened at the sight of her, but he remained somber. "The lava is up over the ledge and continuing to rise. The floor of the passage has several fissures. Steam is coming from them." He sighed deeply and for just a moment, his big, hard body slumped against her. "I think it is only a matter of time now," he said as he straightened, but still held her close, "and probably not very much time at that."

She had known this, yet hearing him say it made the immediacy of danger acutely real. Not trusting herself to speak, lest she betray the depth of her fear, she nodded. But a moment later, all thought of everything but him vanished. A long, ugly burn ran down his right arm.

"You are hurt," she said, almost accusingly. How dare he go off without her and let himself be harmed?

Gavin glanced at his arm. "It's nothing, just a burn. We should leave here."

"Burns have to be treated immediately. At the very least, you have to put water on it to cool it and limit the damage."

Without waiting for his permission, she grabbed his hand and tugged him in the direction of the temple. The luminescent water in the pool might be safe enough, but she did not want to take responsibility for putting it on an injury.

He went with the tolerant patience of a man yielding to the determined desire of a woman. In the temple, she cupped her hands to catch water, then bathed the burn. She was fussing over him and knew it, but it calmed her. For some small snatch of time, the rest of the world was held at bay.

"We must not linger here," he said, a gentle reminder of reality.

He was right, of course, yet she was hard-pressed to leave. So much of such momentousness had happened to her here.

"I saw the statues," she said as she continued bathing his arm. "There is no possibility of taking even one of them?"

"How would we choose? Elena and I discussed it and we agreed it was better to leave them where they have always been."

"I suppose—" She looked to the face peering from the moss-draped wall. "What about that?"

Gavin hesitated. "I thought of trying to take it, but it is part of the cave wall itself. It would have to be cut out, and somehow that doesn't seem right."

The moment he spoke, Persephone realized he was correct. The very idea of cutting the face out seemed a violation of nature.

Gavin leaned back. He looked far more tired than he would ever admit to being. As though in passing, he said, "This is where the trial of selection occurs."

She looked at him in surprise. "Here? Right here?"

He nodded. "I have no idea what it involves, but this is where it happens."

"How do you know that?"

"Atreus told me."

"I thought you said there was never any reason to discuss it with him."

"We didn't discuss it," Gavin said. "He just mentioned it one time when we were down here."

"What did he say?"

"Just that. The ritual has something to do with this temple."

"You weren't curious? You didn't want to know more?"

He shifted slightly, as though he was uncomfortable. She did not think it was his arm that troubled him. "There was no reason for me to know."

"Atreus must have thought there was or why else would he have told you?"

"You read too much into it. It was conversation, nothing more."

"Is Atreus given to idle chatter?" The reputation of the Vanax did not suggest this.

"Of course not, but we were just talking."

"And he told you exactly where the trial of selection takes place. I suppose many people know?"

"No," Gavin said reluctantly, "I doubt they do. It is not spoken of."

"Except to you, by the Vanax himself."

"There is no point to this." Rising, he held out a hand to her.

She took it and let herself be drawn up, but she was not yet done. Pleasantly, as though this truly was mere conversation, she said, "Did you know that some Vanaxes have known who their successor was to be?"

He stopped and stared at her. "What are you saying?"

She pretended innocence, even to the extent of deliberately widening her gaze. "Several books I read mentioned it. They did not go into details. I suppose they really couldn't, but apparently it's not uncommon for the man who becomes Vanax to receive a vision during the trial, and very often that includes who his successor will be."

"That sounds like a legend," Gavin scoffed.

"You mean, like much of our history, which is also legend?"

"I mean, like something people make up when they

don't have real facts. Atreus never said anything to me about any visions."

"Understandably enough, don't you think? Did you know most Vanaxes have left that office because of retirement rather than death?"

He stopped in midstride and stared at her. "What? I didn't know that. Are you sure?"

"Reasonably so. Remember, I had enormous amounts of time in which to read, and most of what I read about was the history of Akora. I'd say fully two-thirds of Vanaxes retired from the office, content to leave it to their designated successors."

"Atreus became Vanax after his grandfather died."

"He was the exception, not the rule. Think of it, if Vanaxes usually died in office, our history would be punctuated by periods of uncertainty and even instability as we waited for a successor to undergo the trial and survive. But Akoran history has very few such periods. What we see instead are smooth transitions, one Vanax handing over power to the next *within his own lifetime.*"

He saw what was in her eyes and rejected it. "I have nothing to do with this. As I have told you, I am for Hawkforte. And that brings me to something I have wanted to say to you—"

There in the temple buried within the earth, he turned to her, drawing her even closer. "Persephone, I think I know how you feel about Akora, but the world is far wider."

"I know that." She could speak. Remarkable. Given

that his touch and the directness of his gaze made her mind feel like a poor, stumbling thing.

"You would like England. Well, perhaps not, there is good and bad, but you would enjoy Hawkforte. It is a beautiful place. When the light hits the shingle beaches below the house in the morning, it is extraordinary. There are moments when a mist drifts over all and it seems as though time itself has no meaning."

"You love Hawkforte." The realization slammed into her. She had not thought of this.

"Yes, I suppose I do, and why not? It is the home of my father's family, going back almost a thousand years. Of course, no one loves it the way my father does. . . ."

"No one?"

"I have a brother."

"I have heard that, but it is said he rarely comes here. What is his name?"

"David, younger than I by two years. He knows Hawkforte better than anyone, other than our father: every hill and glen, every stone and plank. It's really amazing what he knows. We used to explore the grounds when we were younger. David was forever pointing things out to me, showing me things I had never noticed."

"Knowing all that, has it occurred to you that David is meant for Hawkforte?"

To her immense surprise, Gavin said, "I have often thought that David should have been born first. But he wasn't, I was." And therein, it seemed, lay destiny itself.

She could keep silent. They were trapped in a terrible crisis and a good argument could be made that this was not the time for anything else.

But she, too, could be stubborn. And she, too, had a sense of duty.

"Yes, you, firstborn of the Princess Kassandra, who assumed the duties of Vanax and led Akora when Atreus was too injured to do so. Who, some say, made it possible for Akora to survive the greatest challenge it has faced since the Cataclysm itself."

"My mother would be the first to tell you that is exaggerated."

"Whether it is or not, have you ever truly thought about the fact that you are *her* son, not just your father's?"

He laughed, surprising her. "If you knew my mother, you would know the answer to that."

She reached up, her hand resting against the hard curve of his jaw, just below where his life's blood pulsed. Softly, so softly, she said, "I do know the answer, Gavin. Now it is for you to know."

He went very still, as though frozen by her words. She thought he meant to protest, to offer some further objection, but there was no chance to do so, for just then, a long, deep tremor rippled through the cave.

Hard on it, lava poured through the passageway.

CHAPTER XVII

R UN!" WITHOUT WAITING FOR AN ANSWER,
Gavin grabbed her hand and raced from the
temple. They ran through the cave of crystals and beyond, past the statues, reaching the staircase that led
upward to the palace. Before they had gone more than
a few steps, another powerful tremor almost knocked
them from their feet.

Persephone cried out and gripped Gavin tightly. He
did not hesitate but scooped her up in his arms and
continued climbing. They reached the landing on the
ground floor of the palace and stumbled, coughing, out
into the courtyard.

A scene of pandemonium greeted them. People were
running in every direction, but most especially to get
away from the heavy blocks of stone that had tumbled
from the front of the palace into the courtyard.

Fortunately, no one was trapped under them, nor did anyone appear injured by other means. But there was great fear.

Men of the garrison moved among the people. They were not, Persephone saw, immune from the terror, but they were trained to rise above it. They gave direction, imposed order, and brought with them a growing sense of calm.

And they looked to Gavin when they saw him, gathering around to receive his orders.

He set Persephone down gently but kept her near as he said, "There will be more tremors and likely they will grow stronger. Go among the people, see to it that they keep working. We still have time, but not very much."

They heard him and they obeyed.

When they had gone, Gavin turned to her. Still holding her, he said, "I must go."

The urge to plead with him not to leave her was all but irresistible, but she fought it down. "I know . . . I understand."

"But first, where is your boat?"

"At anchor in the harbor. Not at one of the docks—there was no room—but within easy reach."

"Go there tonight, sleep on board, and be ready to leave at once if that should be needed."

"No." Everything in her cried out at the very idea.

"Persephone . . ."

"I mean it, Gavin. I have no notion of how much

time we have together but I will tell you this, I will not leave without you." She who had been so independent, so proudly solitary. The transformation of her life in a mere handful of days might have stunned her had the headlong rush of events left any time to contemplate it.

"That is foolish. There will be great confusion at the end. You will not know if I have gone or not."

"I will know."

His hands ran up her arms, closing on her shoulders. "I must know you will be safe. I cannot go and do what I must without that."

"Then promise me you will find me. We will go out together to the open sea. Promise me!"

"Do not wait for me, Persephone. When you know you must, go."

"I will not." She was being foolish and she knew it. The issue of her own safety aside, it was wrong to leave him with any worry that she could alleviate with a simple promise.

His hands tightened and for just a moment, an expression she had never seen before flitted across his face. Fear. This indomitable man was afraid for her.

"Damn you, Persephone, you must listen to me!"

And damn you, Atreides prince, meant for Hawkforte. Damn you for taking me from Deimatos, from blissful ignorance into a world I never wanted.

The words remained unspoken, for they were, she knew, a lie prompted by her own terrible fear.

Softly, she laid the tips of her fingers over his mouth. "Please, Gavin, let's not argue, not now."

Far in the back of her mind, the thought stirred: She was, after all, an Akoran woman, understanding of the pride and strength of good men whose sense of honor could make them so terribly vulnerable.

"I do not wish to cause you any difficulty," she continued and meant it. "I simply cannot go without you."

"You have to go," he said emphatically. "However hard it is for you, you must do this."

When she did not reply, he drew her to him. Holding her close, his hand stroking her hair, Gavin said gently, "Persephone, you could be carrying our child. If you cannot leave for your own sake, you must for his or hers."

Her immediate impulse was to deny it, but those words, too, were never uttered. Hard on shock came an even more surprising surge of delight. Living as she had, she had never allowed herself to think of having a child. But now—

Fierce protectiveness overwhelmed her, driving out all else. She flattened her hands against his broad chest and glared at him. "A child needs two parents, Gavin Atreides. I know that far better than you, but don't you dare forget it."

His face softened. "I won't," he promised. "I will do everything I can."

"As will I." She took a breath and said what she knew she must. "Now go. There is no time to waste."

He went, but not before drawing her back to him and kissing her long and deeply. It was a kiss not of farewell, but of raw passion and, she had to hope, of promise.

The day took them. What had seemed a frantic pace of activity became even faster and more urgent, halting only briefly when further tremors shook the ground. Horses and mules pulling wagons reacted with panic but were quickly calmed. Those people who were knocked over picked themselves up and went straight back to work.

The sun was slanting westward when Persephone returned from a quick trip out to her boat to replenish stores of food and water. She returned the dinghy she had borrowed to row herself over and had climbed back up onto the dock when she saw Nestor. The elderly librarian appeared white-faced and exhausted, but he straightened when he saw her.

"There you are; I've been looking all over for you. Have you seen Prince Gavin?"

"Not in several hours. Here, come and sit down." Gently, she guided the old man over to a stone bench beside a shop that was closed and empty, as were all the others along the street. Yet even in their haste, people had left things in good order. Flowers in hanging baskets and in the gardens appeared to have been given a final watering. House and shop steps alike were swept clean. No laundry was left hanging on the lines, nor was there any sign of litter. Everything bore the evidence of tender love and care, even at this terrible time.

A nearby wall bore one of the many lovely murals that were common throughout Ilius. It depicted a family—quite possibly the very one that lived in that house—enjoying a meal in the garden. Across the bottom of the mural, painted in careful script, were the words, "We will return."

Nestor grimaced but lowered himself onto the bench. Smiling apologetically, he said, "My knees punish me for giving them no thought in my younger days."

From the way he held himself, a man poised on the keen edge of agonizing pain, she knew he was making light. She also knew he would not welcome sympathy. But she could offer practical help. "Have you eaten?"

"Of course . . . that is, I think so." He sighed and shook his head. "The truth is, I can't remember when I ate last. There has been so much to do and so little time."

"Even so, you must eat. Wait here." Before he could object, she hurried down the street. The women were clearly winding down their efforts to provide food, but there was still bread, cheese, and sweet apple cider. Carrying some of each, she returned to where Nestor was sitting. He welcomed the plain fare as though it were a banquet, but could eat only a little and that in very small bites.

Crumbling a morsel of cheese, he said, "I finally

found the survivors' records that I was looking for. Much of what is in them is of no particular use to us right now, but I did glean some information that could help. Without exception, the eyewitnesses describe earth tremors similar to what we've been experiencing. They worsened in intensity in the days before the eruption. But most importantly, on the very day before the Cataclysm, people were awestruck when an immense column of steam rose from the mouth of the volcano into the heavens. They were still trying to determine what to make of it when, less than a day later, the volcano erupted."

"Do you think we may get the same sign again?"

"It is possible," Nestor allowed. "But I don't believe we should trust our lives to that. Most of us should put out to sea very soon."

Persephone agreed. She was thinking of trying to find Gavin, to tell him what Nestor had discovered, when she saw Polonus at the far end of the street. Calling out to the counselor, she was relieved when he heard her and came quickly over to greet them both.

Frowning at the sight of Nestor, he said, "My dear friend, it is time you sought your bed."

"My bed?" The old librarian looked astonished. "You can't be serious. Have you no idea how much yet remains in the library? I have no intention of leaving it to others to decide what is to be taken. Why, all manner of treasures could be overlooked, irreplaceable documents forgotten, the voices of our ancestors lost forever."

Visibly distraught, Nestor struggled to his feet. Persephone took his arm, helping him up, and spoke to him gently. "Please, you upset yourself unnecessarily. Counselor Polonus means no harm. It is just that we are both concerned for you."

"That is true," Polonus said. "You must realize, people are also our treasure. You, Nestor, are very important to us. We look to you for many more years of wisdom and guidance."

The old man appeared taken aback for a moment, then managed a gruff laugh. "Friend Counselor, you may look all you wish and I certainly will be glad of any time left to me, but I cannot put my life above the heritage of our people. I must return to the library."

"Not alone," Persephone said. She was bound and determined to go with him. Truth be told, he did not try very hard to dissuade her. They parted from Polonus after telling him of what Nestor had learned, and gaining his assurance that he would see to it that the information reached Gavin. From the dock, they hitched a ride on a wagon heading back up to the palace. Once there, Nestor wasted no time in leading her to the library.

Persephone stopped abruptly as they entered the vast room lined with books and set with tables for the scholars. Or it had been lined with books. Now there were only empty shelves. Ranks of librarians, clerks, soldiers, and citizens wound down the stairs from the first level into the stacks below. A steady stream of books and scrolls was being passed hand-to-hand.

Nestor squeezed past the line on the stairs, Persephone right behind him. They descended to the lowest level of the library, where some of the oldest and most precious records were kept. Here the activity seemed especially intense.

"I am telling you," a bald-headed man said, "they are too fragile. Any rough handling and they will come apart."

The soldier listening to him nodded patiently. "Then we will not handle them roughly, but they must go now, if they are to go at all."

"Is there a problem, Ephraim?" Nestor asked.

Recognizing Nestor, the bald-headed man looked relieved. "No, sir, not at all. I'm just concerned that some scrolls we've found may not survive transport."

"They will not survive being left here if the volcano explodes."

"No, sir, as you say—"

Nestor turned his attention to the soldier. "May I suggest you find sturdy wooden crates to load the scrolls into, and use due diligence in moving them?"

"A good plan, sir," the soldier said, and went off quickly to implement it.

Nestor bade Ephraim farewell and continued deeper into the stacks, muttering as he went. "Arguing about such a thing . . . wasting precious time . . . what ails people?"

Persephone doubted he expected an answer, but she offered one all the same. "They don't want to acknowledge what's happening, at least not fully. Even in the midst of terrible danger, they want to pretend that somehow everything is still ordinary."

"Ephraim is far from a foolish man. He knows better."

"I'm sure he does, but he's hardly himself right now, is he? Indeed, are any of us?"

"You're holding up well enough," Nestor pointed out with a smile.

The compliment surprised her. "It's different for me. I'm used to dealing with problems and keeping calm in emergencies."

"Because of your life on Deimatos?"

She nodded. Nestor began going down a row of shelves, selecting items and handing them to her. As they piled up in her arms, he said, "You never spoke of it."

"I was afraid that if I did, you would not let me take books."

He looked at her in surprise. "Did you really think that? I would never have denied you books."

"It was foolish of me," she said with a smile.

"I do admit there were times when I was concerned about you. You never mentioned your family and no one else ever came here with you."

"I have no family."

Nestor shook his head wryly. "You were not hatched from an egg."

Despite herself, she laughed. "That is true."

"But your mother died when you were young, did she not?"

A wave of coldness went through her. "How could you possibly know that?"

"Because mine did, and I went around for a long time braced against the world that had proved so sad and lonely. She was a wonderful woman. I loved her dearly and still do, even though I am now a very old man, the last person alive who remembers her." Piling on another scroll, he said, "You reminded me of that aspect of myself."

"My mother was a good woman," Persephone said softly. "I miss her."

"Of course you do. Did she die on Deimatos?"

"No . . . she didn't." There in the quiet of the long rows of books and scrolls, with only the old librarian to hear her, Persephone spoke of what she had never told anyone. "She was ill, had been for weeks but she didn't want to admit it. Finally, I convinced her that she had to have help. She agreed to go to Ilius but insisted that I stay behind. I didn't want to."

She had argued fiercely that she should be allowed to go, but her mother had stood firm, insisting she remain on Deimatos. With hindsight, she supposed her mother had been unsure of her reception in Ilius and wanted to be sure her daughter remained safe. Or at least that was what she hoped. The alternative was too painful to contemplate.

"You obeyed your mother," Nestor said. "There can be no shame in that."

"Three days after she left, the tide brought the boat back in. There was no trace of her left on it, nor did I ever find any."

Persephone had searched for weeks, walking the beaches of Deimatos and calling her mother's name.

"She was ill, you said, when she left?"

"Yes, seriously ill, although she insisted she could manage the boat."

"She misjudged," Nestor said quietly.

"Perhaps." Or she had chosen to end the life so vastly removed from anything she could ever have imagined for herself. But that would have meant choosing to abandon her child. Much as Persephone did not want to believe that, the uncertainty of her mother's fate still haunted her. It was a bruise on her heart that she had given up hoping would ever heal.

"Let's get these on their way upstairs," Nestor said, gesturing to the books and scrolls she held.

Doing so, she spied a familiar face near the bottom of the stairs. Liam Campbell saw her at the same time and grinned. "Well, now, lass, what's that you've got there?"

"Precious things," she said, passing the pile into his

arms. He, in turn, moved them up the line and continued doing so as the effort went on without cease.

She gave him a quick smile and hurried back to Nestor. Together, they continued making swift, often sorrowful decisions about what to save and what to leave. Persephone took several more armfuls of materials back to the line, exchanging a few quick words with Liam each time.

They were in the library for an hour, not more, and were working in grim, weary silence when the tremor hit.

It came as a rolling undulation from deep within the ground, accompanied by a swiftly growing wave of sound. Persephone froze, then looked to Nestor. "Hold on," she shouted, even as it seemed the world itself convulsed. She had a quick, flashing image of the elderly librarian grabbing hold of one of the shelves that surrounded them in stacks from ceiling to floor. Instinctively, she did the same, but her hand missed, for already the immense rows of stacks were shifting under the force of the tremor. They seemed to be moving in slow motion, drifting away from her even as she tried to grab hold of them.

Tried and missed, for she was falling, sliding across the floor, unable to get her balance. Her head struck a heavy wooden shelf. Pain shot through her, momentarily stunning her.

When she was next aware, she was lying in pitch-darkness and Nestor was calling to her.

"Persephone! Where are you?"

Her first thought was relief that he sounded all right. Hard on it came concern for her own situation. She tried to rise but managed only a few inches before she struck an immovable obstacle. Something very heavy had her trapped.

"Here," she called out. "I'm fine—" This was an exaggeration; her head throbbed agonizingly. "But I'm under something. I can't move it."

Even as she spoke, her nose twitched. The unmistakable smell of burning floated on the air.

"Nestor, there's a fire!"

"I was afraid of that. A lantern must have fallen."

Hardly any had been lit, for safety's sake, but even one could be enough to cause a terrible danger.

"Go!" she yelled. "Get help to put out the fire!"

"You—"

"Never mind, go!"

He went, no doubt realizing her own best hope lay in him returning quickly with people who could put out the fire. In the meantime, she redoubled her efforts to free herself. The smell of burning wood and paper grew stronger. She coughed and pulled up part of her tunic to cover her nose and mouth.

Whatever lay above her, she simply could not move it no matter how hard she pushed and strained. Had it fallen a few more feet, she likely would have been crushed or at least seriously injured. As it was, she was merely trapped, with the fire moving steadily closer.

She could hear it now. The flames crackled almost like the sound of dry leaves being crushed. To die in such a way—

Fear gave her strength she had not known she possessed. Over and over, she pushed at the barrier, twisting over so that she could get up on her knees and try to lift it with her back. It did not budge by so much as an inch.

A sob broke from her. She gasped for air, coughed again and cried out, "Nestor . . . anyone . . . help!"

She heard nothing but the ever-louder sound of the flames coming for her.

What if the old man had fallen or simply hadn't been able to get out? What if no one knew where she was? How much longer could she hope to last?

The smoke was so thick now that she tasted it. Her chest was tight, every breath constricted. Her heart pounded and she could not stop coughing.

Was it true what she had read, that in the terrible years of the Inquisition in Europe, the poor souls condemned to be burned were more often asphyxiated before they were devoured by the flames? Could she hope for a similar fate?

Tears came suddenly. Her life could not end this way, not now when she had only just begun to truly live. She would never see Gavin again, never be able to tell him how she felt—

"Persephone!"

Hope, so perilously close to exhaustion, soared in her. "Here! I'm here!"

"Hold on!"

She would, she had to, but the smoke was very thick now. Her chest was so tightly constricted that she could scarcely draw a breath and when she did, it only made her cough all the more.

But Gavin was there. He wouldn't let her die. She could trust him, rely on him. He wouldn't abandon her.

"Damn, I can't move it!"

He was right above her; she could hear him, hear others rushing to put out the fire. If they did in time—But she couldn't breathe, her lungs were empty of all but stabbing pain. She was lost in darkness cut by swirling lights. Try though she desperately did, she could not hang on to consciousness.

CHAPTER XVIII

I'VE GOT HER." A DEEP VOICE—GAVIN'S—
gruff with emotion.

"Yes, I know you do." Another voice, a man's, with a
thread of amusement.

She was being carried up into cool, sweet air. Strong
arms held her. Persephone breathed once, again, filling
her lungs.

"Gavin—" Was that faint, weak voice her own?

"Sweetheart." He stopped for a moment, staring
down at her with a look in his eyes that made her blink
suddenly as tears threatened. "Thank God!" he said,
and tightened his hold around her.

Minutes later, she was laid on the ground. They
were outside, in the palace courtyard. There were many
people around. She heard voices, some urgent but
calm, others clearly fearful.

"Nestor—" She croaked, only just managing to speak.

The face of the librarian swam before her. "I'm fine, my dear, completely fine. How are you?"

How was she? Gavin was nearby, still holding her. She was breathing. She was no longer trapped in the path of an approaching fire, contemplating the immediacy of her own death. Life was good. "I'm fine," she said, and knew it was true.

For just a moment, Gavin's head rested against the top of hers. Then he straightened and spoke to the large man who stood nearby, observing them. "Thank you, Scotsman."

Liam Campbell grinned. "Happy to help out, Atreides, although I'd wager you would have gotten that pile off her without help if you'd had to."

"Perhaps, but every moment counted. I am in your debt."

"I guess that's better than you wantin' to gut me." Liam inclined his head to Persephone. "Stay out of low places, lass. They're too dangerous to be in now."

"I must agree," Nestor said. "Indeed, given what has just happened, I think we may have very little time left."

"There is so much still to do," Persephone protested weakly. Her normal strength and resiliency seemed to have deserted her.

"Then it must be accomplished in this night," Gavin said. "But with regard for the danger of buildings that are no longer stable and the likelihood of more tremors. The tide will turn shortly after dawn. When it does, the flotilla must go with it."

Liam nodded, clearly approving. "I'll spread the word."

When he had gone to do so, Gavin spoke gently to Nestor. "My old friend and teacher, you must remain out here now. The library is too dangerous."

Nestor looked about to object but stopped when Gavin added, "If you return there, others will go with you. Their respect for you will lead them to do so and that will place them in grave danger."

Sadly, the librarian looked to Persephone. "As you were endangered."

"Of my own will," she assured him.

Reluctantly, Gavin released her. "I must find Marcellus and the others. There will still be preparations to complete before dawn."

"Go," she said and squeezed his hand, telling him silently that she truly was all right.

He went, albeit reluctantly. A healer arrived very shortly, no doubt sent by Gavin. Once convinced that Persephone really was uninjured despite the ordeal she had endured, the young woman turned her attention to Nestor. She coaxed him to come with her to a tent being set up to provide some shelter and comfort for the old and for mothers with young children. He went only when asked to come tell stories to the children.

Persephone was still sitting on the ground, trying to muster her strength to get up and find something useful to do, when Sida swept down on her. "I just heard. Are you all right?"

"Fine, I'll get up in just a minute."

Sida knelt down beside her, frowning. "You're covered with soot, your tunic is singed, and your hair . . . Better we do not speak of your hair."

Persephone couldn't help it, she laughed. All around her, people were struggling to finish what tasks they might still hope to accomplish or were simply sitting, exhausted, waiting for the next tremor to come. A baby who should have long since been asleep wailed. A little boy hugged his sister as both sat, their backs up against the palace wall, watched over by their white-faced mother.

"Sida, I don't think my hair really matters right now."

"Do you not? Foolish girl." With firmness that would not be denied, Sida drew a brush from the bag at her side and set to work. She worked in silence, but her presence alone was a comfort. Long before she was done, all the tension had gone out of Persephone. The terrible incident in the library, the moments when she had truly thought she was going to die, now seemed no more than an unfortunate dream.

"Come along, then," Sida instructed. "You can't sleep here."

"Can't go back inside, either," Persephone murmured. "Isn't safe."

"They're setting up tents."

So they were. A forest of tents appeared to be sprouting throughout the vast courtyard. Men of the garrison were putting them in place. They were far from luxurious, being the tents the soldiers of Akora used on their training maneuvers. But neither were they likely to fall down and crush anyone.

Sida showed her to a small tent just below the outside stairs to the family quarters. She also handed her a bag. Persephone realized with a start that it was the very one she had brought with her from Deimatos.

"I added a few things you seem to have forgotten," Sida told her. She nodded toward a bucket set on the ground. "There's hot water." At the tent flap, she stopped and said, "If we don't see each other again before we leave, you take good care of yourself, Lady Persephone."

"Lady Persephone. Why are people calling me that? It sounds so strange."

"It isn't," Sida said and with no further explanation, went from the tent.

Left alone, Persephone wasted no time. She closed the flap, then shucked off her ruined gown. The hot water was bliss, especially when she added the soap from her bag. When she was clean and dry, she hesitated. The bag held her old tunics, but it also contained another of the lovely gowns. After barely a moment's indecision, she donned the gown, set the bag aside, and sat on the camp bed. It was no more than a thin mattress covered with blankets, yet blissfully comfortable all the same.

She was still sitting there a few minutes later when

Gavin stepped inside. He had to stoop to enter the tent, and once in, his head almost brushed the canvas ceiling. His presence seemed to fill all the available space and left Persephone scarcely able to breathe, this time for far more pleasant reasons.

Brushing a hand through his thick hair, Gavin said, "I thought to get some rest before the tide turns." He looked at her hesitantly, as though unsure whether she might prefer to be alone.

She rose at once and went to him. "Very sensible of you. Here, let me—" Without waiting for his permission, she undid the buckle of his sword belt and took it from him, laying it carefully aside. With a smile, she said, "That's a different kilt, isn't it?"

He raised a brow, never taking his eyes from her. "Different?"

"Than the one you were wearing when you came to Deimatos. The one with the faulty clasp, likely to fall down?"

He remembered then, and laughed. "Oh, that. I made that up."

"To disarm me?"

"Precisely."

"Villain." This said without rancor. Seeing him, being there with him, made her absurdly happy. It also inspired in her a tenderness with which she had little experience. She wanted to take care of him in some way, to give him comfort and ease the burdens pressing down on him, if only in a small way.

Concealing the nervousness that struck her suddenly, she took off his kilt and bent down to take off his sandals. He did not move as she dampened a cloth with the still-warm water and took soap in hand. But he did sigh deeply as she began to wash the soot from his chest and back, his arms and legs. She worked slowly and carefully, helpless against her admiration for the sheer beauty of the man. His body fascinated her. Every part of him was perfectly sculpted of bone, muscle, and sinew. There was no softness to him, yet always she felt within him the check of supreme discipline and, above all, honor, the surety that never would his strength be used to harm the innocent.

Yet for all his strength, he was still vulnerable to worry and fatigue. When she stepped in front of him, she saw the tiredness in his eyes and the gratitude for her simple care of him.

Lastly, very gently, she washed his face, then led him over to the simple bed and urged him down. He went, but drew her with him. She nestled against him as he slept.

Persephone remained awake, savoring from heartbeat to heartbeat every precious moment. She was still awake when the wind picked up and the rain began to fall.

By dawn, when the tide turned, the storm sweeping over Akora had become a full-fledged gale. It came as such storms usually did, out of the west, and slammed up against the Fortress Kingdom with sheets of rain and howling wind.

Shortly, the ground of the courtyard ran with rivulets of muddy water. Rain flowed off the canvas roofs of the tents and joined up in puddles and pools that became impromptu streams. The temperature dropped as the balm of summer turned chill. With Gavin gone to meet with the Council, Persephone threw one of her old tunics over her head and ran for the nearest of the large tents where people were gathering.

She entered to find a subdued group of men and women. The only glimmers of energy or excitement she saw were among the children, who were, for the most part, fidgeting and looking around for something to do.

A few cook fires had been lit and women were working over them, but there were no braziers to warm the air. In the closed space of the tent, they would be too dangerous.

A little girl of perhaps seven, with a spot of mud on her nose, caught sight of Persephone. The child hopped off the bench where she had been sitting, catching her mother unawares, and came over. Looking up, she asked, "Please, Lady, is there anything to do?"

Persephone knew nothing of children, had scarcely been one herself. Yet she was vividly aware of the child's plight. Danger and duty were for adults to deal with. That was as it should be. For the child, for all the children, there should be safety, comfort, and some measure of their normal routine.

"Well," Persephone said, tentatively, "we could play games."

The little girl's face lit up. She nodded vigorously. Without further ado, she grabbed hold of Persephone's hand and urged her toward a group of children who were beginning to stir, curious now that something appeared to be happening.

Abashed, her well-intentioned mother tried to intervene. "Daphne, don't trouble Lady Persephone. I am sorry, Lady. You have enough to occupy you."

"Actually, I don't." Whatever cooking could be done appeared well under way and there was little enough anyone could do until the storm subsided. With a smile for Daphne, she asked, "What do you want to play?"

"Marbles," the little girl replied without hesitation. "Let's play marbles."

Persephone had never played marbles, but she was willing to learn. "All right . . . what do we do?"

"We have to draw a ring first," Daphne informed her and looked around for a suitable location. She pointed to an area where there were no benches. "Over there."

As other children joined in—and Daphne directed— Persephone got down on her hands and knees and carefully drew a circle in the dirt. By the time she finished, adults were beginning to cluster round to watch.

Daphne graciously explained the finer points of the game and demonstrated how to knock one marble out with another. It seemed simple enough, but when Persephone tried it, she found the challenge greater than expected. Even so, it was undeniably fun.

The children thought so, too, to the extent that they clamored for more circles to be drawn. Tables were moved back to make more room, and some of the adults joined in while others stood by and offered encouragement.

Someone produced a flute and began to play. Several other musicians joined in. Sweet, gentle music filled the tent, in counterpoint to the sharp drumming of the rain outside.

Persephone moved back, to make way for a child who wanted to play. She found a seat on a bench beside a woman a few years older than herself, who greeted her with a smile. At some point, a small boy—one of the woman's children—climbed into Persephone's lap and went to sleep with his thumb in his mouth. The woman offered to take him, but Persephone assured her that wasn't necessary. There was something strangely comforting about holding a sleeping child.

She was sitting there, still holding the little boy, when Gavin came into the tent. He stopped just inside and looked round. Seeing Persephone, he came directly to her. A bemused smile lit his eyes as he observed her.

"Who's the little fellow?"

"My youngest, Lord," the woman beside her said. With a murmur of thanks, she took the sleeping child and went to join her husband, who had also just come in.

Persephone rose and brushed off her tunic. She was suddenly self-conscious in his presence. When she looked up again, he was still smiling.

"I heard there was a wild marbles tournament going on in here."

She laughed a little nervously. "Oh, that. The children were bored and needed something to do."

"It looks as though they're occupied now." In addition to the marbles, other games and activities were under way. In one corner of the tent children were busy drawing, while in another a seemingly fierce arm-wrestling competition was taking place. Families were eating together and with friends, old and new. It looked to Persephone as though whatever barriers had existed between the citizens of Ilius and the people who had come in from the countryside in the past few days were breaking down.

"Is the storm lessening?" she asked as she walked with Gavin over to the food line.

"Not yet. We got almost all the boats out into the harbor to ride this out, but two got loose and smashed into the quays."

"No one was on board them?"

Gavin shook his head. "We had to off-load all the animals that were already on board. They couldn't ride this out without being terrified and harming themselves. We'll have to reload them all as soon as it's safe."

She nodded. The storm had cost them dearly. They had lost not only a day, but also a huge amount of effort to protect the animals and ships.

"You must be exhausted," she said quietly, as she sat with him while he ate.

"Not so much. The men are amazing. I know some of them from warrior training and more from visits here, but I never fully appreciated just what they're capable of."

"How is it you participated in warrior training? And you said also that Nestor was your teacher. But wasn't your education in England?"

"It is the custom in England to send the children of the upper class to boarding schools at a very young age. My parents opposed that. They believe it often has a harmful effect." He paused for a moment, then said, "From what I've seen of the British aristocracy in general, I have to agree."

"What about your father? Was he educated like that?"

Gavin chewed a hunk of bread and shook his head. "We've always gone our own way, which might explain in part how we've survived so long."

"So you came here as a boy, to be educated?"

"It was my mother's wish, and my father agreed."

"How did you feel about it?"

He grinned. "I was delighted. Even my brother, David, who loves Hawkforte, enjoyed it. We went through most of warrior training together, although I was always ahead of him by virtue of being older. David spent more time in England than I did, but he had tutors at Hawkforte. Eventually he went up to Oxford, of his own choice, and he did well there."

"You had no wish to do the same?"

"I preferred to study here." He raised a hand, forestalling what he apparently thought would be her obvious response. "I know, I am meant for Akora."

She smiled, caught his hand, and raised it to her cheek. "Perhaps I should just let events speak for themselves."

He turned his head, brushing his lips against her palm, and looked pleased when she shivered. "You've made up for any gaps in your own education with remarkable speed."

"Gaps?"

"Akoran women are well schooled in the management of hapless males. They learn the art at their mother's knee."

"You know that but don't resent it?"

"We manage small spurts of complaint about it from time to time, but they never amount to anything."

"Why not?" she asked a little breathlessly. His hand covered hers, warm and hard.

"We're much too well satisfied. What man with any sense wouldn't be?"

She could think of one. A man who had been satisfied with nothing and who had wanted everything—power, glory, adulation. A man who had destroyed her mother's life and made her own a prison of shame and isolation.

A prison from which the Atreides prince had freed her.

"What is it?" Gavin asked.

"Nothing, nothing at all."

"Something very unpleasant just went through your mind."

"Am I that transparent?"

"No, not at all, it's just that I—I care about what you're feeling."

She looked away. It was that or absolutely disgrace herself. "Do you know how to play marbles?"

"Do I know how to play marbles? You must be joking. I've never been beaten."

She glanced at him skeptically. "Never, really?"

"Not once. In my youth"—he grinned, looking very young—"I was a killer marbles player."

She laughed and stood. "In that case, there's a little girl named Daphne you have to meet."

He went along with her, but cautioned, "Keep in mind, I haven't played in years."

Persephone looked over her shoulder and laughed. "Don't start making excuses now. I'm sure Daphne will go easy on you, at least at first."

For an hour, she had the great pleasure of watching Gavin play marbles. He was good, she had to give him that. He was also kind. Daphne enjoyed the experience immensely, as did all the many children who took turns joining in, watched by their bemused parents.

He did not win this particular game, however. And she loved him all the more for it.

They were still playing when the earth shook again.

CHAPTER XIX

PERSEPHONE STEPPED FROM THE TENT WHERE she had spent a restless night, mostly without Gavin, who was continuing to work with his men. She had only a faint memory of him coming to her in the hours of deepest darkness, lying down beside her and holding her close. The warmth of his body still lingered on hers.

She shaded her eyes, wincing in the bright sun. The wind still blew, but far more gently than it had for a day and night. The gale had passed over and the few clouds that remained were scudding swiftly across the sky.

All around her, people were emerging from the tents and beginning to pack up their belongings. She did the same and joined a group streaming through the lions' gate down to the harbor.

Powerful waves continued to smash against the piles of the docks, but the debris that washed onto several piers showed that the sea had been far more violent during the storm. The garrison, Gavin with them, were bringing vessels in from where they had ridden out the pounding in the safety of the harbor. Already almost all the slips were full.

Animals were being loaded as people waited to board. A tense quiet hung over all. As each ship was filled, it moved away from the quay, making room for another. So it went throughout the morning, as the wind continued to lessen.

Persephone did not wait for her own boat to be brought in. She got a ride out on a dinghy and climbed on board, relieved to find that her vessel had weathered the storm well.

Even so, there was baling to do and she got to it. The work was tedious, but she kept at it without stopping until finally it was done. As she worked, she was aware of more vessels moving up to the quay and away again as they completed loading. All around her the flotilla was forming, as she knew it must be at other locations around Ilius and on the other large island of Leios. The tide would turn again in a few hours and they would have to be ready to leave with it.

By the time she was done baling, her back and shoulders ached and her arms felt as though they had gotten sunburned. She straightened, stretching and looking out beyond the harbor to the distant inlet. It was one of two that connected the Inland Sea to the open ocean beyond.

For centuries sailors from other lands, upon nearing the Fortress Kingdom, believed they were looking at one immense island. Nothing revealed the secret of the inlets, which could not be penetrated while the ever-vigilant Akoran Navy was on patrol. Only those *xenos* fortunate enough to be blown through the inlets during storms had a chance of finding themselves washed up on Akora's golden shores.

Only in recent decades had Akora welcomed closer contact with the outside world. But even so, Persephone noted there were no *xenos* ships in the harbor. They had all been given orders to sail several days before, as Akora prepared to deal with the crisis at hand.

The last ships of the flotilla were at the quay hours later when a dinghy nudged against the hull of her boat. She looked over the railing to see Gavin. A glad cry broke from her as she hurried to greet him.

"I did promise," he reminded her gently.

"You did and I believed you. I'm just so relieved that you're actually here."

He hugged her close, even as he took a quick but thorough look at the condition of the boat. The deck was dry, the sails ready to be unfurled, the oars set in the oarlocks, ready for use if they were needed. "It looks as though you're ready."

Persephone nodded. "How long to the tide?"

"Less than an hour." He stepped back a little but kept his arm around her waist. Together they looked out across the harbor to the now-empty city of Ilius, gleaming in the sun.

On the decks of the ships all around them, thousands upon thousands of men, women, and children were doing the same. Taking what might be their last look at their dearly loved home.

"It is so beautiful," Persephone said softly.

Gavin's arm tightened around her. "I cannot imagine it gone."

"Nor can I." Yet the possibility was achingly real. Once the volcano exploded, there was no telling how extensive the damage would be. Nor was there any escape from the knowledge that the eruption more than three thousand years before had been a true catastrophe, utterly destroying everything in its path.

They stood together without speaking, as the final minutes faded away and slowly but inexorably, the tide turned.

From the lead ship of the flotilla, a cannon boomed out over the harbor. It was the signal everyone had been waiting for. On every vessel, sails were unfurled and anchors raised.

First slowly, then with gathering speed, the ships began moving out toward the open sea.

"It's so strange," Persephone said as she sat beside Gavin, content to let him take the rudder.

"How so?"

"If I let myself, I could pretend this is just a beautiful day and we've decided to go for a sail."

"We should do that when this is over."

It was the first time he had spoken of a future for them. Longing filled her, so intensely that she had to look away. She was just doing that, turning her head to the left, when the world shook again.

The water cushioned much of the impact, but its power was unmistakable all the same. The entire stone quay along the harbor of Ilius—more than a mile long—suddenly rippled as though it, too, had become a wave. Once, twice, it rose in an undulating motion before suddenly cracking apart. Huge blocks of stone fell into the harbor while the rest merely subsided in clouds of dust, a devastated ruin.

Scarcely had she even begun to absorb the shock of that when a sound unlike any she had ever heard engulfed them. Gavin kept one strong hand on the rudder as he grabbed her with the other. Far off in the Inland Sea, in the direction of Deimatos, a vast column of steam rose toward the heavens.

"Nestor told me of this," she shouted above the roar. "The survivors reported it as the last sign before the Cataclysm."

Gavin nodded grimly. "I know. Pray to God the wind holds." For if it did not, they would have to row with all their strength to escape what was surely almost upon them.

The column of steam continued without lessening,

but the wind did hold. Along with the rest of the
flotilla, they were able to move swiftly out of the harbor and along the coast toward the southern inlet. The
countryside they passed was heartbreakingly beautiful.
Verdant hills rose up from the water, dotted with
whitewashed farmhouses, small, exquisite temples, and
orchards. As though in a final stroke of irony, the air
even far out to sea smelled of lemon, jasmine, and ole-
ander—the perfume of Akora that travelers said they
never encountered anywhere else.

As Persephone watched, a flock of small black birds,
hundreds in all, rose suddenly into the air and wheeled
in a wide circle. She was wondering what had provoked
their action when a sudden, hard swell struck the boat.
The sea that had seemed to be calming rapidly in the
wake of the storm abruptly turned rough again.

"What's happening?" she asked urgently.

Gavin put her hand on the rudder and stood, staring
in the direction of the column of steam, which appeared to be increasing in intensity. "I don't know, but
it isn't good."

That it was not. The sea began to buck and heave
like the wildest of horses. The prow of the boat dipped
into the water as waves washed up over the deck.

All around them, the other ships of the flotilla were
being similarly struck. Gavin took the rudder again,
then cursed when he saw two vessels come very close to
ramming each other.

"Spread out!" he yelled. "Keep your distance!"

Men on the ships closest to them heard him and obeyed. They also relayed the orders to others in the flotilla, who continued passing it along. Slowly, with the inertia of a great beast, the fleet dispersed. There were several more heart-stoppingly close encounters, but at least so far as Persephone could see, none of the several hundred ships suffered any damage.

The sea continued to roil. As they neared the southern inlet, the effect seemed to worsen, perhaps because the water was being forced through so narrow a passage. Persephone had the rudder again as Gavin adjusted the sails, when off to port, she saw a small ship beginning to founder.

"Gavin, over there!"

He turned and saw what she did. The ship, larger than their own, looked to be carrying perhaps twenty passengers. It was low in the water, indicating the hold was likely filled with animals. They were close enough now to see that the man at the rudder looked grim and that others were scrambling to take in the sails in a bid to lessen their speed and gain more control.

They were not succeeding. The relentless power of the sea was driving them toward the rocky shore. Within minutes they would crash against it unless something was done swiftly.

No other vessel was close enough to help. Gavin grabbed a length of rope, made sure it was secured to their bow, and nodded to Persephone. "Take us in, sweetheart."

She swallowed hard, all too aware of the trust he was placing in her, and of all that was riding on it. Too close and the ships would crash together with dire results for all. Too far and they would be unable to save the other vessel.

Carefully . . . carefully, struggling to gauge the power of the sea as it communicated itself through the hull and rudder, she narrowed the swath of blue water separating them. Carefully . . .

Gavin coiled the rope in his hands.

Carefully . . . just a little more . . .

"That's good," he said. "Steady—" The powerful muscles of his back and arms clenched as he threw the rope far out over the water. The very end of it fell onto the deck of the other vessel, where it was swiftly grabbed and tied. "Now!"

At Gavin's order, she swung the rudder hard, turning the boat back out to sea and, she prayed, dragging the other vessel with them. If the wind died now, likely so would they.

But the wind did not die. Instead, it seemed to increase slightly, just enough to give the smaller boat all it needed to tow the larger one to safety. A cheer went up from the other vessel as the people on board realized they had been spared. Ahead of them, the rest of the flotilla was pouring out through the inlet, reaching the safety of the open sea.

Gavin cut the rope connecting them to the larger vessel. More cheers and shouts of thanks floated behind as it sped past. Persephone realized with a start that they were the very tail end of the fleet. In some way, she supposed that was fitting. But as they approached the inlet, her whole body tensed. The sudden, stark reality of what she was about to do struck her hard. Even in the face of the greatest danger, how could she leave Akora?

She had never done so and now, faced with the imminence of that departure, she was gripped by panic. Yet she said nothing, only kept her eyes locked on the inlet. There was no alternative; they had to leave. She had known for days this moment would come. She had to be brave and strong. Gavin deserved nothing less.

She had to—

The roar of the steam column suddenly redoubled. At the same time, the small boat bucked wildly. Gavin was beside her instantly, grabbing hold of the rudder, to help her control it. Before Persephone's stunned gaze, the inlet suddenly appeared to be receding from them.

"What's happening?" she shouted above the tunnel of sound in which they seemed to be trapped.

Gavin's face was as hard as she had ever seen it. "The tide's reversed. We're being pulled back in."

"How could that be? I don't understand—"

"It must be the volcano. It's pulling in water from the sea, turning it to steam."

"We've got to get out!"

He knew that as well as she did, but there was

nothing either of them could do. The immense, churning cauldron of energy that had become Akora had them in its grip. Ever more quickly, faster and faster, they were drawn back toward Ilius.

There was nothing to do, nothing to say, nothing left except to hold hard to each other as the valiant little boat hurtled back into the harbor and rammed up against the destroyed quay.

Barely had it done so than Gavin leaped out and pulled her up after him. The boat was taking on water fast. It would sink within minutes. Beneath their feet, the fragments of the quay continued to ripple. Buildings along the harbor were beginning to collapse.

"We've got to find shelter," Gavin said.

"People survived in the caves—"

"No, that temple was on the surface. It was folded into the earth and miraculously they weren't killed, but the caves were filling with lava even before this started. We can't go down."

"Then we go up?" Persephone turned her eyes to the palace high on the hill. From where she stood, it appeared essentially unharmed. But would it remain so?

"Not the palace," Gavin said quickly. "If the tremors are strong enough, it will collapse. Somewhere else—"

He thought for a moment, reaching a swift decision. "Come on, this way."

"Where are we going?" Persephone asked as she hurried after him, her hand still gripped in his.

"Into the mountains. We can't know how high the

lava flows will come. We've got to get as far away from them as possible."

She agreed completely, but if she had not, she had no better option to offer. Behind them, more buildings were collapsing. They ran up in the direction of the palace, but did not enter the lions' gate. The road continued upward, skirting a hillside where the open-air theatre stood, and continuing higher still. Up and up they went as the column of steam continued to roar.

"How far—?" she gasped.

"Very far, are you all right? Do you need help?"

"I'm fine, don't stop, keep going!"

They were out of the city, well beyond any place where she had ventured, and still climbing. The trail they followed led them higher and higher. Ahead lay a rocky crag and beyond that a chasm crossed by a narrow bridge.

Glancing over her shoulder, she saw Ilius spread out beneath her. From her position, the city appeared serene. Nothing moved along the deserted streets, but the buildings and their surrounding gardens seemed to wait for their inhabitants to return. No damage was evident until she strained her eyes to see the harbor, now far below. As she watched, several buildings crumbled in on themselves.

"Where are we going?" she asked as they continued climbing.

"There's a camp high in the mountains. We'll have shelter, water, maybe food."

If they could get there and if the explosion didn't tear the mountain itself apart.

She said nothing of that but kept going, following him along the steep and winding path, climbing higher and higher away from the sea that continued to surge inward, feeding the immense column of steam rising into the sky.

CHAPTER XX

AFTER ALL THE HOURS OF LISTENING to the roar of steam and the rumble of collapsing stone, the awareness of silence slowly crept over Persephone. A pebble rolling away down the trail surprised her because it sounded so loud. She could hear her own breathing as well as the rustle of grasses bending gracefully beneath the now-gentle wind.

The air was pleasantly cool beneath a sky streaked by what she guessed were false clouds, traces of the steam rising into the heavens.

A bird trilled a song at once exuberent and bold. She almost laughed at what seemed its pronouncement—that the world was going along just fine.

And still they climbed, but more slowly now, a little of their desperate urgency gone and fatigue beginning to set in, at least for her. Gavin looked as though he could keep going at top speed all day, but then, he had trained for it, acquiring the stamina and endurance of a warrior in exercises that most likely had taken him into these same mountains.

"Are we going to an army camp?" she asked when they paused briefly. She was bent over, hands braced on her knees, breathing deeply. Sweat fell in her eyes and she was very sure that Sida would not approve of the condition of her hair.

Gavin looked entirely unaffected, but Persephone was not fooled. He was sharply alert, scanning the area all around them, ready to move in an instant.

"Not an army camp," he said. "Something better." When she looked at him quizzically, he said, "Let it come as a surprise."

"I'm not sure I need any more surprises."

He laughed and moved on. She followed him.

A little while later, when they had climbed higher still, Persephone saw movement along the slope of the mountain. A brown goat, grazing on the rough scrub grass that grew at that altitude, paused and stared at the passing humans.

Only domestic animals had gone with the flotilla. There were uncounted numbers of animals left, perhaps many like the small flock of goats who had no apparent sense of danger.

A little while later, they stopped again, this time beside a small spring. Though Persephone suspected they were pausing only for her sake, she couldn't help but be grateful. With a weary sigh, she sat down on a moss-draped rock and dipped her hand into the spring. The water from it might easily be the best she had ever tasted. She drank thirstily, then splashed water on her heated face.

Gavin did the same. He straightened and took a long look around. "It's not much farther."

"We've come miles." She sat up, feeling markedly better. "Up here it seems as though there's nothing wrong." As though to emphasize her words, a black-and-orange butterfly fluttered by.

"Let's hope it stays that way."

On they went, climbing toward a white chalk ridge. All of Akora was spread out beneath them. At the center of the Inland Sea, beneath the column of steam, the islands of Deimatos, Tarbos, and Phobus could be seen. Beyond them, the slight thickening along the horizon indicated the coast of Leios.

From such a distance, the sea looked calm. Only a faint haze of rising stone dust in the direction of the harbor at Ilius hinted at the damage there. Far out beyond the headlands, the open ocean was a deep, dark blue. Small white dots, the sails of the flotilla, shone against it. In the opposite direction, beyond the northern inlet, a similar collection of white dots heralded the presence of the fleet from Leios.

"It looks as though everyone got out," Persephone said. Scarcely had she spoken than a deep, low rumble reached them.

"Tremor," Gavin said. "Powerful enough for us to hear even up here."

A few minutes later, just as they reached the white chalk ridge, there was another roar.

"Keep going," Gavin directed and boosted her over the ridge. Beyond it lay a vast field of wildflowers—daisies, crocuses, violets, irises, poppies, all dancing lightly in the breeze. At almost the precise center of the field stood a small, snug cabin. It was made of logs notched to fit together and roofed with shingles covered with moss.

In front of the cabin stood an enormous bear. Actually, a wooden bear carved from the trunk of an ancient tree, which evoked all bears in a single magnificent image. In the field around the cabin were other large sculptures, some of wood, others of metal, all riveting and evocative.

"What is this place?" Persephone asked.

"Atreus's cabin, his and Brianna's." Leading the way through the wildflowers, Gavin added, "My uncle jokes he wants to retire here someday."

"Why do you think he is joking?"

"A fair point. When he said it, I just presumed he was."

"But now?"

"Now I don't know." He put a hand to the small of her back. "Let's get inside."

The cabin was a single room with two small adjacent spaces, one for cooking and the other for bathing. Persephone was astonished to see that a hot spring ran right through the bathing area. A well, dug directly beneath the kitchen, provided fresh water.

The living area was simply but beautifully furnished with a large carved wooden bed, covered with a weaving that seemed to combine within it all the colors of the sky at sunrise or sunset. There were also several low couches and a carved table. Along one wall was something she had never seen before but had read about.

"A fireplace?" she asked, looking at the brick-lined recess.

Gavin nodded. "It gets cold enough up here to welcome it. I'm going to check the food supply."

"Is there likely to be one?"

"Atreus and Brianna come up here fairly often, so they tend to leave staples. There should also be some fishing and hunting gear."

In the kitchen cupboards they found barrels of flour, salt, and sugar. Clay jars held olive oil and honey. There were also dried peppers, beef, and fruits, as well as a round of cheese and some crackers.

"We won't starve," Persephone observed. She was privately amazed to find such a refuge, for however long it lasted, and even more astonished by the sheer banality of her response. "I can't believe I'm hungry."

"So am I. I'll be happy to help, but honestly, I don't have much idea what to do with any of this."

Perhaps it was the sudden ordinariness of the situation after so many days and nights of fear. Or perhaps she was merely happy to be with him. Whatever the cause, Persephone felt lighthearted and in the mood for a little teasing.

"What did you do when you came up into the mountains during warrior training?"

"Chewed dried beef tough as leather. If we wanted a treat, we caught grasshoppers."

"I don't want to hear about that," she warned.

He relented with a grin but said more seriously, "I'm going to get a fire going, then reconnoiter, all right?"

She assured him that it was. He laid a fire in the stove—very competently, she noted—then found a small box that held wooden sticks. Scraping one of the sticks against the side of the stove produced a spark that turned swiftly to a flame.

"How did you do that?"

"They're called matchsticks." He handed her the box. "They smell terrible, but they do work. Just be careful if you have to use one."

Wondering how a stick could replace the tedious effort required of flint and tinder, Persephone fetched water from the well and put a pot on the fire. She cut thin slices of the dried beef and dropped them into the pot. A further search of the kitchen produced an array of spices that she set aside. While the beef softened, she sliced dried peppers and fruits. By the time Gavin returned, she had all three simmering in olive oil with a bit of honey and a smattering of spices. She had also mixed dough for flat bread, which she cooked on flat pans in the oven.

He sniffed appreciatively. "It smells as though you've worked a miracle."

She tried to hide her pleasure at his praise but knew she did not succeed entirely. They carried the food into the main room and sat at the carved table. As they ate, she asked, "What did you find?"

"What I hoped to. I've only been up here a few times but I thought I remembered it fairly well. The rocks here are different. There's no obsedian at all, but there is a lot of granite."

"Does this mean something?"

"I think it does. This is a part of the original Akora that survived the Cataclysm. There may be a good chance it will do so again."

"That is a comfort," she admitted. Off in the distance, she heard another roar. If she tried very hard, she could almost pretend it was thunder.

"We should get some rest," Gavin said gently.

But Persephone had a different idea. On Deimatos, she had been accustomed to bathing in mineral springs. Since leaving there, such baths were the only thing she missed. When the dishes were cleared away, she decided she could wait no longer.

"I'm going to have a bath." And then, because she

was a woman of courage and passion, an Akoran woman, she added, "Care to join me?"

F OR A MAN SITTING ABOVE A VOLCANO THAT WAS about to explode, Gavin was surprisingly comfortable. Dinner sat well in his stomach, Persephone lay within the curve of his arm, and the bumps and scrapes gathered in several days of bruising effort to save the flotilla from the storm and get it safely embarked were being soothed by the hot mineral spring. All in all, not too bad.

"No wonder Atreus likes this place," Gavin murmured, laying his head back against the rim of the tiled tub, built so that the mineral spring bubbled up into it.

Persephone moved slightly, her body slick and smooth against his own. "It is remarkably beautiful." Her mouth was full and ripe, very close to his own.

He lifted a hand and cupped the back of her head, drawing her to him. His kiss was long and deep as he traced the curve of her lips with his tongue, plunging inward to taste her, savoring her soft sounds of pleasure.

With a gasp, she tore her mouth away and rose above him, her hair freed from its braid and tumbling over them both. In the light of the candles she had set around the spring, her skin looked touched by honey, her eyelashes tipped with gold. He thought suddenly of how readily she laughed, and found himself smiling.

She was a woman to savor with all his senses, a woman to walk beside at daybreak and in twilight.

Her high, round breasts brushed his chest. He clasped her hips, raising her a little more, settling her over him.

The rhythm of their lovemaking was slow and gentle. They were both tired, but more than that, the need was in them to make each and every moment last. When finally the convulsions of release took her, Gavin still held back, waiting as long as he possibly could before his own passion overcame him.

Afterward, they rested in the spring until the cooling air above recalled them to themselves. Rising, he found a drying sheet and wrapped it around Persephone. She murmured sleepily as he carried her to the bed and sat her on the edge. With great care and thoroughness, he dried her, then took the sheet and did the same for himself. Persephone pulled back the covers and they both got into bed. Neither spoke as he took her in his arms, nestling her head against the curve of his shoulder.

Far off in the distance, the thunder of the earth continued.

It could still be heard in the morning. Gavin went out to see whatever he could, while Persephone made coffee from the reserve she found in the cupboard. It was ready when he returned.

"Anything?" she asked. He thought she looked subdued, even a little pale, but put it down to the exertions of the previous few days and the weight of worry.

"The mist is too thick. I walked as far as the chalk ledge, then turned back while I still could."

He took the cup she handed him and drank appreciatively. "I couldn't see but I can smell. There is an odor, very faint, but distinct. I believe it's sulfur."

"Is it possible there could have been an eruption and we wouldn't know?"

"Only if it were very small. There's a stream at the far end of this field. I'm going to catch a few fish. If the mist clears, I'll also do some hunting. We could be up here for a while and I want to be sure we have enough food."

She nodded but did not look at him. "There are berries growing behind the kitchen. I'll pick some, then join you."

He had three fat trout on a string when she did so. Sitting beside him, her feet dangling in the water, Persephone said quietly, "I am not with child."

He hesitated, wanting to respond properly but not entirely able to quell the sudden spurt of disappointment that took him by surprise. The idea of a child of their making drew him powerfully.

"Are you all right?" he asked, for he was a man who had grown up with sisters.

Her cheeks reddened. "Perfectly. At any rate, I'm sure we're both relieved."

"Why do you say that?"

She took a breath, stared down into the water. "You have no duty to me, Gavin."

His hand tightened on the net he'd used to catch the fish. He set it aside carefully. "Do I not?"

She did look at him then, but her eyes were shuttered. He could not see what lay behind them. "No, you don't. With all the responsibilities you have—and all you will have, I believe, in the future—I cannot, will not be a burden to you."

"I never thought you were." The mere suggestion angered him. How could she have thought that, given all they had shared? Did she truly not know what she meant to him?

"The fact is, I am sorry there is no child," he said.

Her shock gave him a small degree of satisfaction, but it faded quickly when she said, "You cannot mean that."

"Why not? I'm a man like most any other. The thought of having children appeals to me."

What would a child of their making be like? A little girl with her mother's valiant spirit? A boy with his father's interest in science? Or something entirely unsuspected, as he had observed children so often could be—a surprise and a mystery yet to unfold.

She sat very still beside him, but her hands were folded in her lap so tightly that the knuckles were white. "It was just a dream."

"What was?" He spoke very gently. He could feel the brittleness in her and did not want to do anything to make it worse.

"When you said I had to promise to leave, even if

you couldn't, because I might be carrying our child. I was so struck by that . . . I let myself . . ." She broke off, staring down at her hands.

"Dream?"

Mutely, she nodded.

He put his hand over hers. "Sometimes our dreams are the best of ourselves."

She sniffed and managed a faint smile, acknowledgment of his effort to comfort her. "Not in this case. Gavin . . . I care for you a great deal. You must have realized that. But when this is over, assuming we survive, we have to go our separate ways."

Tribute to the effectiveness of his training, he replied calmly, even as stark, cold fear ripped through him. Never would he let her go. "And why would that be?"

"Because of who you are . . . who you will be. And who I am."

"Lady Persephone." Let her not think he was unaware of how she was regarded.

She did laugh then, but sadly. "People called me that because they saw me with you and jumped to their own conclusions."

"Really? It is my impression they saw you working alongside them, providing help, guidance, and support. Reassuring them when they needed it, comforting the children, doing everything possible to face danger with courage and resolve."

A tear fell, gleaming silver in the sun, and landed on his hand. She started to get up and he didn't stop her, but he did stand with her, close enough to stop her if she did something truly foolish—such as trying to leave him.

"I'm being ridiculous," she said, angrily wiping her tears away. "Look, there's something you don't know about me."

"I'm sure there's a great deal I don't know, but we have a lifetime to learn about each other." Or so he damn well hoped. The volcano might have other ideas.

"If there had been a child, it would have been a terrible mistake."

He took hold of her shoulders and shook her lightly, for never could he do anything to harm her. That was not merely the law; the very notion of hurting her in any way horrified him. "Don't say that. No child can be a mistake."

"Not even Deilos's child?"

"Deilos—?" He stopped breathing, watching her.

She spoke from the well of deepest grief and shame. "Deilos was my father."

Relief filled him, an incongruous response perhaps, but he was glad all the same to have it out in the open. "I thought that might be the case."

Her head snapped up. She stared at him in disbelief. "What do you mean, you thought? You could not have. You would have said something . . . denounced me. Certainly, you would never have—"

"Become your lover? But I did that, didn't I? Of course I wondered who your parents might be. There you were, living on Deimatos, the island so closely associated with Deilos. How could I not at least speculate that you might have some connection to him?"

As she continued to stare at him, he said more gently, "Then there was your claim to have no family, not to mention your obvious surprise at learning that the prohibition against men hurting women is real, that it genuinely means what it says, and that the very few men who have ever transgressed against it are criminals."

"Even so, you would have said something."

"I did—to Polonus."

"Polonus?" She was white with shock, scarcely able to speak. "Why would you discuss it with him?"

"Because Polonus knew Deilos. He was a follower of his."

Shock heaped upon shock. He held her more tightly lest she fall. "That is not possible," she insisted. "Polonus is respected, honored . . . a member of the Council, your uncle."

"He is all those things and as fine a man as I know, but in his youth—or as he would say, his 'misguided youth'—he was a follower of Deilos. So were several hundred other Akorans, mostly young people."

"Deilos's followers died in battles with the Atreides."

"The traitor warriors among them did, but the vast majority of his followers were reconciled with their families and with society. They went on to lead perfectly ordinary lives or even, as in Polonus's case, lives of great service and accomplishment."

"Reconciled?" Bitterness turned the word sword-edge sharp. "There was at least one family with no interest in reconciliation."

"Your mother's?" he asked gently.

"She, too, was a follower of Deilos, but in her case, she trusted him far too much. When I was born, her family disowned her."

"She fled to Deimatos?"

Persephone nodded. "She wanted nothing to do with the world after that, and she thought I would be better off kept away from it. She believed if people realized who I was, I would be persecuted."

"She was wrong. You must realize that now."

"How could she have been? He is always called 'the traitor Deilos,' as though that was his name for all time. And who can blame people for calling him that? He did terrible things."

"*He* did them, not you. The sins of the father are not visited upon the children. You are not to blame for anything your father did."

"His blood is in me and would be in any child I had."

"What of it? We are not the slaves of whatever it is that flows in our veins. Our lives are our own to make, and whether we use the time we have for good or evil is entirely up to us."

Tears slipped again down her cheeks. She gave up trying to deny them. "Gavin, don't . . . I know you mean well, but don't make me dream again. You are not an ordinary man. You will be called to be Vanax after Atreus."

He stiffened, staring down at her. She had made reference to this, but to hear her say it so starkly was a shock. "You cannot know that." Yet even as he spoke, he recalled her gift, the ability she had to feel the deep inner rhythms of Akora, to understand it on a level very few had likely ever approached.

"I do know it and I am not the only one. I think Atreus knows. Nothing else explains his willingness to be away from Akora at such a crucial time."

"To test me——?" It was a stunning thought, yet it made a certain sense.

"Not just that. To let the people come to know you, to see you as a leader they can trust."

It had the ring of truth. Moreover, it was exactly the sort of thing Atreus would do. All the same, Gavin's mind reeled from the thought. His deepest yearning, the secret sorrow of his life—bound to Hawkforte, denied Akora. But that was all wrong. His life, his future lay here. And not just any life—a life of union with the land itself and dedicated service to its people. It was all he could ever have hoped for and vastly more.

And the woman who faced him so bravely, her face wet with tears, had led him to the knowledge of it.

"Persephone!" Laughing, he seized her up and twirled her around, hugging her tightly, not caring how preposterous such behavior was under the circumstances.

He loved her, he loved Akora, and the world had suddenly opened up grand and glorious before him.

"I don't give a damn about your father and neither

will anyone else. We are meant to be together, Lady Persephone, Lady of Akora." Holding her close, he looked deeply into her eyes and said, "I asked for your help once before. Now I do so again. Let us walk this road together."

She sobbed, crying in earnest, and threw her arms tightly around him. "Gavin, my love . . ."

A hawk screeched overhead, punctuating the stillness. Birds rose from the surrounding trees. A rabbit on the edge of the field near the stream suddenly froze, then scampered frantically into the underbrush.

There was a low, deep rumbling that came up through the earth, all the way through the mountain, shaking the man and woman who still stood within the circle of each other's arms, as one.

The column of steam that had poured into the sky without cease for two days and nights abruptly stopped.

A moment passed . . . then another. The rumbling grew even stronger. The sky itself seemed to tremble.

The volcano exploded.

CHAPTER XXI

A PILLAR OF FIRE ROSE FROM THE SEA JUST
beyond Deimatos, near where the column of
steam had been. At its center, the light was so bright as
to be white. Farther out it turned from hot yellow and
orange to red. Immense flares of flame and sparks shot
off in every direction.

It was beautiful.

What a strange, even bizarre thought, yet Persephone
could not shake free of it. She was witnessing something
few people had ever seen—at least those who had lived,
as she profoundly hoped she would.

Gavin didn't care. She had told him the desperate,
dark secret of her soul, which had weighed her down all
her life and he didn't care. It didn't matter to him at all
that her father had come very close to killing his parents and uncle, had tried to raise a rebellion against his

entire family, had attempted to completely overturn the peace and stability of Akora and destroy everything all the Atreides had worked to protect over thousands of years. Moreover, Deilos had done it with tactics of brutality and cunning that had come perilously close to succeeding.

And Gavin didn't care at all.

The sins of the father are not visited upon the children. He had said that matter-of-factly, as though it was entirely normal to think that way. She knew, from all the vast expanse of books she had read in her days of solitude, that it was not. Through much of the world, vendettas and blood feuds were the order, ancient grudges were lovingly nurtured and old wrongs were never allowed to be righted except with more blood, setting off yet another cycle of brutality.

But not on Akora, and not in the heart of the man who would one day lead it.

Or whatever Akora became when the volcano was done.

"It's amazing," Gavin said quietly. He held Persephone close against him as together they stared out at the display, not of nature's fury, but of its vast, unimaginable power.

Long, arcing jets of molten lava continued to shoot into the sky, where they seemed to hang suspended for a few moments before raining down around the three small islands.

"It doesn't look all that dangerous," Persephone ventured, although no doubt she would feel very differently were she still on Deimatos.

"Unfortunately, I think it's just beginning."

Moments later, it was evident that he was right. A shriek torn from the bowels of hell preceded the eruption of an immense cloud of ash and stone that completely dwarfed the sprays of lava. It climbed so high into the sky that there seemed to be no end to it. There it hung, blotting out the sun and growing with each passing moment.

There was nothing in the least beautiful about it. Indeed, Persephone thought it terrifying.

"We'd better get inside," Gavin said calmly and moved to make it so.

Once in the cabin, they laid strips of cloth at the base of the door and around the windows. Gavin made sure the fireplace chimney was closed. He also filled several buckets of water and set them within easy reach.

She did not ask what they were for. The ash was likely to carry burning cinders. If those reached them, it could set the wooden cabin on fire.

Though it was midday, the light outside faded fast as the sky over Akora turned first gray, then black. Beyond the windows, while there was yet some light, they could see the ash cloud continuing to build. There appeared to be no wind, for the cloud went straight up, thickening steadily.

It was soon too dark to see anything at all. Gavin lit

a small lantern and they sat together on the couch, he with his arm around her shoulders. The air was bitter and acrid, but breathable. Twice he went outside to check on the roof and surrounding area.

When he returned the second time, the cloth covering his face below the eyes was dark with ash.

"How bad is it?" she asked.

"There's a light rain of ash, but it could be worse. There is no sign of fire and best yet, no hint of gas."

"You expected gas?"

"I've read that some volcanoes have emitted fast-moving clouds of poisonous gas. Any people in an area where such a cloud sweeps over are almost certain to be killed."

"You said nothing of this."

"There was no point. People were concerned enough and they realized they had to leave without further persuading. The mountains and cliffs that form the borders of Akora will contain any such cloud, if there is one. Those on the ships will be safe."

She nodded, realizing that she was only beginning to know the full extent of the burden he had carried. He had understood better than any of them the true nature of the danger they faced and how great might be the suffering of their people.

In a bid to distract them both, she asked, "How is the bear?"

That wrung a smile. "He seems fine. A few chunks of pumice have landed in the field, but so far it looks as though a decent rain could take care of the ash." Sitting beside her again, he said, "It's likely to be much worse farther down."

"If the wind were blowing in our direction, it would be much worse here."

He nodded. "Fortune favors us."

So it continued to do through the long, unnatural night. They spoke very little, for the roar of the volcano was a constant reminder of the danger hanging over them. They ate the berries Persephone had gathered earlier in the day and the remainder of the flat bread. Gavin went out several more times, to make sure there was no sign of fire. Toward dawn, something heavy struck the cabin. Persephone jolted out of the light doze she had fallen into. Gavin was already at the door.

"Stay here," he ordered as he wound the cloth around his face again. He stepped out and closed the door behind him.

When he did not return at once, Persephone went after him. It was all well and good for him to go about giving orders—no doubt he was used to doing so—but she saw absolutely no reason why she should obey him. Especially not when every instinct she possessed was screaming that he might be hurt.

Pausing only to protect her own breathing, she pulled the door open and stepped out into a nightmarish world. The cloud from the volcano had lessened somewhat, so that with the rising sun she could see the transformed landscape. Her first thought was that there was no color except gray. Gray over everything: the field, the cabin, the trees in the distance, the bear, all the other sculptures that were at least still standing. Only gray. She stepped forward gingerly, her feet sinking into the soft ash that began at once to fall on her bare arms and her gown.

"Gavin." She called his name urgently, her voice muffled by the cloth around her mouth and nose. When there was no answer, she tried again more loudly. "Gavin!"

He came round a corner of the cabin, holding a large chunk of stone. "I told you to stay inside."

"I was worried about you."

His eyes above the cloth looked amused. Without warning, he threw the stone at her.

She gasped and instinctively put out her arms. The rock settled lightly into them. "What on earth—?"

"Pumice," Gavin said. "Straight out of the volcano's mouth and almost as light as air."

She hefted it tentatively, amazed that anything that looked so heavy could be so light. "Is this what hit the cabin?"

"I think so. The impact came more from speed than weight."

She laughed with relief and tossed the stone aside. Looking out in the direction of the Inland Sea, she said, "The cloud is lessening."

Gavin nodded. "But the lava has returned. It's quite a show."

When she made a move to take a look for herself, he stopped her. "Not while chunks of pumice are still coming down."

She frowned, but relented. Back inside the cabin, she washed the ash from her arms and face. When she returned to the main room, Gavin was standing by a window, looking out.

"Could you see anything below?" she asked, standing close to him but not touching. They had not spoken of personal matters since the eruption. She was glad of that, for there seemed enough to bear, but she was also anxious. Being confined with him was a sweet torment.

"Not much," he said, turning back to her. "At this point, it's impossible to know what damage has occurred."

"We must have faith that everything will be all right or, if it isn't, that we can make it so again."

He did not reply directly, but stood, looking at her. In the otherworldly half-light, he appeared very big and very hard, not a man to be crossed. But he was also the man who teased and cajoled her, drove her to incandescent pleasure, held her in the night and swore that the past did not matter.

Without preamble, she said, "Your family will care, even if you don't."

"What makes you think so?"

She thought it obvious. "They love you."

"They also trust me."

That was hard to argue with, indeed, impossible under the circumstances. Yet she clung to the conviction that he had to be wrong. To do otherwise was to let herself dream again and that could hurt unbearably.

Besides, there were matters far beyond her own concerns to cope with. What had the eruption done? What would the people face when they returned? When could they come back? How much was lost?

Another night and a day they waited to find out. No further showers of pumice came near the cabin. The ground no longer shook. The air lost its acrid smell. When the lava flares ceased and did not return, the time had come.

"I would rather you stayed here," Gavin said with the air of a man who has faint hope of persuading.

"I have had enough of solitude," she replied, and knew it, sadly, to be true. He had to be wrong, his family could never accept her, and she could not bear to come between him and them. Yet the thought of returning to the life she had led before was daunting. Perhaps she could find some occupation for herself in the rebuilding of Akora. But that would mean she would still be near him in some sense and she really didn't see how she could endure that.

"Are you coming?" he asked, standing by the door.

She went out into the gray world. The climb down from the cabin was difficult. Ash masked the trail they had used and forced them to find their way as best they could. The ash was also slick, which made walking clumsy. Several times her feet slipped out from under her, but she was able to regain her balance. The little spring where they had stopped to refresh themselves was clogged with stones.

As they neared the city, the tension became palpable. The volcano had not torn Akora apart as it had more than three thousand years ago. But the damage might still be vast.

Turning round a corner, Gavin stopped abruptly when he caught sight of the palace. "It's standing," he said with heartfelt relief.

Indeed, the immense expanse of the building, carefully maintained and added on to from the days right after the first eruption, did appear to be intact. Ash could be seen on the roof and there were more blocks of stone in the courtyard, but all the pillars stood, and as they walked closer, Persephone could see that the walls showed no signs of cracks.

"It's all right," she exclaimed.

"It might be," he cautioned. "The engineers will have to determine that."

They went farther, arriving at the lions' gate. When Persephone saw the twin lionesses who had stood guard there through the millennia, still upright and whole, she let out a cheer. "Never mind the engineers! The gate stands. What harm could have come to the palace?"

He grinned at her enthusiasm. They continued on, passing homes and businesses that looked blessedly whole, if in need of a good scrubbing. It was not until they were almost at the harbor that they saw the first real signs of destruction. Besides the destroyed quay itself, almost all the nearby buildings lay in rubble.

But it was the sight that greeted them when they looked beyond the harbor that robbed Persephone of breath.

In the direction where once the islands of Deimatos, Tarbos, and Phobos had been—their names reminders of the terror that had come upon Akora long ago—there was only a single, far larger island, covered by lava that steamed harmlessly in the bright day.

"It's gone," she said with wonder. The place of her solitude and her shame had vanished. In its stead was the fresh-born promise of new land that in time would bear new life.

Gavin looked out over the scene thoughtfully. "I never considered that the volcano would create rather than destroy."

"Perhaps we should have considered it." Still, she hesitated. It seemed too much to hope for. "If this is truly over and there is nothing more to come."

"Let's find out," he said and took her hand. Together, they climbed the road up to the palace, entering through the lions' gate into the eerily silent courtyard.

"There's another way into the caves," Gavin said. He went round the palace itself and down a narrow path to a small grotto. Though it, like everything else, was covered with ash, Persephone could see that it was both whole and lovely. Already the small waterfall that streamed down one side of the grotto carried fresh water. They drank from it before going on.

The path continued toward the beach below the palace, but before they descended all the way, they arrived at a small cleft in the hillside. "It's a squeeze," Gavin said, "at least for me, but it leads right into the crystal cave."

"We won't be able to see," she reminded him.

From the sack he carried, he drew a small lantern and the box of matchsticks. "I may not have learned how to cook in warrior training, but I did pick up one or two points about being prepared."

They crawled through the cleft in the earth, Gavin going first, and emerged into the crystal cave. He lifted the lantern and shone it in all directions, its light reflecting off the glittering cones that descended from the ceiling and grew upward from the floor. There were no signs of any damage.

"The statue room," Persephone reminded him.

There they found signs of the volcano's power. Several statues were toppled over and lay in large chunks, but they looked readily repairable. Most remained right in their niches where they had always been.

"I thought the lava would reach here," Gavin said.

"It seems to have taken a different path."

Just how different they realized a few minutes later when they reached the small temple enfolded in the earth. It looked exactly as Persephone had last seen it. The pool still glowed with the luminescent creatures that gave the chamber its silvery light. Moss still softened the contours of the rocks, and she was certain the stone face would still be there.

"This can't be," Gavin said. He moved quickly through the cave toward the passage that led to the lava flows. But here there was great change. Where short days before lava had bubbled up from the earth, spreading steadily in great, flaring streams, there was nothing to be seen but solid ground.

The place where Deilos had died, the hell into which he had leaped, was—like the island where he had plotted—gone.

"It's over," Persephone said softly.

Beside her, Gavin drew a deep breath and let it out slowly. "The last time, several years passed before the first sign of lava appeared."

"And then it took more than three thousand years for another eruption to occur."

The light of the lantern revealed the hard planes of his face and showed his dawning acceptance. "Akora is safe again for a long time to come."

With lighter steps, they went back to the small temple. Persephone hesitated, but Gavin was insistent and she was loathe to refuse him. There on the soft ground where they had lain together for the first time, he knelt and drew her down with him. Holding her hands in his, he looked deeply into her eyes. His voice was rough and deep. He was not a man for poetry, but he spoke from the heart and that was poetry enough.

"Whatever lies before me, it will be duty without joy if you are not there to share it. Be my wife, Persephone. Let go of the past, as Akora itself has done, and let us build the future together."

She was crying, of course. She who had been so stalwart for so long couldn't keep a tear to herself these days. But she was also reaching for him, her mouth on his, her promise the final balm to her healed heart.

"I love you, Gavin Atreides, and always I will be yours."

Beside them, the stone face smiled.

It was sometime later when they emerged from the caves hand-in-hand to discover that they were no longer the only two people on Akora. White sails billowing in the wind, the flotilla sailed back into the harbor of Ilius.

CHAPTER XXII

S IDA WAS ONE OF THE FIRST ONTO THE FLOAT-
ing wooden piers that the garrison wasted no
time hammering together to replace the destroyed
stone docks. She stepped onto the ruined quay, put her
hands to her hips, and took a long look around before
rendering her judgment.

"Not too bad, all things considered."

The men, women, and children crowding the decks
of the ships and pouring out onto the piers behind her
seemed to agree. For some, the shock of seeing their
collapsed homes and shops was difficult, but others offering accommodations and promises of help to rebuild, quickly comforted them.

No doubt it was all the excitement and relief that
accounted for Persephone throwing her arms around
Sida and exclaiming, "I'm so glad you're all right!"

The older woman hugged her back just as fiercely, then stepped back and took a hard look at her.

"I know, I know," Persephone said, "my hair is a mess."

"Actually, I was thinking that you look remarkably well for someone who's supposed to be dead."

Were those tears in Sida's eyes? Surely that couldn't be. "We were terribly worried," the older woman said. "There were reports your boat never made it out of the Inland Sea. People even said they saw it being sucked back in. Word of that spread from vessel to vessel until we'd all heard it. We've been praying for you and Prince Gavin without cease."

"I think your prayers were heard," Persephone said gently. She was deeply touched by Sida's concern, even if it did leave her at something of a loss as to how to respond. She simply wasn't used to people caring about her fate, but she supposed she was going to have to become accustomed to that.

"You are both unharmed?" Sida asked as though it was more than she could hope for.

Persephone took her arm. Together, they started up toward the city. "We're completely fine. Gavin remembered the cabin in the mountains, the one that belongs to the Vanax and the Lady Brianna. We sat out the eruption there. I must say, we had an incredible view of it all."

"We saw the ash cloud," Sida said as they walked, "and coming in, we were all stunned to see the new island where the others used to be. Are there any other big changes?"

"There is no longer any lava under the palace. Gavin's theory is that it was sucked back down into the earth and then ejected by the volcano."

"*Gavin* thinks that, does he? And *Gavin* remembered the cabin?" Sida asked with a grin. "Sounds as though the two of you have gotten friendlier."

Persephone's cheeks reddened as Sida chuckled. "A lot friendlier, and glad I am to see it. Come along, then, let's take a look at the palace."

Sida's notion of taking a look was a thorough examination of a very large chunk of the entire structure. In the process of trailing after her, Persephone saw a great deal more of the palace than she had ever seen before. She also was introduced to dozens upon dozens of the people who worked and lived there. One and all, they greeted "Lady Persephone" with friendly cheer.

Engineers were moving rapidly from one section of the building to another. A few rooms and some corridors were closed off until the walls could be reinforced, but the rest was pronounced safe.

Sida barely waited to hear that before deploying brigades of workers armed with brooms and mops. "Top to bottom" she instructed. "I don't want to see a speck of ash when we're done."

Mercifully, a fair breeze blew up and, with all the palace windows thrown open, helped to move the dust out toward the Inland Sea, where it fell in a barely discernible haze.

Persephone slipped away in late afternoon and went down through the city, finding it pulsing with activity. Women wielding brooms as though they were weapons did battle with the ash, while men hauled out fallen beams and stones from the collapsed houses. In the harbor, the garrison was at work clearing debris. Large cranes were brought in and maneuvered into position to lift the larger blocks.

For a time she stood watching as one of the cranes was used to raise an immense slab of stone from the water directly in front of the quay and hoist it out of the way. She spied Gavin talking with several men she guessed were engineers. They appeared to be working out a plan for clearing the harbor. Certain he was extremely busy, she went away without interrupting him.

Night was coming on quickly. The tired but happy voices of men and women floated on the gathering darkness. Persephone was walking back up to the palace when she saw a familiar face. Rheanne, the young girl who had sought her wayward cat in the tense hours before the flotilla departed, was drawing water from the well in her family's garden.

"Lady Persephone," she called out. Setting aside the bucket, she hurried to the road. "You are well! I heard you were, but it's so good to see you."

"Thank you. It's good to see you, too. How is Mowmow?"

"Glad to be out of the basket," Rheanne said with a laugh. A little shyly, she added, "Can you stay a while? There's a crowd inside and dinner will be ready soon. It would be wonderful if you could join us."

To refuse seemed churlish, and besides, the aroma of grilling meat offered its own inducement. She agreed before she could think better of it and was ushered into the house by a beaming Rheanne. Her welcome was warm, and soon Persephone found herself in the kitchen with a group of women, sharing their conversation and their company.

"Ooohhh," a friend of Rheanne's exclaimed when she learned where Persephone had waited out the eruption. "Up in the mountains with Prince Gavin. What was it like?"

Aware she was the focus of decidedly avid attention, Persephone said solemnly, "There was a lot of noise . . . and ash, a great deal of ash." When the circle of women continued staring at her in expectation, she added, "A big chunk of pumice hit the cabin."

"What did Prince Gavin do then?" a plump, dark-haired woman asked breathlessly.

"He went out to make sure there was no damage."

"So brave," one sighed.

"So handsome," another chimed in.

"It was just a piece of pumice," Persephone pointed out a bit tartly. That made no difference. They had to wax lyrical on the subject of the prince. How wonderful he was. How he had saved them. How they'd always

known, ever since he was a little boy, that he was someone special.

They were still going on about it, while preparing
what to Persephone's eyes looked like astonishing
amounts of food, when Gavin himself arrived in search
of her.

This set off a flurry of excitement unlike any she had
ever seen. The men pounded him on the back and
pressed goblets of wine on him, while the women exchanged eager comments and smiled broadly.

At length, he managed to make his way to Persephone's side. He looked dirty, tired, rumpled, and magnificent. "Sida said someone saw you here," he said after
taking a long drink from the goblet he held. A stray lock
of dark blond hair fell over his forehead. She brushed it
away matter-of-factly and smiled at him. Really, how
could she not? He filled her with smiles.

"I saw you down in the harbor," she said.

"Did you? Why didn't you let me know you were
there?"

"You looked busy, and besides, I was content to
watch you." Perhaps she'd had a bit too much of the
wine herself. Certainly something had loosened her
tongue.

He looked a little startled by that, but not at all dis-
pleased. Food was being laid out on a long table in the
garden. Lanterns swung from low tree branches. Up
and down the street, similar gatherings were taking

place. Although much work remained to be done, people were in the mood to celebrate.

Nibbling on a skewer of grilled beef, Persephone watched Gavin being persuaded to join an arm-wrestling contest. He won against a series of opponents, although not always easily, and he fell at last to a giant of a man—almost seven feet tall—who laughed heartily as he slammed his arm down and congratulated Gavin on lasting as long as he did.

Sometime later, Persephone found herself sitting on the ground with the cat, Mowmow, in her lap, daintily devouring a bit of beef. Gavin was stretched out beside her, snoring softly. All around them, people were in similar condition, asleep wherever relief and revelry had finally overtaken them.

She could have stayed happily enough where she was, but for the knowledge that the coming day would demand yet more labor. Gently nudging Gavin awake, she walked with him, their arms around each other's waists, back up to the palace.

Three days passed in a seamless blur of sweeping, scrubbing, dusting, and mopping. While Gavin worked with the engineers and construction crews, Persephone accepted more and more duties Sida thrust her way. They kept her from thinking about the next crisis, the one looming just over the horizon—the return of the Vanax, accompanied, in all likelihood, by Gavin's parents.

Every time she thought of that, she felt a sick fluttering in her stomach. How could she face the people her father had tried to kill? Had could she dare to stand beside their son and nephew, and tell them she wanted to spend her life with him?

How could she bear the shock and anger she was certain they would feel?

As the days passed and the likelihood of their arrival grew steadily, she became increasingly anxious. Work helped, but only to a point. Gavin was as busy as she herself, with the result that they saw little of each other. Their paths crossed only at rare intervals and never in private. Sleep was snatched wherever it could be found, meals the same.

On the fourth day, the pace began to slow. The first spurt of relief and elation—and the energy it brought with it—was ebbing. Buildings in danger of collapse had been removed, and rebuilding was already beginning. Down in the harbor, several wooden piers were in place and ships were coming in and out.

One of them brought Counselor Goran over from Leios with news that all was well there.

"There's a huge pile of stones that came down along a quarter-mile stretch of beach," he told the eager crowd that gathered round when he was seen, Persephone among them. "And we got plenty of ash. It looks like a few buildings caught fire from flying cinders, but they were only sheds and can be replaced easily enough. All in all, we're greatly relieved."

Seeing Persephone, he left the others and came over to join her. With a nod of his head, he said, "Lady, how goes it here?"

"Very well. The palace had only slight damage and, as you can see, the harbor is being repaired."

Looking round, he nodded. "Truly, we have been blessed." He weighed his words, then said, "I spoke the truth about Leios, but what I didn't say was that there is evidence at least one very large wave moved over most of the island. Every building and field shows the effects of it. There is no lasting damage, but if we had not left and taken our animals with us, the results would have been very different."

"There was wave damage here in the harbor," Persephone said, "and I have heard of some other areas, but nothing like what you're describing."

"Leios is at a lower sea level than you have here. We're almost entirely a flat plain, wonderful for breeding horses, but terribly vulnerable in a situation like this one."

He looked at her directly. "Had you and Prince Gavin not insisted when you did that we begin preparations, many lives would have been lost."

In his quiet words, she heard the recognition of the horror and tragedy so narrowly averted. Her own role in bringing that about did not stir her pride. She felt profoundly humbled by the entire experience. "I am so glad everyone escaped."

They talked a while longer before Persephone continued up into the town. She had promised to join Nestor, who was supervising the restocking of the library shelves now that the palace was judged both clean and safe, and was thinking of that when she heard her name called. Turning, she saw Polonus coming toward her.

It was mid-afternoon. A gentle rain the previous night had left every cobblestone and leaf gleaming. For the first time since the eruption, the air smelled of jasmine and lemon instead of ash. A few fleecy white clouds dotted the otherwise azure sky. The crescent of the pale moon could be seen in the east, out toward the open sea.

A sense of peace stole over Persephone as she absorbed all this. She greeted Polonus with a smile that did not waver as she recalled what Gavin had told her about him. Here was a man who had actually known her father, even followed him for a time. He seemed miraculously untainted by the experience.

"I have been hoping to find you," Polonus said, breathing a little hard from the exertion of catching up to her.

"It's good to see you. Are you well?"

"Quite well, actually. Shoveling ash and helping to move debris seems to have agreed with me." He grinned as he rubbed the back of his neck. "I wouldn't have thought that after all these years, but it's true all the same."

He glanced toward a reopened shop offering coffee, drinks, and small snacks. "The lemonade here is very good. Will you join me?"

They found a table in the back garden, near a trellis of blooming roses. Polonus sat down with an audible sigh of pleasure. After a smiling young woman brought their drinks and a bowl of honey-glazed nuts, he said, "I've done a fair amount of traveling in my life, and enjoyed it for the most part, but when all was said and done, Akora is the only place I've ever really wanted to be."

"How did you come to travel?" Persephone asked.

"Atreus arranged it after Deilos was defeated. He wanted to give me a chance to reassess who I was and how I chose to live my life."

She took a sip of the lemonade, which was very good, and set the glass down slowly. "Gavin told me you were a follower of Deilos's."

"That's right. You look nothing like him."

Her head snapped up. "Do I not?"

"Not in the least." Gently, he said, "But you do have the look of your mother."

Persephone's throat constricted painfully—with shock and with emotions that threatened to swamp her. "You knew her?"

Polonus nodded. "When I first met you, you reminded me of someone. It took me a while to remember."

The serving girl came out to bring them more

lemonade. When she was gone, Polonus said, "You must understand, Deilos was immensely seductive. He appealed to our idealism and our vanity. Listening to him, we believed our country truly was in danger from the Vanax's decision to make us more open to the outside world. We imagined ourselves as the heroes—and heroines—who would save Akora. It was heady stuff."

"My mother told me nothing of this. I only knew he hurt her very badly."

"Your mother was young, but she was also a strong woman. Deilos could not abide that. To those of us he flattered by pretending that we formed his inner circle, he confided his determination to truly enforce the old law about warriors ruling and women serving. He said we would all be better for it, the women included."

"You believed this?"

Polonus sighed deeply. "I was a young man with all the insecurity a young man can feel. The idea of a woman having to depend on me, be led by me, was appealing. I think Deilos singled out your mother because of her strength. He found a malicious pleasure in deceiving her."

"He did more than that. She never overcame her sense of shame and guilt."

"Did she love you?" he asked gently.

Had she? Had the woman who walked with her hand-in-hand along shell-strewn beaches, showing her where the tiny, brightly colored fish lived, who rocked her in her arms in the night, who sang to her and told her stories, who taught her to read and shared the world with her in the pages of books . . . Had that woman truly loved her?

"Yes," Persephone said, very low. As a testament to her mother's spirit, to her courage and strength, to all she had overcome, her daughter proclaimed, "She loved me."

"Then Deilos did not vanquish her." Polonus set aside his glass and stood. Looking down at her, he said, "The man who fathered you is gone, Persephone. There is nothing of him left, not even the island where he plotted his villainy. The woman you are is the greatest proof of his defeat."

Gently he touched her shoulder and then, quietly, he went.

She remained a little longer beside the rose-draped trellis, listening to the doves coo their sweet song as slowly, softly, twilight crept over the land.

Then she rose and went up to the palace.

CHAPTER XXIII

GAVIN PUSHED OPEN THE DOOR TO HIS QUARters with one thought—a shower. He went directly to the bathing chamber, shucked his clothes and sandals off, and turned the valves on full. With his head back and his eyes closed, he stood under the blissfully hot water and let the weariness of the long day wash off him. When at length he felt sufficiently restored, he reached for the soap, cleaning away what grime and sweat remained.

Distinctly improved, he finally turned the shower off, wrapped a towel around his hips, and used another to wipe the steam from the mirror over the sink. He spread soap over his lean jaw and shaved with the straight razor he honed on a leather strap. By the time he was done, his hair was more or less dry. He snapped the towel off, then tossed it along with his tunic into the basket near the sink. The habit of not leaving a mess for someone else was too deeply ingrained in him to be denied.

Naked, he walked into the bedroom. While he was showering, night had descended. A soft breeze blew through the high windows. The covers of the bed were neatly folded at its foot and there, lying on her side, facing him, was an entirely naked and smiling Persephone. Moonlight drifted over her high breasts, sleek flanks, and long legs, over the tumble of her hair freed from its braid and the soft fullness of her mouth. She looked utterly exquisite, just a little shy despite her attempt at boldness, and enticingly feminine.

Weariness dropped away from him, replaced by fierce need and burgeoning joy. For three hard days he had let her be, giving himself up to the work that had to be done and giving her time to work things out in her own mind.

By the look of her, she had done that.

Persephone held out a hand, beckoning to him. "Planning on standing there all night?"

"No," he said as he strode toward her. "I was thinking we could find something better to do."

She moved over to make room for him. "Such as?"

"This," he said, and proceeded to show her.

His lovemaking was slow and deliberate. Neither the raging hunger of his own body, nor her incandescent need would hasten him. He kissed her from head to toe, savoring every inch of her. Long before he was done, Persephone was writhing on the bed, crying out his name, and trying to reach for him.

"Another time," he said roughly, his mouth on hers, "you'll have your way."

"Promise?" she gasped, rising up beneath him, her hips arching to his.

Imagining the sweet torment she would inflict, he smiled. "Promise. But not now. Now—"

He fitted himself to her, thrusting hard and deep. He was very large, but she was exquisitely primed and took him with a sob of relief that turned swiftly to a cry of ecstasy. He rode her, enduring the convulsions of her body until his own need overcame him. His life jetted into her, seemingly without end.

High above, the moon shone over destined lovers and healed land alike.

ALL GOOD THINGS, INCLUDING NIGHTS OF sweet debauchery, must end. Persephone discovered that when she was hurtled from sleep by the blast of a horn that went on and on, seeming to rend the very air.

Hard on it came excited shouts and cries, along with the sound of people running.

Her first thought was that something was wrong. Quickly she discovered how right she was.

"A ship is approaching," Gavin told her. He was out of bed and throwing on clothes as he looked out the window.

"Ships come to Ilius all the time," she grumbled. In a last valiant effort, she hugged a pillow and tried to snuggle back down into the warm bed.

"That horn is the signal the Vanax is returning."

Her stomach did a long, slow flip. It wasn't fair; she had hoped for a little more time. A hundred years or so.

Gavin laughed and pulled her from the bed. She made a genuine effort to kick him, but he evaded her. "I recommend getting dressed," he said, assessing her appreciatively. "Unless you'd rather meet them in all your glory."

Her legs were shaking as she broke free of him and marched into the bathroom. A fiercely cold shower later, she returned to find Gavin gone and Sida waiting for her.

All business, the older woman said, "Sit down, there's no time to waste."

Persephone sat. "There's no hope. I'll never look the way I should."

Wielding the brush through her hair, Sida asked, "How's that?"

Very low, trying desperately not to sound as frightened as she felt, she said, "Like a princess."

"Did I ever tell you about the first time I met the Princess Joanna? She was wearing one of Prince Alexandros's tunics and she looked like a bedraggled ragamuffin."

Persephone's eyes, wide with surprise, met Sida's in the mirror. "She couldn't possibly have." They were speaking of the Lady Joanna Atreides, Princess of Akora and Gavin's aunt, a woman of legend; one of those who had helped to save the Fortress Kingdom.

"I assure you, she did. And then there is Princess Kassandra, who I admit is normally the very picture of loveliness, but who has been known to get herself into a bedraggled state from time to time."

"Gavin's mother is so deeply loved and admired—"

"As she deserves to be, but she is human for all that. As they all are, each and every one, and as they would be the first to tell you. There now, stand up."

Persephone did as she was bid and was surprised when Sida dropped an exquisite gown of deep saffron silk over her head, catching it with ties around her waist so that it fell in delicate pleats to her feet.

It was easily the loveliest garment she had ever seen. Not that her confidence depended on anything so superficial, but the gown did make her feel a bit less anxious.

"That's a good color for you," Sida said. "You should wear it often. Here, bend down a bit."

A necklace of gold set with gleaming green stones appeared around her neck. Persephone fingered it uncertainly. "These aren't—?"

"Emeralds? So they are. Prince Gavin found the stones years ago when he was first beginning to explore the caves." Sida smiled gently. "He gave the necklace into my care when you two came back from Deimatos. He said I'd know when it was time for you to wear it."

Astonishment struck her hard. On the cusp of it, Sida turned her toward the door. "Go on now. Your prince is waiting for you."

As he was, at the base of the stairs of the family quarters. Gavin wore a tunic of the finest white linen. A sword, its hilt inlaid with gems, hung at his waist. Around his powerful upper arms were bands of gold. The sight of him filled her heart and made her step light.

He turned, and seeing her, came up the first few steps to meet her and take her hand. They walked through the vast courtyard, greeted by everyone they passed, and down along the flower-draped road filled with men and women hurrying to the harbor. There, a great crowd had gathered, but a path was made for them so that they could reach the wooden pier where the mighty vessel, its prow carved into the fierce bull's head emblem of Akora, had just docked.

A cheer went up as the gangplank was moved into place. First to leave the ship was the Vanax Atreus himself. In his fifties, he had the grace and bearing of a much younger man. Only the shower of silver in his ebony hair and a fine crinkling of lines around his wise eyes hinted at his true age. Beside him was a woman of rare beauty, his consort Brianna. Dressed in a sky-blue gown that perfectly complimented her vivid red hair, the mother of two and beloved Lady of Akora waved eagerly to friends on the quay.

Atreus's attention was reserved for Gavin. The two

men clasped arms and looked at each other in perfect understanding.

"Well done, nephew," the Vanax said with unconcealed admiration. "My faith in you appears more than justified."

"Kind of you to so say, Uncle. However, I did not act alone. May I present Persephone, who will be my wife."

By now, she really should be accustomed to Gavin's habit of taking the bull by the horns, but she had not been prepared for so blunt a declaration. With a hand at the small of her back, he urged her forward. She took a breath, gathered her courage, and found herself looking into the curious but kind eyes of the Vanax.

"Persephone, thank you for your assistance."

"Not at all, sir. I—"

She never got to finish, for just then, a beautiful woman stepped forward. The coronet of her dark hair wound in braids around her head was set with exquisite, tiny flowers. Her thick-fringed eyes danced with excitement as they settled on the emerald necklace around Persephone's throat.

"Wife? Gavin, is this true? Have you truly chosen a wife?"

The son of Princess Kassandra laughed and hugged his mother. "I'd say we have chosen each other."

Beside her, a tall man with the same dark blond hair as Gavin's and an equally devastating smile, said, "Well put, son." Royce, Earl of Hawkforte, took a long look at Persephone and nodded approvingly. "And well done."

Gavin released his mother and offered his hand to his father. "Sir, we will need to talk. There is much I have to explain to you."

Royce raised a brow. "Do you? Perhaps you will not think so if I tell you Atreus and I have had a conversation about your future. I, in turn, have spoken with your brother, David. He remains at Hawkforte, in charge there during my absence, and sends his warm affection."

Gavin's relief was evident at this crucial step. Explaining to his father that he could not be the future Earl of Hawkforte had clearly weighed on his mind. Now that concern was removed.

Only one remained.

Right there, standing on the pier, Gavin said, "It may interest you to know that Persephone's father was Deilos."

There was silence for a moment, just long enough for her heart to begin to beat with heavy dread. Then Kassandra said cheerfully, "Was he? You don't look like him at all. That's a lovely gown, by the way. Did Sida pick it out? How is Sida—as much a terror as ever?"

She stepped forward, took Persephone's arm, and drew her up the road toward the palace, chatting all the while.

Behind them, the rest of the family followed.

After that, everything became a bit of a blur. Persephone was swept up in the welcome that enveloped city and palace alike. The Akorans had many strengths, but she was beginning to think that their single greatest gift was their ability to celebrate whole-heartedly the joys of life.

In the midst of it all, she struggled to believe—truly believe—that his family shared Gavin's utter lack of concern about the identity of her father. It seemed far too much to hope for, yet both Kassandra and Brianna showed absolutely no hesitation in their manner toward her.

"Atreus told us a few weeks ago what he believed was going to happen," Brianna said as they were touring the palace, both women delighted to discover that everything was as it should be. "I had the sense when we left here for England that something was brewing; even so, it was a shock."

"He was very reassuring," Kassandra said. "It also helped to explain something that has always puzzled me."

"What was that?" Persephone asked softly. She was astonished by how quickly she was coming to feel at ease with the two women.

"As you may know, there was a time when I was 'gifted' with visions of the future. That gift was, in fact, a terrible burden, but it served its purpose when Akora was in danger. Most of what I saw I readily understood, but one vision puzzled me. I saw a dark-haired boy playing on the ancient walls of Hawkforte and knew he was meant to be my son and Royce's. He seemed very important to Hawkforte, very much as though he belonged there. When Gavin was born and grew to look nothing like that boy, I was surprised. It was a shock to realize it was my second son, David, whom I had seen." Quietly she said, "For a time, I feared the vision might mean Gavin would not live to be Earl of Hawkforte. But somehow that fear never seemed right. There was always something else out there on the horizon waiting for Gavin."

She smiled and squeezed Persephone's hand. "I am so very glad my son has found his future."

There were tears then, and hugs and laughter as the last knot of apprehension deep within Persephone un-raveled.

No further affirmation of their acceptance was needed, yet it came all the same when they gathered for dinner. Gavin, Atreus, and Royce arrived a little late, for they had been deep in conference.

Other guests joined them, including Persephone's aunts, Melissa and Electra, the latter she was meeting for the first time. They came with their husbands, and their sons and daughters, all of whom were delighted to meet Persephone. Nor were they alone. At Gavin's invitation, Liam Campbell was also present. It is to be said, however, that perhaps Gavin did not anticipate the bold Scotsman taking the seat next to Gavin's sister, Atlanta, or that the two of them would strike up so pleasant an acquaintance so quickly.

Seated around the table beside the high windows through which the scents and sounds of Ilius wafted gently, the family had almost finished the meal when Atreus looked to Persephone.

"We have been discussing what to name the new island," he told her. "Gavin had an excellent suggestion."

"What was that?" she asked with a smile for the man at her side, the man who would be there through her life and beyond.

"What was your mother's name?" Atreus inquired.

"My mother . . ."

Quietly Gavin said, "Deimatos is gone, sweetheart. The new island is in its place. It is where your mother lived, where she raised her child. We would like it to stand as a reminder that the past, as much as we have always preserved and cherished it, does not determine our future. Only we can do that."

Tears sparkled in her eyes and her throat was very tight. In the face of such overwhelming love and acceptance, she only just managed to say, "My mother's name was Aurora."

"Aurora," Gavin repeated and looked pleased. " 'Dawn'—and so it will be, a new dawn for Akora."

Across the table, the Vanax of Akora said, "Welcome, Persephone, who has shown the way. We are—all of us—honored to be your family."

*L*ET US LEAVE THEM NOW, THERE IN THE PALACE *high on the hill above Akora. But before we do, let us linger* *just a moment longer. Gavin—relaxed, happy, deeply in love—is speaking.*

"By the way, where's Clio? I thought she'd be the most eager of all to return."

Clio, red-haired like her mother, who would fall asleep in the library as she pursued her fascination with Akora's storied history. Clio, who, inexplicably now that he thought of it, had not accompanied her parents home.

"Clio remains in England," *Brianna said softly. She glanced to her husband.* "A young man keeps her there."

And so he did.

But that is another story.

About the Author

JOSIE LITTON lives in New England with her husband, children, and menagerie . . . mostly. Her imagination may find her in nineteenth-century London or ninth-century Norway or who knows where next. She is happily at work on a new trilogy and loves to hear from readers.

Visit Josie at www.josielitton.com.

Read on for a peek
at the next two enticing romances
in the Fountain series . . .

JOSIE LITTON'S

Fountain
OF DREAMS

on sale now

and

Fountain
OF FIRE

coming in September 2003

Fountain
OF DREAMS

on sale now

LIGHTS SHINING IN THE HIGH WINDOWS OF the mansion's ground floor appeared and disappeared among the leafy branches of trees that swayed in the steady breeze off the river. The hour was shortly before midnight. In the walled park surrounding the house, an owl swept soundlessly from its perch. Wings barely moving, it soared over the open ground before descending rapidly to pluck a hapless mouse.

The man waiting in the dark shadows of the bushes saw the catch and smiled faintly. He, too, would hunt soon. Several hours before, he had gotten close enough to the house to confirm that the family was at dinner. He watched them briefly through one of the windows—Prince Alexandros; his wife, Princess Joanna; their nephew, Prince Andreas; and their daughter, Princess Amelia, were all relaxed and in good humor. They had no inkling that their privileged world was about to be shattered.

He had withdrawn to wait and now stirred a little, flexing muscles that would otherwise cramp as he remained concealed behind the thick bushes just inside the high stone walls. The night was cool and damp, but he scarcely noticed. He had known far worse.

He was a tall man, lean and very fit. For this night's work, he was dressed in the garb of a London office worker, a respectable man who earned his portion in a counting house, perhaps, or as a solicitor's secretary. A man neither poor enough nor rich enough to attract attention. His dark trousers and jacket, of plain but sturdy wool, made him all but invisible in the shadows. He had turned up the jacket collar for further concealment and pulled the brim of his felt hat down close to eyes that some had likened to the color of steel.

He was without weapons, although, to be fair, he would still have the advantage against most armed opponents. If the guards found him, he wanted to appear a harmless drunk who had wandered where he should not. For that purpose, he had rubbed dirt on the jacket and trousers such as would result from an inebriated climb over a stone wall, and he carried a half-empty bottle of whiskey in the pocket of the jacket.

By the look of it, the ruse would not be necessary. While it might be true that there was no residence better guarded in all of London, the patrols were at regular intervals, therefore predictable. That was expected. The security around the manor was intended to insulate its inhabitants from the waves of popular unrest that roared through London periodically, not from a lone man intent on gaining access.

Gray eyes flickered in the darkness. He waited, patient and watchful. The lights were extinguished on the ground floor as other lights appeared on the floor above.

The family retired early by the standards of society. They preferred one another's company to the customary round of balls, routs, masquerades, assemblies, and the like. According to his information, they had no social commitments on this night. That suited his purposes perfectly.

The patrol was good; he scarcely heard it coming even though he was expecting it. The three men passed within a dozen feet of him. They did not speak and their steps were almost entirely silent. They were, he knew, part of the military force that was among the most feared in all the world. The warriors of Akora, the Fortress Kingdom beyond the Pillars of Hercules, had maintained that mysterious land's freedom and sovereignty for centuries. Ancient, legendary, and only recently beginning to emerge into the modern world, Akora fascinated many, but not him. He cared nothing for the place and hoped most sincerely to have nothing to do with it.

The patrol passed by him. He took a breath, cleared his mind, and ran across the open space of lawn. In little more than a heartbeat, he reached the bushes beneath the ground-floor windows. Crouching there, he paused and listened intently.

No sound from the house or the surrounding grounds suggested that his presence had been detected. Cautiously, he stood and looked into the now dark dining room. The servants had finished clearing the table and would be going to their own rest soon. Only the guards on patrol and on duty in the hall would be awake.

He moved again, around a corner to the back of the house, and looked up. Directly above him were the windows of what he had already confirmed was Princess Amelia's bedroom.

The patrol was returning. He pressed against the wall

of the house, blending into the contours of stone and shadow, waiting.

When the patrol was gone, he took a length of black cloth from an inside pocket of his jacket, put it over his face, and tied it at the back of his head. Only his eyes remained visible.

He grasped the stones an arm's reach above him, his fingers digging into the mortar between them, and hoisted himself up smoothly and easily. His feet found the narrow indentation that was just deep enough for him to balance on. Steadied, he reached up again. Swiftly, silently he climbed the wall.

There was a stone balcony outside the princess's windows. He swung onto it, dropped, and listened again for any sound that would warn he was detected. When none came, he slowly eased the French doors open.

The room was dark, but he could make out the placement of the furniture, particularly the bed hung with gauzy curtains.

His quarry lay on her side. He could not make out her features, but he knew well enough what she looked like, having observed her for several days as she went about London. She was not precisely beautiful, but her face had a certain unique appeal and, so far as he had seen, there was nothing lacking in her figure. He had also noticed her to be an exuberant woman, confident and outgoing, given to frequent smiles and ready laughter. That seemed at odds with her reputation, namely that she was cold and proud, an unfeeling breaker of hearts, a spinster at twenty-five despite her family's wealth and power.

If the lady's unmarried state troubled her, there was no sign of it. Lost in sleep, she breathed slowly and deeply. For just an instant, he felt . . . not doubt precisely, never that. Just a twinge of regret that he hadn't been able to come up with a different plan.

But he wasn't a man to linger over his shortcomings. In a single movement, he brushed aside the curtains and seized hold of her. She woke instantly with a gasp that was smothered by the covers in which he quickly rolled her. Although she struggled fiercely, within seconds he had the gag in her mouth and a hood secured over her head.

Far from being cowed, her efforts to escape redoubled. She was surprisingly strong. No match for his strength, of course, but still she proved more than a handful.

He might have cautioned her to stop, but he could not risk her recognizing his voice. Instead, he tightened his grip warningly. But not, it seemed, quite enough. To his astonishment, his squirming, struggling captive got an arm loose and promptly landed a solid punch to his jaw.

Only a lifetime of self-discipline stopped him from cursing out loud. He wrapped her ever more tightly in the covers and moved quickly to the door.

The inside of the house was not patrolled. That, too, he had confirmed during his surveillance. The guards were stationed only in the central hall.

He avoided them by using the back stairs frequented by the servants. The going was difficult because the squirming bundle in his arms refused to desist. Trussed as securely as a Christmas goose, the princess continued to struggle. It was all he could do to keep hold of her without actually causing her harm.

He reached the ground-floor landing and paused.

She could not escape him, of that he had no doubt. But neither did he underestimate his potential peril. If she managed to get out more than a muffled Cry . . .

The Akorans would take him prisoner, but he doubted

very much that they would turn him over to the British authorities. Everything he knew about them suggested they would handle the matter themselves in their own way, presuming they didn't just kill him outright.

She'd damn well better be worth all the trouble.

He opened the door and stepped outside. If his calculations were correct, he had not quite five minutes before the patrol passed again. Enough time to cross the lawn, get through the trees, and scale the wall.

Or it would be if Shadow was on post.

He was, as evidenced by the large shape concealed in the foliage of the upper branches of the trees, and by the rope tangling down the near side of the wall. With an inner sigh of relief, he dumped his unwilling burden into the sling at the end of the rope, secured her firmly, and tugged to signal Shadow. Immediately, the sling began to rise. He watched long enough to confirm that his captive was still struggling fiercely, before climbing the wall himself. Settled beside Shadow, who gave him a quick nod, he helped hoist the sling.

Scant seconds before the patrol was due to return, it was done. With his quarry slung over his shoulder and Shadow following close behind, he ran down the road and around a corner to a waiting carriage.

The wheels were turning even before the door was closed.

Fountain
OF FIRE

on sale September 2003

SCRAMBLING AROUND THE DAMP, DANK INTErior of a stone crypt while a thunderstorm raged outside and floods threatened, Clio entertained the thought that she would have been wiser to stay in bed. Not that she could have done so. The floods put at risk the artifacts she had begun to uncover earlier in the day. She would not rest until they were protected.

The crypt was beneath the manor house of Holyhood on the southeastern coast of England. It was a remnant of a much earlier residence dating, she believed, from the ninth century. That alone made it an extraordinary discovery and well worth studying, even if no one else thought so.

Scraping away with the garden trowel, working as fast as she could by the light of a lantern, Clio ignored the muddy water sloshing around her boots and carefully placed a shard of pottery in the basket she had brought along. Several more pieces of what she thought might have been a clay pitcher were still in the dirt. Determined to get them all, she kept digging as the rain poured down and the water on the floor of the crypt continued to rise.

It was up to her ankles when she finished. With a sigh of relief, she grabbed the basket and turned to go, only to stop abruptly. Hesitantly, not really crediting what she thought she saw, she raised the lantern higher and peered into the shadows at the far end of the crypt.

A man was watching her. He had thick black hair to his shoulders, hard features, and a slashing grin. Incongruously, he was sitting on the floor on the other side of the crypt. His long legs, bare below a short tunic, were stretched out in front of him. He appeared untroubled by either the rain or the water he was sitting in.

But then, he also looked completely dry.

A finger of ice moved down her spine. Clutching the lantern in one hand, the basket in the other, and her courage in both, Clio took a step forward. "Sir . . . you startled me. . . ."

The man did not respond. Indeed, now that she saw him more clearly, he appeared to be looking not at her but beyond her, as though something on the opposite side of the crypt in the direction of the stairs commanded his attention.

His keen, intense attention.

The man rose and came toward Clio. He was very tall, well over six feet, and supremely fit. The gleam in his eyes was most disconcerting. . . .

As was the fact that he walked straight through her.

Not around, not past. Through.

Clio screamed. She was not, as a general rule, a screamer. Indeed, if pressed, she could not have recalled the last time she had screamed. She was, however, quite good at it, if the measure of a scream is its volume and duration.

She was still screaming when she gained the ancient stone steps leading from the crypt, took them two at a time, and hurled herself out into the silent garden of Holyhood.

Her lungs finally empty of air, the scream petered out. Bent over, clutching the basket and lantern, she struggled to inhale. Her entire body shook, her heart hammered, and the roiling of her stomach suggested the imminent reappearance of the dinner she had enjoyed several hours before.

That would not do. She was, after all, a princess and princesses do not go about losing their dinners because of encounters with men who are not there.

As reason reasserted itself, she set the basket down and looked back toward the crypt. In the narrow circle of the lantern light, the entrance to it appeared like a black mouth dark against the storm-tossed night.

"Oh, for heaven's sake." Her imagination was running away with her to a disgraceful degree.

There was no man in the crypt. There could not possibly be. And certainly there was no man who could walk straight through her, not there or anywhere else. To do that, he would have to be a ghost.

Clio did not believe in ghosts.

On her native Akora, she lived her daily life in the same places where people had lived for centuries and even millennia. Her private quarters were in a part of the palace that had stood for over two thousand years. Princesses of Akora through all that time had occupied her very bedroom. Their joys and sorrows, triumphs and tragedies had played out within the same walls where she sometimes laid awake at night, wishing the voices of the past truly could speak to her. Not once had she caught so much as a glimmer of a lingering presence.

There was no man, but there had to be an explanation for what she had seen. To find it, she would have to return to the crypt. The choice did not come easily. The echoes of terror still resonated within her, but they were muted by the impossibility of ever yielding to cowardice. Water was dripping off her nose when she moved slowly back in the direction from which she had come.

Holding the light high, Clio descended one step . . . another . . . The stones were slick beneath her feet. She resisted the impulse to call out. One did not address a figment of the imagination. Even so, she breathed a sigh of relief when she found the crypt empty.

No figment there, just muddy ground and the traces of her digging. She was ready to go, satisfied to put the incident down to fatigue and distraction, when a glint of metal caught her eye. Forgetful of all else, she went to investigate it.

AT THE SOUND OF A SCREAM COMING FROM the vicinity of the house, the Earl of Hollister turned his horse away from the stables and spurred the big roan gelding back down the gravel path. It was very late. He was wet, cold, and hungry. So, no doubt, was Seeker, who was as good a mount as a man could want and deserved better than to be turned away from a warm stall. All the same, the scream could not be ignored.

The path led along the back of the graceful three-story

manor built several decades before on the site of a far older residence. Indeed, if legend was to be believed, there had been a manor at Holyhood for a thousand years or more. William gave that scant thought. His mind was on his widowed grandmother, living alone in the house with only her devoted servants for company.

But his grandmother had the sense to be snug in her bed on such a night, and the scream had sounded like the voice of a much younger woman.

One of the servants come to some harm?

He drew Seeker to a halt near the far corner of the house. The storm that had caught him was passing quickly. Behind it, the moon emerged. By its light, he could make out the entrance to what he knew to be a stone crypt under the house. A faint glow emanated from within the crypt.

Swiftly he dismounted, tossed the reins over a nearby hedge, and moved toward the steps leading to the crypt. He was a big man, broad of shoulder and long of limb. Had he not known to bend his head, he would have struck it on the ceiling above the steps.

Descending the stairs, he paused halfway and took the measure of what awaited him. He had played in this place as a child, arranging toy soldiers, imagining long-ago battles. It was a favorite hideaway on the hot summer days that could sweep over Holyhood despite the nearness of the sea. So far as he knew, no one else ever went there.

Certainly no one would venture there in the midnight hour of a storm-filled night.

Which explained his surprise at the sight of a woman on her knees not far from where he stood. She wore a cloak that draped her body. Her head was bent, but he could see that her hair was long, loose, and a deep, rich red. She was digging furiously.

"What are you doing?"

The woman froze. Very slowly she raised her head and looked at him. The glow of the lantern, the light of which had drawn him into the crypt, fell fully on her face.

For a moment, William neglected to breathe. The woman was . . . beautiful, certainly, but beautiful women abounded in his world. Here was something more. Her features, clearly and delicately formed, appeared illuminated from within. Her eyes were very large, all the more so for being very wide. Her mouth was enticingly full, her chin firm. Stillness settled over her as she looked at him.

"Who are you?" she asked.

"William, Earl of Hollister. Who are you?"

To his surprise, she looked immensely relieved. Quickly, she got to her feet and made a futile effort to brush the mud off her cloak. "William . . . I know you. Or at least I did."

"You have the advantage, madam." Yet there was something about her that was familiar, if only to a small degree. It was years ago . . . a little red-haired girl playing in the garden of Holyhood. She had come with her parents, the Vanax Atreus, ruler of the legendary kingdom of Akora, and her mother, the Lady Brianna, who was related to his own family.

That child grown to such a stunning woman? It didn't seem possible, yet nature was known to work such wonders.

He came to the bottom of the stairs without taking his eyes from her. Close up, she was even lovelier, for all that she was clearly wet and bedraggled. "Princess Clio?"

Her smile was immediate and genuine. "Please, just Clio. You know we are not so fond of titles on Akora as people are here in England."

He did know that, or at least he had heard it, for all that he had never been to Akora. His grandparents had made several trips there over the years, but they were among the very few outsiders invited to visit the legendary Fortress Kingdom, which was situated in the Atlantic beyond what the ancients called the Pillars of Hercules.

"Clio, then. What are you doing here?"

"Digging," she said as though it should be obvious. When he continued staring at her, she elaborated. "I have been digging for several days and I've found some wonderful things. When the storm started, I was afraid those still left on the surface or near to it would be damaged, so I came down to get them."

Later he would try to understand why a lovely young woman—a princess, no less—was digging in the dirt floor of an empty stone crypt and what sort of "wonderful things" she could possibly have discovered. Just then, he had other things on his mind.

"I heard you scream."

Her creamy skin brightened as though a tongue of flame had moved over it. "I'm terribly sorry. I was . . . startled."

"By what?"

He half-expected her to mention a rat or something of the sort, when she surprised him. "A man, or at least what I thought was a man. There wasn't actually anyone there." Hesitantly, she added, "When I saw you on the steps, I thought you were him again."

"The man you saw looked like me?"

"There was no man, and no, he didn't look like you, not really. He was as tall as you and fit the way you are, but he was dressed very differently and his hair was much darker. Yours is auburn, his was black and somewhat longer."

"This man who did not exist?"

She made a small gesture, whether waving away her own inconsistency or his persistence, he could not tell.

"I was asleep when the rain woke me," she said, "and I realized the artifacts I had found could be endangered. When I got down here, I think I was still less than fully awake. Under the circumstances, it is not so surprising that my imagination overtook me."

"Perhaps not. What are these artifacts you speak of?"

Proudly she held out her basket. He peered into it and frowned. "Those are broken bits of pottery."

"A clay pitcher, I think. There is writing on them."

"That signifies? . . ."

"I am not absolutely certain of the script, but I think it is Anglo-Saxon, from the era of Alfred the Great."

"That would be old, indeed, but why would it interest you?"

"It's what I do . . . dig up the past." When he did not reply, she sighed. "I don't expect you to understand. People think the only objects from the past that matter are great monuments and the like, not the remains of ordinary life."

"You believe otherwise?"

She nodded and gestured to the basket. "From these, I may be able to confirm that this crypt is as old as I think it is and even what it was used for."

"Storage," William said.

"What?"

"It was used for storage, except for the time when it very briefly became a prison for captured Vikings."

"How could you possibly know that?"

He shrugged. "It's an old story, part of the lore of Holyhood. This is not the time to speak of it. You are soaked through and covered with mud."

She gathered her cloak more closely around herself. "I am aware of that."

"Then you must also be aware that you should retire." He offered his arm.

Briefly, she considered refusing. The glint of metal that had drawn her attention came from an iron bar that was revealed by the water washing down into the crypt. She was eager to examine it more closely, but she knew by experience that being metal, it was likely to come apart in flakes as soon as she tried to move it. Excavating it safely would be a delicate process, not best undertaken by lantern light when she was already weary.

Instead, she covered it again with soil, carefully marking the spot before accepting William's assistance. As they emerged from the crypt, she caught sight of Seeker and smiled. "He is yours?"

"Or I am his. We have not settled the matter." He took the reins with his free hand. The gelding followed them.

"How do you happen to be here at so late an hour?" Clio asked as they approached the back entrance of the house.

"I was delayed coming down from London."

Something hovered beneath his words, but she could not place it. His sudden appearance had shocked her. For just a moment, she truly had thought she was looking at the same man she had seen before. But that was not the case. Besides the difference in dress and hair color, the features were different. Yet both men bore the stamp of strength and determination. Both reminded her of the men of her own family and the men of Akora in general, good men, to be sure, and warriors to the bone.

"Your grandmother will be thrilled that you are here. Have you come for Racing Day?"

"Yes . . . I have. How is Grandmother?"

"Well, I think. She was very kind to invite me."

They had reached the door. He opened it for her and stood aside. His voice was deep and low. "Good night, Clio."

She came only to his shoulders and had to look up to see his face. In the shadows cast by the moon, his features looked hard and unyielding. There was a bleakness about his eyes that surprised her. She glanced down and saw that the left sleeve of his jacket was torn and there was a dark stain of some sort on it. The thought passed through her mind that perhaps he was not as well cared for as he might have been. Softly she said, "Good night . . . William."